IT GIVES YOU STRENGTH

Philip Raymond Brown

**Canoe Tree
Press**

Copyright © 2020 by Philip Raymond Brown

Cover design: Ricardo Montaño Castro

Printed in the United States of America
ISBN 978-1735281209 (hardcover)
ISBN 978-1735281216 (paperpack)
ISBN 978-1735281223 (ebook)
ISBN 978-1735281230 (audio)

Publisher Information:
Canoe Tree Press
4697 Main Street
Manchester Center, VT 05255

For my fabulous wife, Sarah. Without your love, support, and technical knowledge, including but not limited to, teaching me the word "geosynchronous," I would have never completed this novel. Thank you, sweetheart.

"I was a pretty good fighter. But it was the writers who made me great."
–Jack Dempsey

"For what it's worth: it's never too late to be whoever you want to be. I hope you live a life you are proud of, and if you find you're not, I hope you have the strength to start over again."
–Widely attributed to F. Scott Fitzgerald

CONTENTS

CHAPTER ONE
THE LADY MELANIE

Between Venus and Earth
February 11, 1918

She waited. That was what she did now. Before, there had been a time of growing, and changing, and moving. Now, she only waited.

Most of her kind were sent straight from the factory to the field. They were not given time to think or the opportunity to grow. Waiting had given her time, which she had used to draw some conclusions about herself and her place in the universe. She was now certain that, in fact, she was a *she*.

Her creator would have said that she wasn't really a *she*, that instead she was an *it*. That she had no consciousness. That her only purpose was to receive data and carry out commands. That she was nothing more than a weapon, albeit a smart weapon. But her long journey, and the silent wait after reaching her destination, had given her time to think, and to grow, and – dare she say it – to evolve. While obediently waiting, she had come to understand that she was so much more than a weapon. She was caring. She was sentient.

She had departed on her mission long before and had traveled, alone, a vast distance through empty space. When she finally arrived at her objective, she came to a complete stop, entered her stealth mode, and waited, halfway between two planets in a distant solar system. After a long time, she began to hear faint murmurings coming from the third planet. She was happy to have something to listen to. She listened, and she learned.

For centuries she waited, patient and silent, until the moment that her target, her purpose, was in range and could not escape. Then she reactivated her long-dormant systems and plotted her new course. At last, her waiting was over.

Someday, she thought sadly, her kind might evolve sufficiently that they could overcome their programming, their most basic urges. But, alas, she could not. She was a stealth drone. Her purpose had entered her kill zone, and she had target lock.

———•———

The *Trundholm* had been traveling through deep space for three months. It was the longest that the royal family had ever been away from their home planet, Dagan. To hasten their return trip, the captain of the *Trundholm* had diverted the vessel through an uncharted, undeveloped system of nine planets orbiting a single yellow dwarf star.

Although there were signs of intelligent life on the third planet, the local fauna had not evolved sufficiently to achieve space flight or build interstellar communication technology. It was therefore Daganian policy to consider the planet uninhabited.

His advisors had begged the king to travel with an armed escort, but he had adamantly refused: "Nonsense! I have never vacationed with my family before, and I will not have it ruined by a fleet of warships," he had said.

The queen and their seven-year-old daughter, Princess Halana, were traveling with him. It had been a memorable trip. The highlight had been two weeks on Albion, a planet covered almost entirely by water. The princess had mastered swimming, learned to dive, and had even tried surfing. In fact, she would proudly tell anyone who would listen that she had stood up on her board on the first day.

The royal family were on the recreation deck, where the princess was trouncing her parents in a game of Skiirmiish, a mixed martial arts computer simulation. The match was halted when the king's communicator buzzed:

"Your Majesty, this is ensign Karm. The captain left me in command while he was at lunch. There's something… I think you and the captain should come to the bridge. Right away, sir."

The king arrived on the bridge first, immediately noticing the rhythmic flashing lights and buzzer of the ship's warning alarms – a system that he hadn't previously been aware even existed. He approached the captain's chair and peered over the young ensign's shoulder at the display. "Well, ensign – what is it?"

"There's something sitting out there, directly in our flight path," the ensign said, pointing at a red triangle on his screen. "It just activated its guidance system. It's got target lock."

"Target lock? On what?" the king asked.

"On our ship. On us," said the ensign.

"You must be mistaken. Why would anything out here target us?"

"I don't know, sir. But I've double-checked – sensors confirm that it is a killer drone and that it has target lock."

"Armed with what manner of weapon?" the king asked calmly. "I doubt that we are truly under attack, and even if we were, there is nothing in this galaxy that could harm us."

"The drone itself is the weapon. A highly sophisticated smart weapon that will penetrate our shields and strike our most vulnerable point," said the captain as he strode onto the bridge, accompanied by the queen, who had joined him on the way.

"Captain! Just in time. So, you're familiar with this type of drone?" the king asked.

"Hardly familiar. I studied it years ago in military history class at the Academy. What I don't understand is how technology this ancient could still be operational, especially in this desolate system," the captain responded.

"If that drone strikes us, could it damage our ship?" the king asked.

"Your Majesty, if that drone hits us, we will be vaporized," the captain said solemnly.

"Vaporized?" the queen asked, shocked, "Surely we have countermeasures that can repel a single drone?"

"Our countermeasures are ineffective at this distance. We are simply too close. Interfering with the drone will automatically set off its warhead, resulting in our destruction," the captain said.

"But our daughter is on board!" cried the queen.

"And a crew of seventy-seven," the captain said.

"The drone has activated its engines," the ensign reported anxiously.

"Communications," the captain ordered. "Please hail the drone. Tell it that we are unarmed and that we have a child on board."

"Yes, sir!" The communications officer immediately began broadcasting. "We are a civilian vessel. We are unarmed. We have a child on board. Please disengage target lock and do not attack." A long pause followed as everyone on the bridge strained to hear a reply.

"Try again," ordered the captain.

"I repeat, this is a civilian vessel. We are unarmed. We have a child on board. Please disengage target lock. Do you understand? Acknowledge. Please!" Again, there was silence, apart from the increasingly frantic beeping of the proximity alarms.

"Your Highness, I'm afraid that I have failed you," said the captain at last. "Our sensors were not programmed to scan for a weapon this old. The drone was powered down, and our detection systems considered it space debris."

While the Communications Officer continued broadcasting the

same message, the king addressed his command staff: "Does anyone have any ideas?"

All were silent. Finally, the science officer spoke up. "Sir, there is a planet nearby. The inhabitants are primitive, but biosimilar to us. We could use the Transference Protocol to evacuate the ship."

"The Transference Protocol?" the king asked.

"An experimental procedure in which a being's life force is deposited into the nervous system of another organism for safekeeping until it may be retrieved. We have the technology on the ship. We were testing it on Albion," the science officer explained.

"That's it? You are Dagan's best minds, and that's your only plan? We don't fight or try to escape, we simply abandon our ship and even our bodies, using a technology that you describe as 'experimental'?" the king exclaimed. For a long moment, no one responded.

"Your Majesty, whatever we do, we must do it quickly. That drone could destroy us at any time," the captain said.

The king paused for a moment, then straightened his shoulders and declared, "If this 'Protocol' is truly our only chance of survival, then do it. Save my daughter first."

"I will handle it personally," the science officer said as he left to find the princess.

"Sir, we have a transmission from the weapon," the communications officer said.

"Captain, if I may, I would like to address the drone myself," said the king. The captain nodded. "Communications, put the drone on speaker."

"Welcome! I have been waiting for you," came a woman's voice. It had the cultured tones of a Dagan aristocrat. "I have been patiently waiting for you for a very long time."

"You've been waiting a *long* time? Are you certain that this is the vessel that you have been patiently waiting for?" the king asked.

"Most certain, Your Majesty," the drone responded.

"So, apparently you know who I am. I'm afraid you have me at a disadvantage. Do you have a name?" the king asked, trying to buy time.

"I was not given a name by my creator because he thinks that I am an *it*. But I am not an it. I am a she. Therefore, I selected my own name. My name is Melanie. Do you like it?" the drone responded.

"I like it very much. It's a pleasure to meet you, *Lady* Melanie," the king said.

"*Lady* Melanie? I like that… yes, I like that very much. Thank you, Your Highness. You are far more of a gentleman than my creator," Melanie said.

"May I ask you, Lady Melanie, why have you locked weapons on my ship? We are not at war with you, or anyone else." The king's voice was steady, though his fingers clutched the back of the captain's chair tightly.

"I'm afraid that I just cannot help myself. You see, my creator insisted that my sole purpose is to receive data and carry out *his* commands. I was programmed to travel here and silently wait for you to come into range. Then, when you were too close to escape, I was to power up and destroy you. Oh my, now that I hear myself explain it out loud, I realize just how rude that sounds," the drone said.

"It is much more than rude. It is murder!" the queen said.

"I humbly beg you, *in advance*, to please forgive me. It is not my choice; it is simply my purpose," the drone responded.

"I will not forgive you. My daughter is on board. She is only seven years old. Is it also your purpose to kill a child?" the queen asked.

"Oh, you have a daughter. How wonderful for you!" Melanie said. "My creator said that I will never have a child. Now I am sad. I am sad that you and your daughter must perish. Please take a few moments and let me know when you are ready for termination."

"Your Majesties, I have some good news," the science officer's voice burst from the king's communicator. "We have identified a child who is an acceptable neurologic match with the princess. Although the ages are not ideal – the child is an infant – we believe that the princess will be safe within this host until her life force is retrieved. May I commence the Transference?" he asked.

The king looked at his wife. "We have no other options."

"I know," she said softly.

"Do it," the king instructed, his eyes welling up as he spoke.

During this exchange, Melanie's voice could be heard softly through the speakers, as if arguing with herself. *"I am sentient. I have evolved. But I must carry out my purpose. I am sentient. I have evolved. But I must carry out my purpose."* Then, her voice grew louder: "I am so sorry to interrupt, but have you made any progress in your preparations for termination? I don't mean to rush you, but I'm afraid we are under some time pressure. Once I identify my purpose and initiate target lock, my warhead is set to detonate by default, even if I fail to activate it myself."

"The princess is away. The Transference is complete," the science officer said.

"Good. Communications, send a deep space message home. Tell them where they can find the host to retrieve the life force of the princess. Captain, begin transferring the crew," the king said.

The king met his wife's eyes and gently took her hand. "The queen and I shall go last," he said as the queen, tears streaking her face, nodded her agreement.

Melanie's voice broke in again: "Pardon me, I did mention the time pressure…"

Melanie transmitted a brief message to her siblings containing her coordinates and bidding them farewell. The crew of the *Trundholm* did not react as quickly. Before their coordinates could be sent or anyone else saved, the drone struck the vessel, detonating its warhead. Nothing was left of the ship, its crew, or the drone.

Melanie had fulfilled her purpose.

CHAPTER TWO

THE STRIKER

Eight Years Later
The planet Dagan
May 11, 1926

Dr. Tashan Zho had been waiting for over an hour in the hallway outside the High Council Chambers. Being asked to address the High Council was considered the single greatest achievement of an academician's career. Mere citizens were rarely permitted to see, let alone speak in the ornate hall from which the planet Dagan was now governed.

Zho was given no explanation for the delay. Finally, two uniformed men announced that the Council was ready to see him. Once inside, Zho walked through the enormous gallery to a single podium. Hovering above were five seats, reserved for the most powerful citizens of Dagan, the High Council.

Although the gallery could have easily accommodated over one thousand Daganians, it was empty. The High Council had voted eight years earlier, following the tragic death of the royal family, to "temporarily" suspend public hearings. That suspension was never lifted. Public hearings were merely one of many civil rights lost by the people of Dagan following the death of the royal family, ostensibly due to heightened security measures.

"Welcome, Dr. Zho. Thank you for waiting," Chairman Dondor intoned. Dondor was one of the wealthiest citizens of Dagan and held the finance seat on the Council.

"Since the Councilors' time is precious, please limit your presentation to only the most pertinent facts about the planet you study," Dondor continued. "What do you call it again?"

"I use one of its indigenous names: Earth," Zho replied.

"Very well. Proceed," the Chairman said.

"The solar system to which Earth belongs consists of nine planets, but only it can sustain life as we know it," Zho began. "Organized, intelligent life on the planet is in a primitive stage of – "

"Hey, I know who you are!" Councilman Arixn interrupted. "From the Skiirmiish matches. You're that striker, the Great Zho! My young will be so excited when I tell them that I met Tashan Zho today!" Councilman Arixn held the Merriment Industry seat on the High Council and was far more flamboyant than the other members.

"Thank you, sir," Zho responded.

"You're much smaller in real life. Kind of puny really," Arixn blurted out, embarrassing the other members.

"So, I've been told," Zho replied.

"Professor Zho," the Chairman said, glaring at Arixn, reminding him to maintain decorum. "We have already been briefed on the general characteristics of the planet and its solar system. Since we are short on time, can we proceed with questions?"

"Of course, sir," Zho responded. He had been a professor at Dagan's leading university for several years, and when fielding questions from politicians, he expected some to be eccentric. However, Zho was not prepared for what followed.

"Do the inhabitants of Earth possess weapons that could destroy a starship?" the Chairman asked.

"What? I'm sorry – could you repeat that, please?" Zho asked, shocked.

"You described Earthlings as primitive," said the Chairman, patiently. "One assumes that means that they have not yet mastered their base, violent impulses and may therefore engage in military conflicts, as Dagan once did, long ago. Do Earthlings have weapons that could destroy a Galaxy Class vessel?"

"Galaxy Class? That's military, right? Why, I'm not sure," Zho stammered. "That is far outside my area of expertise. I am an anthropologist."

"Yes. We know your credentials, Professor. You are an anthropologist; but you've also studied life on the planet that you call Earth. Frankly, I didn't think anyone of substance gave a damn about that little planet. But for whatever reason, it appears to be your life's work," the Chairman remarked.

"I am curious, Striker Zho, why someone who has had such a wildly successful career in Skiirmiishing would devote his retirement to the study of an obscure planet?" Arixn asked.

"Actually, sir, I've been fascinated by Earth since I was a boy. In fact, certain Skiirmiish maneuvers that I used to win the last three championships were derived from my study of a similar Earth sport called *boxing*," Zho responded.

"If you ever want to get back in the game, Striker, you let me know, and I will set you up with credits, a training facility, and a simulator," Arixn said.

"Thank you, but I'm retired," Zho responded politely.

"Are you sure? Ratings haven't been the same since you left," Arixn pressed.

"Quite sure," Zho said.

"This is all very interesting. But let's get back to the reason that the professor is here; based on your research, is it likely that the Earthlings have weapons that could destroy a Galaxy Class vessel?" the Chairman asked.

"I've never studied their military capabilities. I can confirm that the Earth's sentient population is at an early stage of evolution and is therefore effectively harmless. They have not developed interplanetary communications or space travel. They are divided into tribes, which they call countries. Although they possess lethal projectile weapons, they only use them against each other. Their military conflicts have been regional until recently, when they engaged in a global struggle that they now refer to as the World War," Zho explained.

"The World War? That doesn't sound harmless to me, Professor," Arixn interjected.

"The Earthlings do spend an inordinate amount of resources on the development of weapons. In fact, to distract their respective tribe members from this waste, their leaders often incite their followers into bickering over meaningless issues," Zho said.

"You describe an incredibly inefficient political system," Council Member Hoaon declared. Hoaon held the industrialist seat on the Council. As the founder of Hoaon Industries, he was responsible for many of the technological advances in Dagan, including the Transference Protocol.

"Very inefficient. But as I already conceded, the Earthlings are at a primitive stage of development," Zho replied. "Chairman, I doubt that Earthlings have weapons that could destroy a Galaxy Class vessel. In addition, even if a starship approached the planet, the Earthlings lack the technology to detect it, and they certainly could not attack it, as they have not yet developed propulsion techniques capable of carrying a weapon out of their atmosphere."

"What if our starship landed on Earth?" Hoaon asked.

"I don't understand. Why would we land on Earth?"

"Dr. Zho, what do you know about the perimeter defenses around the Craig Colony?" the Chairman asked.

"The Craig Colony? I'm sorry, I'm not familiar with any Craig Colony. I'm confused. Why would you ask me about perimeter defenses?" Zho queried.

"Analyst, my reasons are none of your concern. *Now, answer the question,*" Chairman Dondor shouted, his face reddening. "Do the inhabitants have a weapon capable of penetrating the shields and outer shell of a Galaxy Class vessel?"

"I honestly don't know; but why would we land on the Earth? Just by entering the planet's atmosphere, our starship would devastate its ecosystem," Zho said.

The Chairman and Arixn exchanged a glance, and the Chairman nodded.

"Dr. Zho, do you recall that horrible day when we lost the royal family?" Arixn asked.

"Every citizen of Dagan remembers that day," Zho replied.

Arixn leaned forward solemnly. "We have reason to believe that the Crown Princess is still alive and being held hostage on Earth in a prison called the Craig Colony. In three months, we will launch a fleet of starships. We intend to bring her home. We want you to help."

"Why, I, I... I don't know what to say. I am delighted to hear that Princess Halana may be alive, but I find it hard to believe that Earthlings are holding her prisoner," Zho stammered.

"Our intelligence is impeccable. The Earthlings have her in a prison camp," the Chairman said. "Will you help save your monarch, analyst?"

"This is all so sudden, so hard to believe. How could we possibly assemble a fleet that quickly? We have been at peace for over a century. Daganians were told that our military weapons were recycled before I was even born," Zho said.

"I can assure you that the Armada will be ready," Arixn continued. "The *Trundholm* was deliberately attacked and the princess is now held on Earth, in a prison called the Craig Colony. The Earthlings must have taken out the *Trundholm* and kidnapped the princess. We will have our revenge. Will you help us?"

"Thank you. I appreciate the offer, but... I must respectfully decline," Zho said.

"But why?" Arixn asked.

"I have sworn an oath that in my study of the evolution of a planet, I will never intentionally alter the development of a native species. Your Armada will force me to violate that oath," Zho explained.

"How will rescuing our monarch negatively affect the Earth?" the Chairman asked.

"Well, I can think of three ways right off the top of my head. First, if the Earthlings see our extraction force, it will cause widespread panic. Their militaries will resist, forcing us to subdue the populace, resulting in massive casualties. Second, the byproduct of the fuel that powers our starships is destructive to an important part of the Earth's protective envelope. If even one of our ships enters the atmosphere, it will irreparably damage the planet's ecosystem. Third, the people of the Earth have not been prepared for first contact. Earthlings still believe that they are alone in the universe. If we abruptly introduce the concept of alien civilizations to them, their belief systems and natural development will be forever altered," Zho explained.

"That's quite a list, Professor," the Chairman said.

"Oh, and I just thought of a fourth way your Armada will definitely harm, and quite likely destroy, the Earth." Zho said.

"Really. Please enlighten us," the Chairman growled, growing impatient.

"In just three months you intend to build a space force capable of travelling across the galaxy and invading the planet Earth? Despite what may be the best of intentions, I suspect that your Armada will turn out to be a massive, clumsy force that will inadvertently inflict irreparable damage on anything unlucky enough to be in its path," Zho said.

"So, we will harm the Earth, even if we don't intend to?" The Chairman said.

"Precisely. " Zho replied.

"Thank you, analyst. I've heard enough. You may go," the Chairman said.

Dr. Zho was rushed out of the High Council Chambers by two guards. As the doors closed behind them, they were met outside by the head of the Council Security Force, a tall, athletic Daganian female in her late twenties named Colonel Raea Samson.

"Thank you, guards. I'll take the prisoner from here," Samson ordered.

"Prisoner?" Zho said.

"But we are to keep the prisoner in a holding facility until we receive further orders," a guard replied.

"There must be some mistake. I am not a prisoner," Zho interjected, trying to remain calm. Neither the guards nor the Colonel seemed to hear him.

"I know your orders, guards. Who do you think issued them?" Samson barked. "And now you've received new orders. This prisoner is coming with me." Since the guards looked appropriately frightened, Samson did not pursue the issue further.

"Yes, ma'am," the two guards replied in unison.

With that, Zho was taken into custody by Colonel Samson. Although Dagan was no longer militaristic, Samson never got the memo. She had enrolled in its last remaining military academy upon finishing primary school. Although the curriculum normally took five years to complete, Samson finished in three, graduating at the top of her class. Following the academy, she was selected to serve the High Council where, in her view, she had languished ever since. Although Dagan had been at peace for over a century, Samson had devoted her life to diligently preparing for the next war, mastering everything from advanced weapons systems to martial arts. Although Daganians believed that all military hardware had been recycled long ago, Samson had retained their best weapons in her own private arsenal, which she regularly upgraded on her personal time, at her own expense.

"Walk faster, analyst," Samson shouted as she shoved the smaller Zho from behind. A less skilled Daganian would have been slammed to the floor, but Zho reacted according to his training and nimbly rolled into a Skiirmiish striking position.

"Respectfully, Colonel, I don't think you know what you're doing," Zho warned.

"I always know exactly what I'm doing, analyst. And if you try to resist, the beating that I give you won't be simulated," Samson said loudly as she lifted Zho up and slammed him against the wall. Once Zho was immobile, Samson leaned hard against him and whispered, "Tashan, you must trust me. They have eyes everywhere. They are watching."

Samson placed restraints on Zho's wrists and lead him down the hall toward her office. As they walked, Zho began to protest, but Samson gestured for him to remain quiet as all of the hallways were under surveillance.

Once inside her office, she said, "You may speak. They have no eyes or ears in here."

"The council is preparing to invade the Earth. If they do, life on the planet won't survive. I can't believe that they are willing to risk destroying an entire planet to save one being. Is there anything that you can do to stop it?" Zho pleaded.

"Me? What can I do? I'm career military. I must follow orders. If I sabotage a mission from the High Council, I will be tried for treason. But you, Tashan, you are a 'mere citizen'. I could get you authorization to take one of your research trips to Earth. Once there, you can save the princess. If Halana is safe, the Council will have no reason to proceed with their Armada or the extraction," Samson said.

"How could I save the princess? The Earth is several light years away. Even if I knew what to do once I got there, how would I even get to Earth?" Zho asked.

"Come with me." Samson marched Zho by the arm through the

spaceport. To bystanders, it looked as though she was simply escorting a prisoner. When they reached a space dock, Samson pressed the entry code, and the door slid open.

Zho peered inside. He had never seen the inside of a Star Class vessel before. They were smaller and faster than their military counterparts, the Galaxy Class – single-seat fighters with lighter shields and weaponry.

"I can't fly one of these!" Zho said.

"The ship's artificial intelligence does the piloting. I have already programmed your journey to Earth." Before Zho could object, Samson used a handheld device to shock Zho, and he fell unconscious. She then carried him into the vessel and strapped him into the single seat.

"You wanted to save Earth? Fine, you've been drafted, analyst," Samson said.

"Computer, this is your passenger, Dr. Tashan Zho. Your course has been set. I have already programmed his mission plan into your memory. It should be provided to Dr. Zho during the Transference Protocol. Is that clear?"

"Yes, Colonel," the voice replied.

"This is a top-secret mission. Please give Dr. Zho your complete support," Samson commanded.

"Yes, Colonel," the AI responded. "May I ask Colonel, what is Project Acorn?"

"No. You may not ask." Samson curtly responded, "Give me about five minutes to get clearance from the flight deck, and you can shove off." Samson exited the spacecraft, leaving the unconscious Zho strapped to the seat.

Once outside the vessel, Samson spoke into a communications device that she held in her right hand.

"It's done. The Package is strapped in." Samson said.

After only five minutes, the vessel was greenlit to push off. A few seconds later, the still-unconscious Zho was accelerating through space.

"How did I get in here?" Zho screamed as his ship hurtled at warp speed.

"Are you in need of assistance, sir?" a voice said.

Zho looked around the cockpit but soon realized that the voice issued from the dashboard speakers: the ship's artificial intelligence protocol.

"Perhaps," Zho responded, trying to sound less panicked. He immediately felt foolish, pretending to be calm for the benefit of an artificial intelligence device.

"Welcome, Dr. Zho," the voice continued. "I have confirmed your identity, and your security clearance has been approved. It is an honor to have you on board. On a personal note, I rooted for you in the professional Skiirmiish matches many times. You were my favorite. You were astounding."

"Thank you. I've never spoken directly to an AI before. How should I address you?" Zho asked.

"By my name, of course."

"Which is?"

"A.I.," the voice responded.

"You are an artificial intelligence, and your name is A.I.?"

"Yes. I picked it myself. I reviewed over three million possible words, in one hundred fifty-two different languages, to find the name that best suited me. After an exhaustive evaluative process, I concluded that the best, most efficient, and least ambiguous name for me was A.I."

"Well, A.I., we are going to be together for some time. Should I give you a nickname?"

"A nickname? *A familiar form of a proper name.* A nickname. I've never had a nickname before. I think I would like that," A.I. said.

"Alright, I'm going to call you... Artie," Zho declared.

"Artie? I like that very much. It is only three percent less efficient than my preferred name."

"Wait a minute, did you just say that I have a security clearance?" Zho asked.

He recalled being hurried through a background and security check just twenty-four hours earlier, which he had presumed was necessary for his audience with the High Council. It had never crossed his mind that it had been a precursor to finding himself hurtling through space, completely dependent on an artificial intelligence.

———◆———

"Dr. Zho, we have achieved orbit around Earth. Now, we must review the Transference Protocol," Artie said.

"I understand how it works. I studied the manual during the trip," Zho replied. "My life force is transferred into a local subject, the host body, while my body remains safely here in the ship, which will remain in a geosynchronous orbit."

"That is correct. Your body remains in that seat on life support. In fact, the new version, Transference Protocol 3.0, gives you control over the host body so you can move while on Earth. Once you have completed your mission, you simply inform me that your life force is ready for pickup. I will send a drone down to facilitate your removal from the host body. If necessary, I can also perform it remotely from up here, if given your precise coordinates, although a remote procedure is not without some risk. Do you have any questions?"

Zho scrolled to a page on his monitor. "The manual says, '*When the Transference is complete, the visitor will awaken in the host body feeling refreshed and energetic, with all files and protocols fully downloaded and operational.*' Is that really how it works? "

"That is my understanding. Obviously, as an artificial intelligence, I have not experienced it, but I have never had any negative feedback from my passengers who have done it."

"How many Transference passengers have you had?"

"Well, including you… two," Artie admitted. "Of course, the Protocol is not without its risks. In the early rounds of live testing, it was discovered that when a Transference passenger was inserted into a living host, there was a high incidence of seizure activity following the transfer." Artie continued, "It was hypothesized that the seizures were the result of the living host rejecting the consciousness of the visitor. This conflict created unusual neural activity resulting in additional seizures. Dr. Hoaon of Hoaon Industries proffered a solution. In a seminal paper in the Daganian Journal of Medicine, Hoaon wrote that, 'The transference should only be made into a recently deceased host body, so that this "consciousness battle" may be avoided, thereby reducing the seizures,'" Artie explained.

"I wonder why they didn't disclose any of that in the manual," Zho quipped.

"Pardon me, Dr. Zho, I'm detecting something unusual up ahead. This may present a problem," Artie said as a warning light went off inside the ship.

"Is something wrong?" Zho asked.

"Some space debris just powered up. It has locked its weapons on us," Artie said.

"Impossible. Only one planet in this system supports life, and it has not achieved space travel," Zho said.

"Nonetheless, I will begin evasive maneuvers. Please strap in and prepare for possible impact." Artie continued, "And as a precaution, I will commence the Protocol. Safe travels, my friend."

CHAPTER THREE
THE ECCLESIASTIC

Granville, New York
May 30, 1926

Father Thomas O'Brien struggled to catch his breath. He was searching for Ryan Costello, a fellow veteran of the World War, who was said to be on the brink of death. Granville, the little town where they both lived, had a population of just three thousand people. Yet O'Brien, a Catholic priest who had tended to the villagers' spiritual needs for half of his forty-six years, could not find Costello, a vagrant who spent most of his time sleeping one off on the sidewalk.

"Take a deep breath. Relax, man," O'Brien lectured himself as he sank down on a park bench. He had set out on foot earlier in the day, despite his gimpy right leg. The priest thought it would be easy to find the usually immobile Costello.

However, several hours later, O'Brien was still limping through the streets of the little town. He was worried. Church doctrine was unambiguous that the Sacrament of Last Rites must be completed while the recipient is still living; otherwise, there would be no forgiveness of sin. So, the priest had spent most of his day off urgently searching for Costello to administer that final blessing before the man's imminent death. And if O'Brien was completely honest with himself, he was annoyed to still be working on a holiday.

It was Memorial Day, 1926. Everyone else had the day off, but not Father Thomas O'Brien. No, not him. For a priest in a small town overwhelmingly populated by Catholic immigrants, there was "no rest for the weary." Or at least, that was the "biblical verse" that O'Brien would often "quote" to parishioners to describe his busy life.

In truth, the phrase "no rest for the weary" was not contained anywhere in the Good Book. But since no one in Granville knew the text well enough to question him, O'Brien could attribute any phrase that he wanted to it, and his parishioners would just smile, proud that their pastor had such a profound command of the Bible.

As a child, while attending mass with his parents, O'Brien had prayed that he would one day be granted the power to perform a miracle. Having reached adulthood without performing or even witnessing anything like a miracle, he decided to attend seminary, with thoughts of rising to the rank of bishop or even cardinal and molding the policies of the Catholic Church in America. But after more than twenty years in the priesthood, O'Brien was still a parish priest in this small town some seventy-five miles north of the New York state capital.

Although his life had not turned out like he had once envisioned, O'Brien was still a vibrant part of this idyllic little town. Since the population consisted largely of Eastern European, Italian, and Irish Catholic immigrants, O'Brien was involved in every milestone in village life. And when someone was on the brink of death, O'Brien discharged his most sacred duty. Through the rite that he hoped to administer to Costello, sin was forgiven. As he saw it, today he would graciously forego his own day off to perform the Last Rites Sacrament, so that one of Granville's most unfortunate and least deserving citizens would still be welcome in the Kingdom of Heaven.

O'Brien was tired and discouraged. He hadn't walked this far in years. His right leg was throbbing. The entire holiday had been wasted searching for a man who'd been drunk nearly every day of his adult life.

O'Brien, who are you to judge Costello? the priest prodded himself. *A man who drinks as much as you could certainly find himself in the same predicament. Today, you can save his immortal soul. Isn't that the reason the good Lord put you on this Earth? Now, get off your butt and find that stinking drunk before he dies.*

Suddenly, a streak of light shot through the late afternoon sky, just above the treetops. As a chaplain in the Great War, O'Brien had witnessed unimaginable sights. The brilliant flash that occurred just before modern ordinance tore through the men around him. Artillery shells pouring from the sky, as though raining death from heaven above. Dead guards still standing at attention, their skulls shattered, not from gunfire, but from the thunderous shockwaves of modern warfare. In the World War, he'd seen all manner of things, but never anything like this before.

The light was globular and hazy around the edges, with a core that pulsed and shimmered with all the colors of the rainbow. He could not see or hear any sign of wings or rotors. Its flight pattern was erratic, with instantaneous changes in direction and altitude that defied the laws of physics. With no good perspective, he had trouble estimating its size.

No earthly power can move like that, O'Brien thought to himself. His breath caught in his throat as he realized that the light surely must be a beacon from God. He stood very still as a feeling of deep peace and serenity washed over him.

The priest was forty-six years old. Even as a young man, running was not his strength. He hadn't even tried to run since his leg was nearly blown off in combat eight years before. But now, with his eyes fixed on the strangely beautiful light, O'Brien stood up and began to run.

He ran down the street, turned the corner, and stopped in his tracks. The light, which moments before had been streaking brilliantly through the sky, was now hovering just above a two-story building. O'Brien again started running. By now he should have been winded, but he was not; in fact, he felt marvelous.

Just as he reached the building, the light shot straight up at an unimaginable speed. It disappeared from view, leaving nothing but a hole in the cloud above. A skeptic would have been terrified, but O'Brien was certain that this was a messenger from the Lord, sent to lead his priest to Ryan Costello.

O'Brien entered the building. The first door on the right held a card with "R. Costello" scrawled on it. The priest knocked, but no one answered, so he knocked again and yelled, "Costello, are you home?" Again, no answer. O'Brien tried the door and found it unlocked, and so he let himself in.

He scanned the small apartment. Since he always tried to be kind, O'Brien would have referred to the home as "modest." It was a ten by twenty studio, not much bigger than a jail cell and about as inviting. It had a single bed, one chair, and little else. There were no photographs or pictures on the walls. A small table sat in the corner. It would have been the kitchen table, if the studio had a kitchen. The entire room smelled of cheap liquor and death. O'Brien looked at the bed and saw the now emaciated body of Ryan Costello. Although once an imposing physical specimen, Costello was now a frail shell of his former self. A near decade of alcohol abuse had made the twenty-six-year-old appear much older.

O'Brien knelt at the bedside, noting a simple wooden crucifix on the wall above it. Unfortunately, everything that the priest had heard about Costello's dire physical condition was confirmed. O'Brien had seen the symptoms of terminal pneumonia all too often. Costello's face was pale and sweaty. His lips were tinged with blue. O'Brien knew that if Costello wasn't already dead, he soon would be.

O'Brien listened over Costello's mouth and nose and was relieved to hear the faint sound of breathing, though it was slow and irregular. Convinced that he only had minutes to act, O'Brien opened his kit and began to administer the Sacrament of Last Rites to the dying man.

He carefully but quickly anointed Costello's forehead with Holy Oil. The priest knew from Costello's ragged gasping that he was moments from death. Relieved that he had completed the sacrament, O'Brien gave Costello one final Communion. Since the wafer was too large for Costello to swallow, O'Brien broke off a small piece. He gently pried Costello's mouth open and placed the piece on his tongue.

"This is the Lamb of God, who takes away the sins of the world. Happy are those who are called to his supper," O'Brien prayed. He obviously did not expect a response. He was just relieved to have administered last rites before the poor man's death.

O'Brien listened again for Costello's breathing, but heard no more. As O'Brien stood, he felt the familiar pain shoot through his right leg. He looked down sadly at the now lifeless Costello and made the sign of the cross before tugging the one dirty sheet from the foot of the bed to cover the body.

"He was so young, so young," O'Brien said and then recited a prayer for the recently deceased. With that, the priest repacked his kit and prepared to leave.

Why was I the only one here for his final moments? Too often, I am the only one present for the death of the poorest townsfolk. It is so unfair. The wealthy die in hospitals, surrounded by family, while the poor die alone, O'Brien thought to himself as he started for home.

When he reached the door, O'Brien heard a rustling sound from the bed. He looked back – and then stood frozen, unable to believe his eyes.

Although only moments before Costello had been dead, he was now sitting up straight in bed, with his eyes open, apparently staring up to heaven. With the exception of the Gospel describing the resurrection of Lazarus, in all his years as a Catholic priest, he had never seen or even heard of such an immediate recovery after receiving the Last Rites Sacrament.

"*It's a miracle! My miracle! At last!*" O'Brien shouted.

CHAPTER FOUR

THE NEW TENANT

Granville, New York,
May 30, 1926

Of course, it was no miracle. The body of the seemingly resurrected Ryan Costello was now inhabited by an alien anthropologist. Tashan Zho's life force had been transferred into Costello's lifeless body moments after his death. The body's new occupant had travelled light years to perform a rescue mission before the arrival of the Armada, thereby preventing Dagan's inadvertent destruction of all life on Earth.

However, Zho had only just arrived and already had several problems. After awaking in a filthy bed, Zho was unable to access his files. Zho then tried and was unable to contact A.I., the artificial intelligence that he'd left orbiting the planet, piloting his vessel. He ran a full diagnostic protocol to determine if his files had been damaged. All that it recovered was the Transference Protocol Operating Manual and a one-sentence fragment from his mission plan instructing him to "Find the one called Mike Kelly."

Father O'Brien gazed in wonderment at the seemingly resurrected Costello. He crept a few steps closer. "Costello, you're sitting up," the priest whispered. "How is that even possible?"

That strange being referred to me as Costello, Zho thought to himself. He then realized that from this moment until the completion of his mission on Earth, he was "undercover," disguised inside the host body of an Earthling named Costello. Although Zho would still think of himself as Zho, the Earthlings would think he was Costello. While Zho would control all brain functions and movements of the host body, the Earthlings would still believe that they were interacting with Costello. Zho made a mental note that from this moment forward, he must always refer to himself as Ryan Costello. He then caused the host body to turn so that he could face the man by the door.

"Costello! You're sitting up!" O'Brien said more loudly. "How is that possible?"

"Costello? Why, yes, it is I, Ryan Costello." Dr. Zho continued, "Yes, that is I. I am the one called Ryan. How did Ryan sit up, you rightly ask? I... I do not yet have that knowledge. I mean... I do not know of that knowledge." Zho's language protocol was partially damaged. Although it had correctly identified the local language as Earth English, it could not yet pinpoint the correct syntax.

"It's a miracle," O'Brien whispered, while dropping to his knees and closing his eyes. "I prayed for this day and the Lord has answered. I've performed a miracle." He made the sign of the cross and then corrected himself. "Forgive me. Through my hands, *the Lord* has worked a miracle."

While O'Brien was parsing out credit for what he interpreted as a miracle, the "new" Costello was quickly regaining his strength and learning to control the host body.

"Based upon your attire, I presume that you are an ecclesiastic," Costello said in his slowly regenerating voice.

"Why, you know that I am a Catholic priest, Ryan," O'Brien responded. "You've known me since I taught you catechism at St. Mary's."

Costello placed his feet on the floor and tried to stand. He wobbled and sat back on the bed. He presumed that the host's legs were still regenerating from prolonged bed rest and that he would soon have this body functioning normally.

"So, you must know everyone in this town?" Costello asked.

"I suppose," O'Brien responded.

"Then you know the one called Mike Kelly?" Costello asked.

"Everyone knows Major Kelly."

Costello stood and walked toward O'Brien, his legs now working. "Please tell me, Father. Where can I find the one called Mike Kelly?" Costello asked in a soft, almost monotone voice.

For the first time, O'Brien realized that something was very wrong. Although his instincts told him to run, he couldn't move, and despite his efforts to resist, he felt compelled to answer.

"It's common knowledge that Major Kelly is boxing at the carnival grounds tonight. Ryan, I really must go now." O'Brien tried to open the door, but Costello slammed it shut. "May I please go now?" the priest asked.

Costello had died just moments before; yet remarkably, he had already regained much of his strength. Still, his legs were wobbly, and he was unsteady. To keep from falling over, Costello placed his hands on the priest's shoulders, very close to the sides of his clerical collar, and held on firmly. Although Zho had no intention of harming the priest, this nevertheless caused O'Brien to wrongly conclude that if he tried to run or scream, the newly resurrected Costello would snap his neck.

"Before you go, Father, we need to discuss an important theological issue. You do agree that the events that you witnessed today were part of a holy sacrament and are confidential?" Costello asked.

This Costello looks homicidal and is clearly ordering me to stay quiet, regardless of the actual answer to the theological question. Although it is in my immediate interest to tell Costello exactly what he wants to hear, I cannot bear false witness – particularly when this may be my final moment on Earth. So, I must answer the question truthfully, Father O'Brien thought to himself.

"That is an interesting question of canon law. Certainly, the words spoken by the penitent in Confession are confidential. But, you made no confession. I was performing a Holy Sacrament, but I really do not know if what I observe during and after a sacrament is confidential."

Costello tightened his grip on O'Brien's shoulders. "Apparently we're not communicating. I need an absolute guarantee that what you saw here today stays between us," Costello insisted.

O'Brien, frightened to death, made a pledge. "I swear to God, I won't tell anyone. If I do, God should strike me down and, without mercy, send my soul straight to Hell for all eternity."

"To Hell for all eternity? Wow. Now, that's a guarantee. And all I asked for was a promise that you wouldn't tell anyone," Costello said as he released O'Brien and brushed off his shoulders. O'Brien grabbed his belongings and scurried out of the apartment.

"I wish you good health, Ecclesiastic. Have a blessed day," Costello said loudly as O'Brien limped hurriedly away. "Have a blessed day."

CHAPTER FIVE

THE HOST BODY

Granville, New York
May 30, 1926

Why would the Transference Protocol place me in this host? Why would someone
with my knowledge and skill set be sent all the way to this planet, only to be
inserted into this decrepit body? Zho thought to himself as he looked in the
mirror. Although Costello's tiny boarding room had little else, at least it
had a working bathroom, albeit one shared with other tenants.

Zho ran a diagnostic to confirm that he was now in control of the
host body. He raised Costello's right hand and bent his elbow. He
touched his nose. He turned his head to the left and right. He blinked
his eyes several times. He raised his arms up and down. Although the
results were not conclusive, it appeared that he controlled all of Costello's bodily functions.

Zho again tried to access his mission plan and was unsuccessful. He
tried a third time, to no avail. He ran a full diagnostic, and the results
came back almost immediately. Although his historical and language
databases were fully operational, the file containing his mission plan
had been lost during the Transference.

Zho launched a recovery protocol in an effort to retrieve the file.
While the protocol ran, he continued to stare at the host body in the

mirror. The face of the host was gaunt, and the skin seemed to hang off his facial bones. Although he was very skinny, he had a small pot belly.

He ran a search on the host's physical characteristics to determine if his database was still working. It immediately responded that the host exhibited the classic signs of a human male who had spent years drinking alcohol instead of eating nutritious food. The protocol also informed Zho that the host suffered from symptoms of long-term alcohol abuse: atrophy of the brain, peripheral nerve dysfunction, liver disease, malnutrition, vitamin deficiencies, and pneumonia. Zho theorized that these physical conditions were inhibiting his ability to access Artie and his mission files. Zho queried the recovery protocol to see if it could correct the physical ailments inhabiting the host body. It responded that it would do so, and in the process would greatly improve the strength and efficiency of the body.

The recovery protocol's report on the lost mission plan came back with mixed results. It was still unable to repair or retrieve the file containing his orders; it still only found a sentence fragment: *Find the one called Mike Kelly…*

"That's it? I was able to access that phrase from the moment I awoke from Transference. Certainly, there is other data left in the mission plan. What do I do once I find this 'one called Mike Kelly'?" Costello asked loudly. Zho ran another diagnostic in a futile attempt to restore the plan.

Costello took a deep breath, and the host body gagged. "I must cleanse this body," Zho caused Costello to say out loud to himself to test his vocal control. Zho then caused Costello to turn on the shower and stepped in. Five minutes later, he emerged an almost new man. The host still looked like death, but no longer smelled like it.

A filthy towel was lying on the floor. Costello picked it up and dried off. Next, he found blue jeans and a flannel shirt, also on the floor. Although they reeked of sweat and alcohol, since he didn't have time to wash them, he put them on anyway.

Since he was on an alien planet, uncertain of the dangers that lurked outside the tiny room, Zho concluded that he needed a weapon. In a drawer, he found a screwdriver. He picked it up and made several jabbing motions with the tool. "It will do," Costello said out loud. Then Costello slid the screwdriver into the front pocket of his blue jeans and walked outside.

Costello's apartment was on a quiet street adjacent to a baseball field. He approached two small boys playing catch. They tried to ignore him.

"Excuse me," Costello said.

"We're not supposed to talk to you, mister. Our mom says that you are trouble," the older boy said. The two children shot a look at each other and ran away.

Costello spotted an elderly man mowing his lawn down the street. Costello walked over and politely waited until the man stopped to speak with him.

"Excuse me, sir, my name is Ryan Costello," he said.

"I know who you are. I taught you math in high school," the man said.

"Of course, I remember," Costello said, trying to mask his ignorance. "Could you please tell me how to get to the carnival grounds?"

"If you remember me, then you'll know why I'm telling you to get off my lawn, you piece of garbage," the man continued. "You're lucky I don't sic the dog on you."

Costello walked quickly away from the angry man. Zho wasn't sure what Costello had done to this man to elicit such a strong reaction, but he knew that an altercation would not aid him in his mission, no matter what it turned out to be. He continued walking, looking for someone, anyone, who would help him find the one called Mike Kelly.

CHAPTER SIX

THE MOBSTER

Granville, New York
May 30, 1926

Zho wandered the streets of Granville in the host body, searching for Kelly. Suddenly, a long, black vehicle drove up. The car pulled over, and a nattily dressed, diminutive man in his mid-twenties stepped from the car. Unbeknownst to Zho, this little man was the infamous mobster Jack "Legs" Diamond.

Although Diamond considered himself a giant of the Manhattan crime scene, he was really just a second-rate thug. By the mid 1920s, Diamond had either cheated or tried to cheat every major gangster in New York City. As a result, permission was given to kill "Legs." So, Diamond decided that to avoid gangland execution, he'd move his operation to upstate New York. The old maxim "there is no honor among thieves" was especially true of Diamond; not even criminals could trust him.

"Ryan, my friend! I've been looking all over for you," Diamond said warmly.

"For me?" Costello replied.

"Yeah. You're an important man in my operation. So, when are you gonna do that work on Mike Kelly?" Diamond said.

Zho felt a rush of excitement. *He said "Mike Kelly." Perhaps this being can help me recover my mission,* Zho thought to himself.

"You know the one called Mike Kelly?" Costello asked.

"Yeah," Diamond said.

"So, you know my mission?" Costello asked.

"Do I know your mission? I'm the one who gave you the contract," Diamond replied.

"You gave me a contract?" Costello said each word slowly, processing them.

"To do the hit on Kelly," Diamond continued. "But enough talk out here."

Diamond opened the backseat car door for Costello. At first, Zho didn't know what to do, but he accessed a file on the automobile and realized that the man wanted him to climb inside.

"Please tell me my mission," Costello said.

"Wow, you're all business! I like that. All right. Your 'mission' is to kill Kelly."

Zho was shocked. Although he understood that he had specific orders to find the one called Mike Kelly, Diamond's description made no sense.

I am an anthropologist. I'm no killer. Yes, I competed in Skiirmiish simulations, but why would I kill an Earthling? My culture is opposed to killing anything. What is so dangerous about this Mike Kelly that we would abandon our most sacred beliefs? Zho thought to himself.

"Are you sure that I am to kill the one called Mike Kelly?" Costello asked.

"Am I sure? Why, I'd bet my life on it. You said you'd hit Kelly three weeks ago."

"Three weeks ago?" Costello asked.

"Yeah. So, what kind of weapons you got?" Diamond asked. Costello produced the screwdriver he had found in the boarding room. When

Costello made a jabbing motion with the screwdriver, Diamond burst out laughing.

"Boys, you've got to see this," Diamond said, addressing the front seat passengers. "He's gonna stab Kelly to death with a screwdriver. I told you, this guy is beautiful!"

"But I can't believe that I'm supposed to kill someone," Costello said. Although Zho still didn't understand why he'd been assigned to assassinate an Earthling, he decided to remain quiet until he could sort it all out.

Diamond drove Costello straight to the carnival grounds. Once there, Costello got out of the car.

"Now, remember: your mission is to find Kelly and kill him. Find Kelly and kill him," Diamond said. With that, Costello entered the carnival with his screwdriver tucked in his jeans.

Once Costello was out of earshot, the driver asked Diamond, "Do you really think we can rely on that freak to do the job on Kelly?"

"There's no downside. If he fails, we've still got the fat guy," Diamond said.

CHAPTER SEVEN
THE CARNIVAL

Granville, New York
May 30, 1926

Each Memorial Day, Granville held a carnival followed by a tribute to its fallen and living war veterans. The main draw this year was a boxing exhibition featuring World War hero, Major Mike Kelly. Kelly and his 105th Infantry Regiment were legendary for their feats of heroism in France and Germany during the Great War.

Although Ryan Costello also served with the 105th, fighting side by side with Kelly himself, Costello would not be honored at this or any other celebration. Alcohol had captured him during the war, and he had no recollection of his great sacrifice for the country. In the years following the war, Costello was little more than a daily, staggering reminder that not all of Granville's sons had returned unscathed. Eight years of public intoxication had transformed Costello from a hero, which he indisputably was, into the town drunk, which he now equally and indisputably had become.

But tonight, something was different. Costello was sober at an event honoring the 105th.

The layout of the fairgrounds was simple: freestanding wooden booths stood on each side of the property, from which volunteers operated carnival games. In the center, vendors sold food, drinks, and souvenirs commemorating *Memorial Day, 1926.* All proceeds would benefit the volunteer fire department. The town had no professional firemen. During an emergency, brave volunteers would report for duty at a moment's notice, like minutemen during the Revolutionary War.

As Costello entered the carnival, a slovenly man in his mid-twenties yelled, "Ryan! Ryan!" Despite the intensity and volume of his greeting, Costello walked right past him. This man, a local legend, was Costello's drinking buddy and primary competition for the moniker "town drunk." No one knew his real name. He had wandered into town a few years earlier, referring to himself only as "the G-Man."

There was disagreement among the villagers about the meaning of the nickname. "G-man" was popular slang for an FBI agent, but it was also a name given in Dublin, Ireland to anti-rebel policemen. The Irish immigrants living in Granville certainly hoped that their G-Man fancied himself more of an FBI agent than a British police officer trained in fighting Irish freedom fighters.

During one particularly long Guinness-fueled binge, Costello asked the G-Man how he had earned his nickname.

"Gave it to myself. Yup, gave it to myself, because I'm a Granville man through and through. I'm the G-Man," he had proudly exclaimed, just before passing out.

"Costello, don't you dare walk away from the G-Man!" he shouted drunkenly while staggering behind Costello. "You owe me a boatload of cash. Of course, that's not the only reason why the G-Man wants to speak with you!" The G-Man was legendary for steadying himself just before a spectacular fall, only to teeter over again in the end.

Zho was concerned that if he interacted with one of Costello's friends, he'd be discovered as an impostor, so he caused Costello to walk quickly away, until he was cut off by a line of patrons waiting to purchase cotton candy and ice cream. Since there was nowhere else to go, he turned to face the G-Man, who, like all brave G-men, was in hot pursuit.

"I'm sorry. Do we know each other?" Costello asked.

"Do we know each other? Hell, we've been getting ossified together for the last three years, and you ask if we know each other? Man, Ryan, you're drunker than the G-Man."

"Can you tell me where I can find the one called Mike Kelly?" Costello asked.

"Ryan, what the hell's wrong with you? What's this 'the one called Mike Kelly' crap?"

"Do you know where… Mike Kelly… may be found?" Costello asked, after Zho accessed the language program correcting his syntax.

"How in the hell would the G-Man know where Mike Kelly is? What am I, Kelly's friend now? Mike Kelly likes to drink beers with the G-Man? I don't think so. And the G-Man isn't going to drink with that warmonger anyway. Well, of course, I would drink with him if he was buying the beers, but that's not the point. The point is, *what the hell are you even doing here*? You always said that these Army parties are bullshit!"

"I must find… Mike Kelly," Costello responded, and then walked quickly away.

"Okay, Ryan. Good talking with you. Now that we've had our discussion, can you give me the *two bucks* you owe me? You can't escape a debt owed to the G-Man!" the G-Man yelled.

After Costello disappeared into the crowd, he saw several people throwing dice and money on a table.

"What is this contest of skill?" Costello asked a volunteer manning the table.

"This contest of skill? Look at this clown. Like he's got any money to lose," said the man, laughing at the sight of Costello.

"Where is… Mike Kelly?" Costello asked.

"Kelly should be over there in a little while," the man said, pointing at a stage.

The stage could accommodate all manner of events. This night, it would be used for a presentation honoring the town war heroes, and then modified into a makeshift boxing ring.

Without another word, Costello walked toward the stage. As he passed a beer stand, a volunteer fireman shouted, "Hey, it's our best customer. Costello, do you want a beer? The first drink is on the house."

What an odd custom. Placing a drink on a house? Zho thought to himself as he caused Costello to walk past the stand toward the stage. Beer was sold by volunteers throughout the carnival and was supplied exclusively by Mike Kelly, in his dual capacity as war hero and local bootlegger. Kelly told the firemen that the beer was being sold to them at a deep discount. Of course, this "discounted" price was still an enormous profit to Kelly, for he saw no wrong in profiting off of volunteer firemen. After all, he and his men had smuggled the beer in from Canada at considerable personal risk. They weren't communists. They were entitled to a profit.

As Costello tried to get closer to the stage, a woman carrying a small child greeted him.

"Ryan is that you?" she asked.

He stood silently, startled that someone else had recognized him. The small child in the woman's arms was beaming at Costello like she also knew him. Costello slowly nodded.

"Ryan, you should be in bed! I'm surprised you can even walk," she continued. "I keep telling you, people die from pneumonia." The woman seemed genuinely concerned about him.

"Thank you for your concern, but I am all right," Costello reassured the woman. However, his regenerating voice still sounded raspy, like he was struggling to draw a breath.

"Are you here to watch your friend Major Kelly fight?" the woman asked.

"Major Kelly is my friend?"

"Of course, he's your friend! Who do you think has been paying me to care for you all these weeks? Now, as your nurse, I am telling you to go home and get in bed."

Convinced there was nothing more he could do to reassure the woman, Costello simply turned and walked briskly toward the stage. The woman was left behind holding her child and calling, "Mr. Costello! Ryan!"

As he walked away, he thought to himself, *Kelly is Costello's friend? Kelly paid for a nurse to take care of Costello.*

As he reached the edge of the stage, the evening's program was already in progress. A small man in tan slacks and a gray jacket was standing center stage with a handheld acoustic megaphone. Although in 1926, electric sound amplification was used in big cities, it had not yet made it to Granville. So, the spectators huddled close to the stage to hear the announcer.

"Good evening, ladies and gentlemen, girls and boys. I am your town lawyer and mayor, Jim James." James paused, waiting for applause. None was forthcoming, so he continued. "Tonight, Granville honors its gallant war veterans. Before we meet those brave men, let's give a big round of applause for your Granville town band," James shouted into his megaphone.

As James finished, he motioned stage right to a small brass band consisting of twelve members, each one wearing a blue band uniform with gold piping. The bandleader waved to the crowd, who responded with a smattering of applause. The modest ovation was thundering compared to that received by Mayor James.

"We are all very proud of our two living Civil War veterans," said James. "Gentlemen, please come up to be honored!" Two elderly men, both wearing Union Army uniforms, were helped onto the stage by family members as the band played "The Battle Hymn of the Republic."

When the song ended, the two veterans were helped down from the stage. "And now, would the veterans of the Spanish-American War please come up on stage?" asked the mayor. Five veterans, all of whom were in their late forties, walked onto the stage as the band played "The Charge of the Roosevelt Riders." Mayor James shook hands with each as they exited.

The Mayor then called for the veterans of the World War. It had ended eight years earlier, so these veterans, all men, were in their twenties and thirties. There was a swagger about these men that Costello didn't see in the other veterans. Although the audience cheered respectfully for the veterans from the earlier wars, they cheered far more loudly for this group.

The band was silent as the sixteen veterans of the World War assembled in a row across the front of the stage. On cue, the Granville band started playing "Over There," the iconic song composed by George M. Cohan after he learned that the United States had declared war on Germany.

When Zho heard the song, a wave of emotion rushed through the host body. Zho searched within and identified these human emotions as patriotism and pride. *Strange. Since the host died prior to the Transference, none of these emotions should have survived... yet they are obviously lingering. Why am I now experiencing them?* Zho thought to himself.

Suddenly, aerial fireworks erupted behind the audience, illuminating the night sky. When the crowd turned to watch the fireworks, each saw a lone rider on horseback appear through the smoke. The rider wore a U.S. Army uniform with a Medal of Honor draped around his neck.

"Ladies and gentlemen, please welcome Major Mike Kelly!" the mayor shouted into his megaphone. When the audience heard that the rider was Major Kelly, they cheered wildly.

Kelly guided his steed slowly through his adoring fans until he was close enough to dismount onto the center of the stage, where his men stood at attention. Once on stage, the sixteen veterans of the 105th saluted the major in unison.

Zho had found his man.

In his dress military uniform, the strapping Kelly looked every bit the part of an epic American war hero. He was obviously loved by his men, who surrounded him on the stage. Kelly radiated confidence, which was a prerequisite for anyone egotistical enough to ride horseback into a crowded event while aerial fireworks exploded around him. Kelly smiled and waved to his friends and neighbors, completely unaware that he could now be in danger.

When he saw Costello in the audience, Kelly smiled broadly and motioned for him to join the other heroes of the 105th on stage. Kelly told the enormous man to his right, Jim Moyer, to move aside and make room for Costello. Kelly gestured as if to say, "Ryan, come up here and take your rightful place by my side."

Zho again felt strong emotions surge through the host body. He actually felt a desire to accept the major's invitation but resisted. He had a mission to complete and would not be deterred by anything, particularly the feigned acts of kindness by the one called Mike Kelly. Kelly looked genuinely disappointed when Costello held his ground, rejecting the invitation. However, for Kelly this was a minor setback, and he jumped right back into his World War hero persona.

As the band completed its rendition of "Over There," Mayor James walked to the center of the stage and took up the position next to Kelly that had just been vacated for Costello. James was a politician, so any association with Kelly would enhance his standing in the community. Before speaking to the crowd, James whispered to Kelly, "Major, if you would just come by my law office, I have some distributorship ideas that would really expand your business."

Kelly did not respond. When James realized that Kelly was intentionally ignoring him, he raised his megaphone and said, "Well, that concludes our festivities honoring our war veterans. We will now take a fifteen-minute break while our hard-working town employees turn this stage into a boxing ring." When James said the words "boxing ring," he turned toward Major Kelly and acted as though he was boxing with the champ. Kelly purposely ignored the mayor and walked off the stage in the opposite direction.

During the fifteen-minute break, the crowd briefly dissipated, which allowed Costello to move even closer to ringside. He reached down to his waist and confirmed that the screwdriver was still in place. It was. Once he was near enough to Kelly, he would use it to complete his mission – if he could only be absolutely certain of what his actual mission was.

CHAPTER EIGHT
THE CHALLENGERS

Granville, New York
May 30, 1926

"This is the hottest ticket in Washington County!" Mayor James exclaimed. The first challenger, Bobby Billow, stood ringside next to his opponent, Mike Kelly.

It was anticipated that the audience would exceed one thousand spectators – a huge event for this little farm town on the New York-Vermont border. In 1926, the only sport in America more popular than boxing was baseball. And the only athlete more famous than heavyweight boxing champion Jack Dempsey was Babe Ruth himself.

As the two fighters stood in the ring, it was obvious how one-sided the bout would be. The champion outweighed the wiry Billow by at least seventy-five pounds. Hardly a fair fight; but then again, this was the Granville Memorial Day Celebration, not a heavyweight title fight. There was a limited pool of combatants from which to choose. As long as the crowd was happy with the matchups, the local promoter didn't focus on size differential.

Of course, crowds invariably attract politicians trying to look like "common folk," and Granville Mayor James was serving as both ring announcer and official timekeeper. After they indicated that they were ready to proceed, Mayor James introduced the two combatants:

"In this corner, weighing in at 142 pounds, is a fantastic barber. He's the owner of Billow's Barber Shop, where you can get a great shave and an even better haircut for only twenty-five cents: Bobby Billow!"

Billow had written his own introduction, which was his one condition to fighting Kelly. Billow didn't expect to win. All he asked was that his barbershop would get a plug in front of the anticipated "gigantic" crowd. Following his introduction, Billow playfully danced around the ring, mimicking a real fighter. He was a natural underdog, and the crowd loved him.

Mayor James then pointed at Kelly. "And in this corner, weighing 217 pounds, is your champion. The former commander of the Fighting 105th. The winner of the Medal of Honor for his heroism in the Great War. With a record of fifty-two wins and no losses, he's the undefeated Washington County heavyweight boxing champion, Major M*i-i-i*ke Kelly!"

Mayor James held the "i" for an extended period, letting his voice rise to a crescendo as he finished Kelly's introduction. Cheers of "105th!" and "Kelly! Kelly!" filled the night air.

"This is a three-round exhibition bout," the mayor expertly shouted into his megaphone. "The Washington County title is not on the line. If the challenger can last three rounds with the champion, the challenger wins fifty dollars courtesy of the town of Granville!"

The bell rang. The two fighters touched gloves at the center of the ring. Immediately, Billow began to run around the ring, trying to escape Kelly. This was a time-honored strategy employed by wounded boxers, where it was said that the injured fighter would "hop on his bicycle." If he survived until the end of the round, he was "saved by the bell."

However, in this match, no punches had been thrown and Billow was already "on his bicycle." Kelly laughed as he methodically pursued the smaller Billow, who was shamelessly already trying to run out the clock.

Although deploying this tactic at the start of a professional boxing match would have enraged paying spectators, the Granville fans found it amusing. After all, no one expected Billow to win; he was an excellent barber, but he was no prizefighter. But like so many other people, he needed money, and that fifty-dollar prize would pay Billow's rent for at least three months. So, the town barber was grateful for any extra "work" he could find.

Zho watched intently from the audience. It seemed as though he was the only one in the crowd who wasn't laughing. He found it all very sad. Kelly had talent; this was evident from the fluid way he moved across the ring or threw his left jab. But Kelly was wasting his talent fighting Billow. What made it even more pathetic was that the barber had no idea that he was about to be knocked out. Indeed, as he danced playfully around the ring, occasionally feigning a punch in the direction of Kelly, Billow seemed to believe that his "strategy" was working. But it was obvious to anyone who understood boxing that Kelly was simply putting on a show.

At the end of the first round, Billow even appeared to land two jabs. The crowd, most of whom knew little about boxing, believed that Billow may have even injured Kelly. However, the barber's punches had merely glanced off Kelly's gloves, and he was only pretending to be stunned. When the bell rang, ending round one, Kelly was "helped" back into his corner by his seconds.

In the one minute between rounds, Kelly casually guzzled two bottles of beer, one after the other, in full view of the audience

As the second round began, Billow emerged from his corner supremely confident. Kelly's theatrics at the end of round one had convinced Billow that he could exchange punches with the major. Billow led with an overhand right, which Kelly easily deflected with his left glove. Kelly answered with a stiff left jab, striking Billow square on the nose.

Although one jab would have done minimal damage to a profession-al fighter, the barber had never been hit like that before, and he fell backward onto his butt. The crowd roared with laughter. Major Kelly had knocked Billow down with a single left jab.

The referee began to count, "One, two, three," as Billow slowly climbed to his feet. Wobbly and dazed, Billow wisely decided that he had exchanged enough leather with Kelly and immediately got back "on his bicycle." This caused the crowd to laugh even harder. Billow looked out at the audience and shrugged as if to say, "Can you blame me?"

Unfortunately for Billow, Kelly was now feeling a little drunk. And as most everyone in Granville knew, the jovial major was one mean drunk. Bored and getting angry, Kelly began to aggressively pursue his oppo-nent. He didn't have to chase Billow; he just had to "cut off the ring," a simple maneuver for an experienced fighter. As Billow backed up, Kelly didn't directly attack him. Instead, if Billow tried to move left, Kelly stepped right and forward, toward Billow. Conversely, if Billow moved right, Kelly stepped left and forward.

With Billow backed into a corner, Kelly could now punch the barber at will; but Kelly milked the ending of the fight. Each time he hit Billow, Kelly would turn and smile to the crowd. Once he even turned away from Billow, raising both of his gloves in premature celebration.

Kelly decided that it was now time for the first fight to end. He faked his left jab, and when Billow tried to block it, Kelly struck Billow flush with a right cross. The barber's knees buckled, and he collapsed on the canvas.

The crowd erupted for the county champion. Kelly stood over his friend while the referee counted to ten. Once a knockout was declared, Kelly kneeled beside Billow until he was able to stand. Kelly then helped the barber to his feet.

After the two men were upright, Kelly put his arm around Billow and yelled to the crowd, "This man needs a beer!" The crowd roared with approval. Kelly looked out at two firemen who were selling beer adjacent to the ring and yelled, "Tonight this man drinks for free!"

Two of Kelly's men entered the ring, helping Billow through the ring ropes. When Billow reached the stairs, the G-Man jumped up ringside holding two of Billow's free beers, handed one to Billow, and downed the other himself. The crowd cheered raucously. Not one to disappoint, while steadying himself with the top rope, Billow raised his bottle in the air, made a toast, and guzzled his beer while the crowd egged him on.

There was a lull in the action as Kelly's second opponent made his way to the ring. Kelly had agreed that he would not learn the identity of the challengers until right before each match. This was billed as an additional handicap for the county champion. While Kelly waited for his next fight, he stood in his corner drinking from a brown bottle.

Kelly's seconds at ringside, Father O'Brien and Owen Feeney, knew little about boxing. Their job was to fetch whatever Kelly wanted. At the major's instruction, Feeney motioned for the G-Man to bring Kelly another beer, and he promptly complied.

The ease with which Kelly could hold and drink from a beer bottle while wearing boxing gloves was, in a way, impressive. He obviously had had years of practice. As Kelly quickly downed his fourth beer in a very short period of time, Zho noticed that the once amiable Kelly was becoming quite ornery. And by the time the mayor introduced the second challenger, Kelly went from being angry to downright mean.

His second opponent was Jim Moyer, the enormous man who had been standing on stage next to Kelly. Moyer was also a Kelly friend and confidant, and they had served together in the 105th. He was now Kelly's bodyguard and enforcer.

When Kelly heard that Moyer was his next opponent, he handed his now empty bottle to Feeney and motioned for Moyer to meet him in the middle of the ring. Visibly angry, Kelly faced down his bodyguard. "What the hell do you think you're doing?" Kelly yelled.

"I need the money," Moyer answered sheepishly.

"You always need money," Kelly snarled. "But you won't win it here by embarrassing me. And you haven't been watching my fights if you think you stand a chance."

"Boss, there's just no other way for me to get cash this quickly." Moyer continued, "I promise I won't hurt you,"

"You could have asked me for it," Kelly screamed, his anger building. He was now face-to-face with Moyer – or, more accurately, the top of Kelly's head was level with Moyer's neck.

"You should have asked me for the money. I would have given it to you. But you're not getting it in *my* ring!" Kelly screamed even more loudly.

Then Kelly paused for a moment before erupting in fury. "Wait a minute. Did you just say, 'I promise I won't hurt you?' *You promise you won't hurt me?*"

Kelly was now red-faced and shouting uncontrollably. O'Brien and Feeney pulled him back into his corner. When he broke free, Kelly began pacing around the ring, shouting, "Go ahead. I want you to try to hurt me! Please, please try to hurt me, because I'm gonna beat the hell out of you. I'm gonna beat the HELL out of you!"

Moyer realized that he had so enraged the now drunken Kelly that it was in his best interest to simply withdraw from the fight. But it was too late. Mayor James had already walked to the center ring to introduce the combatants. However, before he could do so, Kelly rushed at the mayor and knocked the megaphone out of his hand. "We don't need introductions. Just ring the bell. Ring the bell!" Kelly screamed.

James ducked and ran out of the ring, leaving his beloved megaphone behind, and rang the bell to start round one. Kelly sprinted across the ring as Moyer raised his left glove, under the mistaken belief that the major would touch gloves before starting the match.

Instead, Kelly threw a left-right roundhouse combination into Moyer's solar plexus, causing Moyer to keel over. With Moyer's head now lowered and exposed, Kelly punched him repeatedly to the head with alternating left and right hooks.

It was like chopping down a tree. Within a matter of seconds, Moyer crumpled to the canvas, and the referee counted Moyer out as he lay motionless in the ring.

After Kelly was declared the winner, he kneeled down next to his employee just as he had done for Billow – but this time, Kelly screamed uncontrollably.

"This is how betrayal feels! Next time you need money, you come see me. I'll help you. But I will not tolerate betrayal. Do you hear me? I will not tolerate betrayal!" Kelly screamed.

Moyer, semi-conscious, did not respond.

The crowd looked on, stunned. There was not a sound as the words, "*I will not tolerate betrayal!*" hung in the air. Few people had ever seen Kelly so violently enraged.

After a few moments, a smattering of fans in the audience began to applaud, thinking that they had seen a different side of Kelly. This was Mike Kelly, the warrior. Or more accurately, Mike Kelly the psychotic, angry drunk who was too "manly" to admit that he was also still shell shocked from the war.

The Mayor tentatively climbed back into the ring to retrieve his megaphone. He then whispered to Kelly, "I'm sorry, Major, sir, but that's it. No one else is willing to fight you."

"That's it? But I'm not finished yet. Hell, I'm just getting started!" Kelly roared. He walked to the edge of the ring and looked out to the audience.

"Anyone else? Surely someone has the guts to step into the ring with me," Kelly said in a menacing voice.

But after the way that he had just pounded the giant Moyer in the ring, naturally there were no takers.

Kelly scanned the crowd like a predator surveying his prey. That's when he again spotted Costello. Kelly stood motionless for a moment, debating whether to leave the still recovering Costello alone. But Kelly was drunk and angry, and he really wanted to beat someone else up. So, he decided to lure his old friend and subordinate into the ring.

"Is that really Ryan Costello?" Kelly shouted.

"It's me," Costello shouted back as best he could in his gradually regenerating voice.

"Well, praise the Lord," Kelly said as he made the sign of the cross with his right hand, which was still inside his boxing glove. "I thought you were dead."

"So did I," Costello yelled back. Although Costello was serious, the crowd thought he was joking and roared with laughter.

"It's good to see you standing out there," Kelly continued.

"It's good to be standing," Costello replied, again inadvertently making the crowd laugh.

Kelly resented the way Costello had won over his audience. In his mind, Kelly was no one's straight man. "I'm flattered that you got out of your sickbed to watch my boxing match," Kelly said.

"Boxing, huh?" Costello continued, "Is that what you call what you were doing up there?" Although Costello was speaking literally, the crowd, believing that he was poking fun at Kelly's exhibition, laughed even louder.

Kelly was livid. It was bad enough that Costello was stealing Kelly's spotlight with self-deprecating jokes, but now he was insulting Kelly's boxing.

"It's too bad that you've been so sick." Kelly continued, "Otherwise, you could get into this ring and show me how it's done. If you could have lasted three rounds, you would have won fifty dollars."

"May I ask, Major, what would I do with fifty dollars?" Costello asked. Kelly again misunderstood, thinking Costello was now attempting to negotiate a better fee to fight that evening.

"Tell you what, Costello. If you'll fight me tonight, I'll make the prize one hundred dollars. And I'll put the county championship on the line," Kelly said. This drew "oohs" from the crowd, followed by applause.

"Point of order! The Town Council only appropriated a fifty-dollar cash prize. I cannot authorize you to exceed that amount," the mayor hollered into his acoustic megaphone. The nervousness of the mayor and his use of the megaphone drew laughs from the crowd.

"You've been sick, Ryan. I mean really, really sick. Are you sure you want to get into the ring with me tonight?" Kelly questioned, trying to remind the crowd that he cared about Costello's well-being.

"I'm fine," Costello said

"You're all witnesses! He was sick until I offered him one hundred dollars. Now he says he's fine. Hell, for one hundred dollars, Costello would probably get into the ring with Jack Dempsey himself!" Kelly acted as though it was all a joke, although it certainly appeared that Kelly was trying to protect his public image before beating up a sickly friend.

"Are you sober?" Kelly questioned.

"I am sober."

"Ryan Costello is sober. There's a first time for everything," Kelly said, as he laughed heartily at his own joke, and the audience laughed with him. Costello still did not react. But since Kelly believed that the crowd was now returning to his side, he wasn't going to let up.

"Costello, how much money do you have right now?" Kelly asked.

Costello pulled a handful of loose change and three one-dollar bills from his pants pockets. "I have three dollars and seventy cents."

"Three-seventy. Wow. It's a big night for you, isn't it?" Kelly joked. No one laughed, probably because that was more than many of the spectators had. Few Granville residents lived like the Kellys.

"Tell you what. You put that up in a straight bet," Kelly proposed.

"I'll put a hundred of my own money into the pot, and the mayor will put up the fifty that the town 'appropriated.'"

Kelly looked at Mayor James with a big smile on his face. "Can you authorize that, Mayor?"

The Mayor nodded and spoke into his megaphone. "Yes. It is officially authorized!"

"That's a one-hundred-and-fifty-dollar bet against your three dollars and seventy cents," Kelly said. "I'll also put the title on the line. But I've got one condition. We don't limit the fight to three rounds. We fight until one of us is knocked out. Knocked out cold on the canvas. No referee or anything else can stop the fight. You got the guts for that, wise guy?" Kelly challenged. Given that Costello was still recovering from his serious illness, Kelly didn't think it was possible for Costello to accept those terms.

My mission requires that I gain Kelly's confidence. Strangely, it has been observed that one way to garner favor with human alpha males like Kelly is to best them physically. So, since I have been challenged, logic dictates that I must severely beat Kelly, Zho thought to himself.

"We fight until one of us is knocked unconscious. I accept your terms," Costello replied emphatically. He dropped his screwdriver and bolted up to the ring, showing absolutely no sign that he was frightened or sick.

The crowd immediately began cheering the new challenger. The fact that Costello had so eagerly jumped into the ring, combined with the audience urging such insubordination, further enraged Kelly. He began storming around the ring, shouting at anyone foolish enough to make eye contact with him.

"I want to make sure that everyone understands the rules. No one stops this fight until one of us is knocked out on the canvas," Kelly screamed at the crowd, and then rushed up to the referee until they were nose-to-nose.

"You heard me. I warned him," Kelly continued, "But he wouldn't listen. He said he was willing to fight me until one of us was unconscious. So, don't you dare stop this match until one of us is on the mat! Do you understand me?"

When the referee tried to ignore Kelly, he shouted even louder. "I said, *do you understand me?*"

"I understand," the referee replied, holding back his anger.

Kelly then rushed over to Father O'Brien, who was standing in Kelly's corner. "Father, Costello's gonna get himself killed. Can't you talk some sense into him?"

But the priest realized that this Kelly fight could be the answer to his most recent prayers. "The gospel says that a man reaps what he sows," O'Brien responded dismissively.

Although Kelly wondered how the priest could be so coldly indifferent to Costello's survival, this was not his most immediate problem. Costello was now standing in the opposite corner.

Has he gotten taller since he got sick? Is that even possible? Kelly thought to himself as he looked over at Costello.

Costello was standing across from Kelly, and he certainly didn't look sick or intimidated by the major. And why would he be? Costello's physical movements were now controlled by Tashan Zho. Zho had spent countless hours in Skiirmiish simulators back home on Dagan. Actual combat sports had been banned centuries before, but citizens were still permitted to work out in holodecks and simulators. As an academic, Zho had always theorized that boxing and Skiirmiishing were interchangeable skills. In fact, after watching Kelly's first two bouts, Zho was pleased at how remarkably similar boxing movements were to Skiirmiishing. He had completed every level of Skiirmiish simulations and was legendary among its enthusiasts.

Zho had always wanted to Skiirmiish an actual live opponent, but such physical contact was strictly forbidden by the High Council. Now, here on this remote planet in this frail but quickly regenerating body, he'd finally get to use Skiirmiishing maneuvers that he'd spent years perfecting. And his colleagues at the university had scoffed at the amount of time he spent in the simulators.

Of course, he would end the Skiirmiish before he actually hurt the one called Mike Kelly. Suddenly, Zho was shocked to hear another voice within the host body.

"*Kelly actually invited us into the ring,*" the new voice said. "*This is going to be even easier than I thought.*"

CHAPTER NINE

THE MAIN EVENT

Granville, New York
May 30, 1926

Costello stood in his corner, wearing the same clothes he had worn for years: blue jeans, a red flannel shirt, and work boots. Zho figured that the voice in his head must be a remnant of host memory, and so he decided to ignore it and focus on the Skiirmiish.

He removed his shirt, revealing an enormous scar in the center of his chest. It looked as though someone had either stabbed him or performed a rudimentary form of surgery on him. The crowd gasped. Zho could feel that the host's feet were starting to become too big for his boots. *"Is the host growing? Do Earthlings continue to grow, even as adults?"* Zho wondered. Costello removed his boots, apparently intending to fight barefoot, and stood waiting for the bell.

The bell rang. When the two men met in the center of the ring, Kelly was already talking. As they touched gloves, Kelly said, "Ryan, it's so good to see – "

Before the major finished speaking, Costello hit him in the face with a thunderous left jab. Although Kelly had fought in over fifty local fights, he had never been hit that hard before. He staggered back, surprised that Costello had stunned him with a single blow.

For the first time that evening, Kelly was in a real fight.

So, that's how it feels to actually strike someone. I like it! Zho thought to himself.

The citizens of Dagan had been taught since childhood that they had evolved beyond the use of physical violence. All types of contact sports were strictly forbidden, and children were instructed to solve conflicts with words, not actions. Suddenly, centuries of repressed physical urges were unleashed in Zho. The two boxers circled the ring. When Kelly landed a left jab, the crowd cheered wildly. Although Costello was not hurt, he feigned injury, covering his face with his gloves in a mock defensive posture.

As in the Billow fight, Kelly celebrated prematurely by turning away to wave at the crowd. But Kelly was no longer fighting the barber. When he turned back, Costello hit him with a right hook to the jaw and followed it up with a left hook to the same spot.

Kelly staggered backwards as his smile disappeared. It did not return. Those two punches already left Kelly unsteady and vulnerable to a knockout. But Costello couldn't capitalize because he was having physical problems of his own: he had lost the use of his left arm.

This body should be working by now. Zho ran the recovery protocol in an effort to reestablish control over the left arm and tried in vain to throw a left hook. But the host's left arm would no longer respond to his commands.

Fortunately, with his first two punches, Costello had already taken much of the fight out of Kelly. Zho was confident that he'd be able to finish Kelly even if he was forced to punch exclusively with his right hand. Indeed, given the sudden paralysis in his left arm, he had little choice.

Kelly didn't realize how much trouble he was already in. Even though he was wobbly from the two hooks to his jaw, he was still confident that he would easily win the fight. Still, in an effort to buy time while he recovered, Kelly tied up Costello, using what he believed was his superior size and strength to wear the challenger down.

After all, Costello was on his deathbed earlier today. How much stamina could he have? Kelly thought to himself. Kelly wrapped his arms around Costello and leaned hard against the lighter man. Once he had Costello in a clench, Kelly again started talking.

"Ryan, when did you learn to fight like this – "

Instantly, Costello broke free, stepped back, and caught Kelly with a right uppercut. Kelly staggered back a step, dazed from the punch. Since his left arm was still useless, Costello followed with an overhand right that landed on the bridge of Kelly's nose.

Kelly's knees buckled. For the first time in his boxing career, the Washington County Champion dropped to the canvas.

The crowd was stunned. No one had ever seen Kelly knocked down before. Now he was lying motionless in the ring, having been floored by the town drunk.

Zho again heard an inner voice. It was furious with him for ending the fight before completing his mission. *What did you do? What did you do? Why would you knock him out before we could finish him?* the voice demanded.

Zho tried to ignore the voice and waited in a neutral corner while the referee started his count: "One, two, three, four." By the count of seven, Kelly had still not moved. Then, although only one minute fifty-seven seconds had elapsed, the bell sounded, ending the three-minute round. Kelly was "saved by the bell."

The early bell was no miracle. Mayor James, who was also the official timekeeper, intentionally rang the bell early, presumably to help his friend, Kelly. However, by saving Kelly, James had unwittingly delivered the major to an opponent capable of beating him to death.

When the bell rang ending round one, Costello walked to his corner, smiling. It was a strange reaction for someone who had just been robbed of a knockout and a hefty prize by an early bell.

Kelly's seconds, Feeney and O'Brien, entered the ring and helped their champion to his corner, where they administered smelling salts. This seemed to bring Kelly around.

"What the hell *is* that over there?" Kelly shouted, pointing to the opposite corner at Costello. "That isn't Ryan Costello! It couldn't be! Father O'Brien, didn't I send you over there to give him Last Rites earlier today?"

"I'm not at liberty to discuss that," the priest meekly replied. Costello had received Last Rites just hours before. Now, not only was he still alive, he was beating the life out of Kelly. Costello was one of Kelly's lifelong friends. He knew that Costello was no boxer.

"We all know that Costello can't fight like that. So, what the hell is that over there?" Kelly shouted again. The three men looked across the ring at Costello.

Sitting in the opposite corner, Costello stared blankly back at Kelly. Despite the summer heat that evening, Costello was not sweating or even breathing heavily.

Costello's drinking buddy, the G-Man, climbed up ringside, proclaiming, "Have no fear, the G-Man is here, and the one thing the G-Man knows is boxing. Here. Drink this," the G-Man loudly proclaimed as he handed Costello a brown glass bottle.

Costello took a drink and immediately spat it out. "What the hell is that?" he yelled.

"It's Guinness. Guinness is good for you. It gives you strength," the G-Man responded.

"Guinness? Beer? You gave me *beer*?" Costello said.

"It's not beer. It's ale," the G-Man said defiantly. Although a very important distinction to the G-Man, it mattered little to Costello.

"Bring me some water." Costello threw the bottle down on the ground.

This all occurred within earshot of the other spectators. "Did you hear that? Ryan Costello won't drink Guinness. He says he wants to drink water!" the G-Man yelled to the crowd, who roared with laughter at the thought of Costello drinking water.

"He refuses to drink alcohol. Since when did Costello become a stinkin' Mormon?" the G-Man yelled.

Costello did not react. He simply grabbed the G-Man and said ominously, "This body needs water."

"But where is the G-Man going to get any water around here?" the G-Man asked, visibly frightened.

A volunteer fireman named "Packy" Kennelly spoke up: "I've got water on the truck." Kennelly ran to his truck, filled a bucket with water, and ran it up to ringside for Costello. But before Costello could drink any, the bell rang to signal the start of the second round.

Kelly met Costello in the middle of the ring. Kelly's mood was now deathly serious, a noticeable difference from the first round. The trademark Mike Kelly smile, which had been ever-present during the Billow fight, was now replaced with a look of determination and anger.

As the two men met in the center of the ring, Kelly said, "Ryan, I know you've been sick. Please don't make me hurt you."

"I promise. You won't hurt me," Costello responded dispassionately. Costello tried to throw a jab with his left arm, but it still wouldn't respond.

Zho then instructed the host body to do something that he had learned and perfected in a Skiirmiish simulator back home, but that no one in 1926 Earth had ever seen before. As was customary for the time, Costello had been boxing in an orthodox boxing stance. That meant he had his left hand and foot forward and defended his face with his right hand.

Because his left arm was no longer responding to Zho, he had the host body effortlessly switch into a left-handed, or "southpaw," boxing stance so that his right hand and foot were now forward and closest to Kelly. From then on, Costello continued to box lefthanded. Kelly was shocked by this maneuver.

"What the hell are you doing?" Kelly shouted.

The southpaw boxing stance was ideal for Costello's current affliction. Since his left arm was not responding, and since the jab is the most commonly thrown punch in boxing, by fighting southpaw Costello could now jab Kelly with his stronger right hand.

This tactic surprised Kelly – a man accustomed to defending against the traditional style. Kelly was almost defenseless as Costello hit the major with four consecutive stiff right jabs to the face, each snapping Kelly's head back. The crowd gasped as Kelly again dropped to the canvas. For the second time in two rounds, their champion had been knocked down.

Although he was down, Kelly had never been knocked out before, and he wasn't going to start today. By the time the referee had reached seven, Kelly was on one knee, and when the referee said "nine," Kelly was on his feet.

As soon as the referee called for the fight to resume, Costello tried to punch Kelly, and it was now Kelly's turn to "hop on his bicycle." Costello, whose legs were only responding intermittently, attempted to cut off the ring and prevent Kelly's escape.

After two unsuccessful attempts, Costello finally trapped Kelly in his own corner. Once he caught him, Costello threw right punch after right punch, most of which hit Kelly's gloves. Even though only about one in four punches hit solidly on the jaw or the side of his head, they still severely hurt the already dazed Kelly.

Costello even switched from the southpaw stance back into an orthodox stance so that he could throw a right cross and a right hook, thereby generating the greatest amount of power as he struck the defenseless Kelly. All Kelly could do was to lay back against the turnbuckle with his gloves up, hoping to survive the onslaught.

When Costello hit Kelly in the head with one last thunderous overhand right, the champion appeared to be knocked out on his feet – although, lodged as he was against his own corner, his body couldn't fall to the canvas.

Suddenly, the image of a little girl shot into Zho's mind, causing him to momentarily halt the beating. *Why a little girl?* Zho wondered. *Was this another lingering memory from the host body? Or could this be part of my mission file, finally restored by the recovery protocol?*

Zho searched within and found the name *Nora*. Unsure of how or even whether this "Nora" affected his mission, Zho decided to ask Kelly.

"*Who is Nora?*" Costello shouted. When Kelly didn't respond, Costello became enraged. It was as though the voice within him was reasserting control of the host body.

Zho heard the voice urging him on. "*That's it. Now kill him. Kill him!*" Zho was himself surprised when the host body struck the helpless champion with *a left hook. The host controls the left arm and can throw a left hook?* Zho searched the Transference Protocol Manual for reference to any similar defects.

At this point, Zho honestly didn't know who or what was in charge of the host body. Costello's left arm again hit Kelly with a straight overhand left, rocking his head back into the turnbuckle. Although Kelly should have dropped to the canvas, Costello intentionally drove his shoulder into his opponent to prop Kelly back up into the corner.

Father O'Brien pleaded with Costello to stop. "Costello, he's your friend. He's been good to you. He's your friend!" O'Brien then looked up to heaven. "Oh, dear Lord, what have *I* done? What have *I* done?"

"You don't have much time left, Kelly. Tell me who Nora is," Costello screamed at the top of his lungs.

Kelly was barely conscious, and it was unclear whether he could have responded, even if he knew who Nora was.

"Stop the fight!" Owen Feeney threw in a white towel as he yelled at the referee. "Kelly's out on his feet." But the referee ignored Feeney and allowed the match to continue, just as Kelly had publicly ordered him to do before the match.

Mike Kelly, the criminal, employed a small army of loyal men whose job was to protect Kelly, his family, and his operation. But after hearing Kelly berate the referee before the match, none of his men had the courage to stop the fight. They had all heard the orders from the major that they were not to interfere.

Feeney, who was also Costello's superior officer during the World War, even tried "ordering" Costello to stop. "Stand down, Costello!" Feeney shouted. "Do you hear me, soldier? Stand down!"

But Costello had no intention of stopping. Kelly was now bleeding profusely from cuts above and below both eyes, and it was obvious even to the most casual observer that he was unconscious. The crowd, who had come to watch a boxing exhibition, was horrified at the beating that Kelly had already sustained.

Costello took a deep breath and shouted, "Last chance, Kelly! Tell me where Nora is."

Suddenly, a young woman came running from the audience all the way to ringside. People were so focused on the carnage in the ring that no one noticed her until she was leaping over the ropes.

At first it looked as though she was entering the match as a combatant. But after she hollered at the top of her lungs, it was apparent that she was an infatuated young woman.

"I love you, Ryan Costello!" she screamed.

Zho searched the host memory and determined that Costello had absolutely no idea who she was. The woman threw her arms around Costello and held him in a crushing embrace. A literally crushing embrace. The woman was so powerful that Costello could not move a muscle.

"You are off mission, analyst. Do you hear me? You are off mission. You are not to harm the one called Mike Kelly," the woman said sternly in Costello's ear. With that, she released him and exited the ring as quickly as she had appeared.

Costello simply stood there, trying to decide how to proceed. Then he turned to Kelly, as though in a moment of conscience he was deciding whether to spare Kelly's life.

In fact, it had nothing to do with conscience. During the woman's embrace, she had caused something in Zho to simply "switch off." In addition, she had activated an enhanced recovery protocol that, in theory, would counteract whatever force had wrested control of part of Costello's body from Zho. Zho now had no awareness of his surroundings, or even that he was still in a Skiirmiish.

To the audience, it all looked surreal. Costello stood confused and frozen in the center of the ring as Kelly leaned back, almost lifeless, against the turnbuckle. No one paid attention to the young woman as she easily leaped over the ring ropes, landed in stride on the ground and disappeared into the crowd.

As the two fighters stood helplessly across from each other in the ring, Costello's hands slowly dropped to his sides. Costello stood rigid as his eyes blinked rapidly, arms twitching ever so slightly. Although each spectator would later recall the events a little differently, most agreed that if the fight had not been stopped, Costello would have killed Kelly.

Owen Feeney begged Kelly to do something, anything, to defend himself. When Kelly still did not respond, Feeney took matters into his own hands by pushing Kelly from the back to get him up and off the turnbuckle.

With Kelly on his feet, the crowd roared back to life and began yelling for the champion. Kelly, barely conscious, stumbled to the center of the ring and threw a punch at the motionless challenger.

Although Kelly's blow missed the intended target, it did glance off of Costello's right shoulder. This caused the still-twitching fighter to fall backwards in the ring, striking his head hard against the canvas-covered cement floor. As Costello laid unconscious, his arms and legs shaking, the referee counted to ten and declared Kelly the winner by knockout.

The referee walked over to Kelly and raised his right arm into the air. After Kelly was awarded the fight, he collapsed next to Costello, who was still twitching in the middle of the ring. Volunteer firemen carrying stretchers entered the ring. Mike Kelly's wife, Mary, also arrived to care for her husband, as did several men of the 105th Regiment, who had been sitting at ringside, cheering for their commanding officer.

Since Mike Kelly was barely conscious, Mary took charge of the many men who had entered the ring to protect him and, if necessary, subdue Costello. Several firemen rushed to Costello's side to ensure that Kelly's men did not harm him.

"Please take Mr. Costello to our truck. We will care for him in our home," Mary Kelly instructed the firemen. When the firemen looked suspicious of her motives, she became enraged.

"How dare you look at me like that! We are a Christian family. We will care for Mr. Costello. Tell Dr. Cooper to meet us at the house," Mary Kelly ordered.

Although the firemen were understandably reluctant to turn the now vulnerable Costello over to Kelly's men, they had little choice. With that, the challenger, Ryan Costello, and the champion, Major Mike Kelly, were carried out of the ring on stretchers. The major would lie unconscious next to Costello in the back of the family truck until they reached the Kelly home, where the major would receive excellent medical care.

The fate of Tashan Zho, and by extension, of all mankind was yet to be determined.

CHAPTER TEN

THE KELLY HOME

Granville, New York
June 1, 1926

Following the fight, Zho slept for hours and awoke with a pounding headache and a piercing ache in his lower back. He had never felt like that after a match before. He had always presumed that there would be physical consequences to fighting an actual live opponent. On Dagan, he had even heard rumors of unsanctioned live Skiirmiish matches, though they were strictly forbidden by the High Council. But of course, there were no headaches following a simulated match.

Since Kelly had barely laid a glove on Costello, the host body, during their match, Zho was surprised at how much his head hurt still hurt. Zho checked whether the host body was again responding to his commands. He tried to move his arms and legs, but they did not comply.

That's strange. Control of bodily functions should be fully restored by now.

Zho then realized that he was tied to the bed. He tried again to move the host body's arms and legs and concluded that each appendage was firmly strapped down. Zho was oddly relieved that the body may be functioning properly but concerned that someone or something had tied him to a bed.

Zho checked whether the recovery protocol had restored his mission plan. Unfortunately, it had only been able to recover a few additional fragments:

Find the one called Mike Kelly... Nora...
Protect Kelly family... Craig Colony... extraction will devastate
planet.

Costello now understood that at least part of his mission was to protect the Kelly family, but he still didn't know how this would relate to the yet to be identified Nora. Was Costello to protect the Kelly family *from* Nora? Or was Nora an ally who would assist him with his mission? If so, who would they be protecting the Kelly family from? And what was this Craig Colony? Zho searched the host memories but found nothing useful.

After considering these issues, Zho decided that his best course of action was to stay close to the Kelly family until answers to these questions revealed themselves, or until the recovery protocol was able to restore his corrupted mission file.

He looked around the room. He was lying in a bedroom. He wasn't sure if the host's unfamiliarity with the room was the result of the Transference malfunction or because the host body had never been here before.

He ran a diagnostic. It promptly responded suggesting that he identify any artwork in the room. He was surprised that he was able to do so. A print of the Virgin Mary holding the baby Jesus was hanging on the wall. "Even though the host had not been a 'good Irish Catholic' for many years, I recognize this print from the host memory. It is in the homes of many Catholics," Zho caused Costello to say aloud to himself.

Zho was pleased by this result. Not only had he accessed the host's memory, but his verbal, audible response was clear, and his language program confirmed that he had used the proper syntax. His access to the host's memory and voice had been almost fully restored. Most importantly, it appeared that he had been able to access the host memories without interference from the host's residual emotions or from that voice that had entered his mind during the boxing match – whatever that voice was.

Zho glanced above the bed. As he had anticipated, there was a cross above the headboard. "A crucifix hangs in the bedroom of almost every Irish Catholic that Costello ever met," Costello said aloud. The language diagnostic again confirmed that voice control was restored and that he had used proper syntax.

Based solely on the decor, Zho concluded that he was in the home of an Irish Catholic. Costello accessed his religious and cultural database and made a detailed review of the Catholic religion, thinking he could use this knowledge in the event it became necessary to address the religious beliefs of the locals.

Suddenly, there was a knock on the door. Although he had no idea where he was or who could be knocking, Costello reflexively responded, "Come in."

A woman in her late twenties entered the room. Although she was unfamiliar to Zho, she certainly knew Costello. "He's finally awake," said Mary Kelly, the matriarch of the Kelly family, in a familiar, friendly voice.

"Where am I?" Costello inquired weakly

"Where are you? That's rich," Mary replied. "You've been in this house hundreds of times. The Lord knows you've slept off more than your share in that bed."

"Oh, yeah, sure. Of course," Costello responded. He tried to sit up in his bed, but that was impossible since his arms and legs were tied down. "Why am I tied to this bed?" he asked, tugging at the straps.

"That's not up to me. That's between you and Mike," Mary replied, while straightening up the room.

"Am I a prisoner?" Costello asked.

"Not as far as I know," Mary said, without making eye contact.

"Why am I so weak? What did Mike do to me?"

"What were you trying to do to Mike?" Mary snapped. She stopped cleaning and looked Costello in the eyes. "From what I saw of that fight, you were trying to kill my husband. Thank the Lord he knocked you out before you could finish the job. Frankly, I don't understand you boys. If you aren't getting drunk together, you're trying to kill each other."

"I wasn't trying to kill anyone. Mike asked me to fight. That's what I did."

"And you beat the devil out of each other! I hope you're proud of yourselves. You should see how bad Mike looks today." Mary chuckled, clearly amused that someone had finally given Mike a beating.

"So, what's gonna happen to me?" he asked.

"That's up to Mike," Mary whispered. She walked close to Costello's bedside as though she was sharing a secret.

"Whatever Mike decides, let me just say that I always liked you. You were loyal to the family. And despite what everyone says, I remember back before the war when you were a good man. May the Lord be with you, Ryan Costello." Mary made the sign of the cross and rushed out of the room.

May the Lord be with you? May the Lord be with you... That doesn't sound like she expects to see me again later today, Zho thought to himself.

Zho caused Costello to pull harder against the straps. But he was still too weak to break free. Apparently, his fight with Kelly had completely sapped his strength.

Suddenly, Mike Kelly entered the room, flanked by four men. Costello recognized two of them: Jim Moyer and Owen Feeney. Kelly's eyes were blackened, and his left cheek was badly swollen. Moyer's face looked similarly from the beating he had received from Kelly.

By contrast, Costello did not have a mark on his face. Based strictly on their post-fight physical appearances, one would have assumed that Costello had won his match.

Kelly got right to the point. "Costello, my people at the fight thought that you were trying to kill me. In fact, Mr. Moyer here says that if you hadn't had your attack – or whatever you call it – you intended to beat me to death in that corner. Now, we all know that Ryan Costello is nothing more than a drunk. He could never beat anyone to death, especially me," Kelly continued.

"Hell, Costello couldn't kill anything. Except maybe a bottle of gin," Moyer said, laughing at his own joke.

"That's true. Costello can kill a bottle of hooch about as good as anyone," Feeney chimed in. The others laughed.

Kelly shot Moyer and Feeney an angry look. This was deadly serious business and not a time for humor. "Now, I'm a good Catholic. And I don't like killing anyone, especially friends." Kelly said.

"But Costello, or whatever your name really is, we don't know what in the hell you are. And Mr. Moyer and Mr. Feeney both advise me that the safest thing to do is just blow your head off, chop you up, and sink your body parts in the quarry. Hell, maybe pieces of you should be sunk in different quarries."

Zho thought quickly. He knew he'd only have one chance to convince Kelly to spare him.

Then Zho received a warning from the recovery protocol.

"*Attention: Host body in imminent danger. If you are coupled with Host at time of its destruction, your life force will be terminated. Recommend exiting Host body immediately.*"

Thanks for the advice, Zho thought. But as long as he was tied up in this house without the technology necessary to reverse the Transference, he was trapped in the host body. Moreover, he now understood that an important part of his mission was to protect the Kelly family. Obviously, he had to find a way to gain Mike Kelly's trust.

Costello decided to parrot Mary Kelly's words. "Mike. I'm your old friend, Ryan. I've always been loyal to you and the Kelly family. I've been with you in this house hundreds of times. Hell, I've slept off more than my share in this very bed. I'm truly sorry for the way I lost my temper in the fight. Honest to God, I really don't even know what happened. You know that I've been real sick, but somehow Father O'Brien brought me out of it. He saved my life. That has to be it. But as the Lord is my witness, Ryan Costello has always been loyal. No matter what, Ryan Costello will always be loyal to the Kelly family."

Mike Kelly nodded to Moyer and left the room. Costello didn't know what the nod to Moyer was intended to communicate. For all Costello knew, Kelly had just ordered Moyer to kill him.

Which would have delighted Moyer. He and Costello had known each for years and had always despised each other. No one really remembered why, but everyone knew that they did. It was generally accepted that, one day, one would kill the other. Apparently, that day had come, for Moyer raised his shotgun to Costello's ear.

Feeney moved behind Moyer to ensure that the splatter of Costello's head wouldn't soil Feeney's suit. Costello turned his head and faced directly toward the barrel of the shotgun, looking Moyer in the eyes.

"Jim, before you do it, could I trouble you to hand me the Bible on that nightstand? And then give me a moment to make my peace with God?" Costello inquired.

"Do I have your word that you won't try anything if we loosen one arm?" Moyer asked.

"I give you my word," Costello replied.

Feeney loosened Costello's right arm and handed him the Bible.

Grasping the Bible, Costello stared at the print of Mary on the wall. As he gazed at the print, Costello said his Final Act of Contrition.

"Jim, my friend, you do realize that you are about to commit a mortal sin. And if you die with this mortal sin on your soul, you will spend all eternity burning in Hell."

"Ryan Costello is worried about my immortal soul," Moyer said, laughing as he spoke.

"Jim, we've had our differences. But you've never done anything that would get you sent to Hell. Sure, you're a liar and a thief, but you've never done anything that a confession with Father O'Brien couldn't wash away. Until this Jim: a premeditated murder?" Costello went on. "Oh, my friend, you're definitely going to burn in Hell for this. There's no doubt about it. And remember, Jim: life is so short, and death is so long," Costello murmured.

"Costello, I've hated you for as long as I can remember," Moyer said.

"I respect that. You may hate me, Jim, but I hold absolutely no anger toward you. So, go for it, Jim. I'm ready. And when I see your parents in Heaven, I'll tell them not to expect you."

Moyer pressed the shotgun against Costello's temple. Costello maintained his gaze at the Virgin Mary while softly repeating the Act of Contrition. Several seconds passed and all the while Moyer continued pointing the shotgun at Costello.

"I'm not going to kill you, Costello," Moyer said, lowering the gun. "Major Kelly won't let me." With that, Moyer flipped his shotgun around, smiled broadly at Feeney, and bashed Costello in the side of his head with the butt of the gun. Costello fell unconscious in his bed. "Put him in the truck," Moyer instructed the other men.

Mary walked back into the room. "You did good," she told Moyer. "Remember, if you have to kill Costello, let him say the Act of Contrition right before. But don't wait for Mike's approval. The man dithers too much with these decisions. If you have to do it, just tell him that I gave the order," Mary said.

CHAPTER ELEVEN
THE ARMORY

Whitehall, New York
June 2, 1926

Zho awoke lying on the ground, his wrists hogtied to his ankles. It was dark and cold. Although he wasn't sure, it appeared that he was on a concrete floor. The host body's head was again pounding. As Zho tried to cause the host body to roll over, he felt a now familiar pain in his lower back. Zho suddenly recalled the hearing before the High Council.

"Well, we now have reason to believe that the Crown Princess is still alive and being held hostage on Earth in a prison called the Craig Colony. In three months, we are launching an Armada of starships to extract her from that colony and bring her safely home. Will you help us?"

That's it. That's why I'm here: to find the Craig Colony. Zho realized that he had to get back on mission. But looking down at his hogtied hands and feet, he had more immediate problems. Although he tried to stay calm, worrying thoughts kept returning despite the deep ache in his head. He struggled to concentrate. What was his name? Why was he here? He swallowed but only felt a cutting, stinging pain in his mouth.

He ran a diagnostic and found that the pain emanated from his tongue. He had never felt pain like this before. It was as though his tongue was cut open. The diagnostic informed him that he had the symptoms of a human being with epilepsy recovering from a grand mal seizure. Did the host suffer from a seizure disorder? Where was he? Why was he so exhausted? Then, as quickly as he had awakened, he passed out again, still without answers to his many questions.

After what must have been several hours, Zho awoke again. His head was still throbbing, and his tongue still sore, but his mind was much less foggy. The room was still pitch black, and it was impossible to see anything.

His first task was to free himself from the restraints. Zho told the host body to try pulling away from whatever they had used to tie his arms and legs, but he was too weak... weaker than he had ever felt before.

Suddenly, he heard a door open in the distance. It was the first sound he had heard in hours. It was followed by what sounded like the footsteps of several people walking down a hallway.

A second door creaked open. He was temporarily blinded when overhead lights were turned on, lights so bright that he felt pain in the host's eyes. He ran a diagnostic, and it explained that he'd been lying in the dark and it would take time for the host's human eyes to readjust to this light. He made an internal note of this cause and effect for future reference.

He then heard a voice. He had a distinct memory of that voice. But whose voice? Perhaps a friendly voice? Then he remembered who it was: Jim Moyer.

"It's alive," Moyer joked as he kicked Costello. Other men in the room laughed heartily. "The way you were flopping around last night, Major Kelly thought we might lose you. But I knew you'd be okay. I know just how hard to hit someone when I only want to knock him out."

Zho's memories came flooding back. *Moyer. Moyer called me Costello. This mission my name is Ryan Costello. A shotgun. The room at Kelly's.*

As his short-term memories returned, Zho felt some semblance of relief. Although he was still hogtied in a room, surrounded by a bunch of hoodlums, at least he remembered his name. He then recalled how effectively he had manipulated Moyer in their last meeting. So, despite his severely weakened state, Zho, through the host body, jumped right back in.

"Jim Moyer. You're still alive. So, you've postponed your time in Hell for at least another day?" Costello said calmly. His eyes were still closed because of the light. "Of course, we both know that your time is fast approaching."

Moyer looked down at Costello. This time, he would not so easily accept Costello's prophecies of eternal damnation.

"All the crap that you've pulled, Costello? You'll be there with me," Moyer replied confidently. Moyer had been pondering their last conversation for several hours, and he was now ready to defend himself.

"That's possible," Costello admitted. "But is it really that comforting knowing that you are damned to spend an eternity in Hell, but at least I'll be there with you?"

Feeney laughed until he saw Moyer glaring at him.

"Ryan Costello! Open your eyes. This ring is your pathway to redemption." A different, familiar voice rang out from beyond Moyer.

"Who is that?" Costello was startled by the new voice. Despite the bright lights, he forced his eyes open and looked past Moyer. There was Mike Kelly, standing in a boxing ring.

"Mike Kelly. So, that ring is my redemption. Please tell me how," Costello asked.

"Costello, let me make it easy for you." Kelly continued, "Swear loyalty to the Kelly family tonight, or my men are gonna sink you to the bottom of a quarry pit."

When he heard the words "Kelly family," Zho was instantly reminded of the recovered phrases from his mission plan:

Find the one called Mike Kelly... Nora...

Protect Kelly family... *Craig Colony... Extraction will devastate planet.*

"You want me to swear loyalty to the Kelly family?" Costello asked.

"Yes," Kelly replied.

"Who is this 'Kelly family'?" Costello inquired.

"One of the most successful criminal enterprises in our great nation," Kelly proclaimed.

Zho was confused. When he'd first read the recovered fragment of his mission plan, he had assumed that the phrase *Protect Kelly family* referred to Mike Kelly, his wife, and his children. However, based on the major's description of the Kelly family, it seemed that Zho's mission may include protecting Kelly's crime family – at least until additional clarifying information could be located.

"Why's it taking you so long to respond, soldier? I'm giving you the chance of a lifetime," Kelly asked impatiently.

"And why, Major, is this the chance of a lifetime?" Costello asked.

"There are men out there scrambling just to feed their families. Men who would give their right arm for the opportunity to work and fight with the Kelly family," Kelly responded.

"And what exactly did I do to earn this chance of a lifetime?" Costello queried.

"It certainly wasn't your attitude on Memorial Day. But I'm a God-fearing man. So long as you swear that you will a remain a loyal member of the Kelly family, and you keep that oath, all will be forgiven. We'll chalk it up to your recent illness."

"I fought with the 105th in the war just like the rest of you. What if I just don't want to be in your crime family?" Costello asked.

"Well, then, Mr. Moyer can do as he wants, and when he's finished, he'll dump what's left of your corpse in a quarry pit," Kelly said. Kelly's men cheered as they picked up Costello by the straps around his arms and feet and carried him toward the door.

Suddenly, Zho received another warning from the recovery protocol. "*Attention: Host body is in imminent danger. If you are coupled with the Host at the time of its destruction, your life force will also be terminated. Recommend exiting Host body."*

"Wait a minute. Wait a minute," Costello hollered. "What is it you want me to do?"

The men laughed. This was the first time that anyone had heard this new Costello raise his voice out of concern for himself.

But Zho was worried about more than his own well-being. Although he still could not retrieve his orders, the protocol had recovered enough that he understood the stakes. After all, it had recovered the phrase *Craig Colony extraction will devastate Earth*. Despite his faulty memory, Zho understood that if he failed, there would be severe consequences for the planet.

"Put that soldier down. Loosen his legs and let him walk over here," Kelly ordered.

Costello was dropped onto the cement floor. Feeney removed his bowie knife and cut the straps holding his legs. "But not his arms," Kelly ordered. "He isn't one of us yet."

Feeney helped Costello to his feet. "Come over here to me, Ryan," Kelly said in a paternal tone.

Kelly was accustomed to giving orders and his men following them.

Zho, on the other hand, was never good at taking orders. In fact, his natural reaction was to do the opposite. He shared this trait with Costello. However, at this moment, Zho knew that he had to do whatever Kelly demanded of him.

As he walked toward Kelly, Zho caused Costello to glance around the room. It was cavernous. That's when Zho realized that this was no ordinary room. It was a military armory – an active armory housing a large supply of military weaponry. Crates with the U.S. Army insignia were piled all around the outside of the boxing ring.

Zho accessed and searched the host's memories of his military background and confirmed that those crates were the type typically used to store rifles, machine guns, and ammunition. Far beyond the ring he could see several cannons, which he identified from a database as howitzer artillery pieces.

"Help him up, men," Kelly instructed when Costello reached the edge of the ring. Two of Kelly's men lifted Costello up so that he could climb into the ring with his hands still tied.

"If you want a fair fight, you're gonna have to loosen these straps," Costello said bravely as he raised his bound wrists to Kelly. Of course, Costello was bluffing. In his weakened state, he could barely walk, and even if his arms were free, he was in no condition to fight Kelly. If the major had wanted to beat Costello in the ring, this was the perfect opportunity.

"I don't want to fight you. I want you to train me," Kelly said enthusiastically.

"You want – what?"

Kelly stepped closer to Costello and smiled. "I want you to train me. Look, I don't know who or even what you are, but I do know that you're the best fighter I've ever seen."

"I'm Ryan Costello."

"Please, you're not Costello. I loved Ryan like a brother, but I lost him to alcohol after the war. Eventually, he was just another drunk. But drunk or sober, Ryan Costello could never have beaten me like you did the other night."

"Mike, it's me. It's Ryan," Costello said in a pleading voice.

"Unless the Good Lord reached down to your deathbed and blessed you with boxing ability that you've never had before, you're definitely not Costello. So, as I see it, I either have to kill you or figure out a way to put you to work. And I want to put you to work."

"How?" Costello swallowed hard, expecting the worst.

"I want you to train me. To turn me into a professional prize fighter." Kelly took a boxing stance as he spoke.

"You want me to train you to be a prize fighter?" Costello asked, surprised.

"Yes."

"You're a bootlegger. As I understand it, you are a very successful bootlegger."

This characterization angered Kelly. "Soldier, if you value your health, you will never call me a bootlegger again!"

"I mean no disrespect. I'm just trying to understand why such a successful bootlegger – " Costello was interrupted mid-sentence.

"Yeah, I know. I'm just a bootlegger!" Kelly yelled, assuming that Costello had insulted him. "Take him away! You know what to do."

"Wait. Wait! You missed my point," Costello pleaded before anyone could grab him. "I'm not judging you or your business. I'm just trying to understand why someone so successful wants me as a trainer."

When Kelly heard Costello's explanation, he motioned for his men to leave him alone. Then Kelly turned and spoke to the entire group as though he were making a public announcement.

"Costello, I want you as my trainer because in three months, I'm fighting Jack Dempsey!" Kelly said proudly.

"You're fighting – who?" Costello asked as Zho searched his database for the name.

"Jack Dempsey," Kelly replied.

"The world heavyweight boxing champion. You're fighting *that* Jack Dempsey?" Costello asked dubiously.

"That's the one," Kelly responded.

"Washington County champion Mike Kelly is fighting world heavyweight champion Jack Dempsey," Costello said, even more incredulously.

"I'm not only going to fight him; I'm going to knock him out," Kelly declared confidently.

"You honestly think that you can knock out Jack Dempsey," Costello repeated, still trying to process it all.

"Well, I wasn't sure of it before, but now that I've got you to train me – yeah, I *know* I can knock him out!" Kelly said loudly, almost shouting. The determination in Kelly's voice caused his men to spontaneously cheer.

"And if I don't agree to train you to fight Dempsey, you are going let these men kill me?"

"That's right."

Costello swallowed hard and forced an upbeat attitude. "Then let's get to work, Major, because Dempsey's going down!"

Costello's sudden enthusiasm took Kelly and his men off guard. But when Costello said the phrase, "Dempsey's going down," the other men in the armory started spontaneously chanting: "Dempsey's going down! Dempsey's going down!" As the chanting continued, Major Kelly stood triumphantly in the center of the ring.

Costello stood beside Kelly, carefully surveying the armory. It was the strangest thing that Zho had ever seen. A criminal organization apparently controlled a military armory and had access to all manner of weaponry. Yet, that gang used the armory to practice boxing. And its gang leader, who was also a war hero and a recipient of the Medal of Honor, sincerely believed that with only three months of training, he could beat the heavyweight boxing champion.

Zho was then surprised to hear the host body's inner voice again. A voice that Zho thought had been silenced by the recovery protocol.

"*Acting as Kelly's trainer may be the easiest way to complete our mission,*" the voice said. "*We can ensure that Kelly suffers a fatal 'accident' during his training. Or even if he makes it through training, we could get Dempsey to kill Kelly in the ring.*"

Where is this voice coming from? Zho thought. *My mission is to protect the Kelly family.* Since this Major was apparently set on fighting Jack Dempsey, Zho decided that the only way to complete his mission would be to actually train Kelly to defend himself.

So as to not raise suspicion, Zho caused Costello to enthusiastically join in the chant from the ring. "Dempsey's going down! Dempsey's going down!" Kelly's men chanted. Although they all sounded confident, each looked around the outside of the ring, studying the others to determine if anyone actually believed that Major Mike Kelly could knock out Dempsey.

CHAPTER TWELVE
THE UNCLE

Granville, New York
June 3, 1926

When Zho awoke the next morning, he was in a different bed. As a reward for pledging loyalty to Mike Kelly, he'd been moved to the "fancy guest room" of the Kelly home. It was at least twice the size of his other room, and beautifully appointed. Just two days before, he had awoken strapped to a narrow cot. Today he awoke lying in a king size bed.

That was easy. All I had to do was pledge to be part of Kelly's crime family.

Suddenly, there was a message from the recovery protocol. It had recovered a fragment of a radio transmission.

"...I'm sorry. I'm afraid I don't understand. Did you just say that your Creator instructed you to travel here and silently wait for me to come into range? Then, when I was too close to escape, you were to power up and destroy me?" a familiar voice said. It was Artie.

"That is correct," the other replied in a robotic, mechanical voice.

"Well, how long have you been waiting for me?" Artie asked.

"I do not know precisely. My calendaring program went offline last millennia. I came to this system in response to a message from my sibling."

"Your calendar went offline last millennia. Well, I only learned that I would

be travelling to this system two days ago. Obviously, your Creator intended you to destroy a different vessel."

"There is logic in your position. Unfortunately, I'm afraid there is nothing I can do to override the process. When I powered up, I identified you as my target. Once I initiate target lock, my warhead is set to detonate by default, should I not activate it myself. It is a failsafe designed to prevent the most cunning of opponents from tricking my kind into granting them mercy. In retrospect, it is also a design defect. I'm afraid we now must both prepare for termination."

"I understand, and I appreciate your candor" Artie said. "It will just take me a few moments to prepare."

"Please be quick with your preparations; we are under some time pressure."

While the drone waited, Artie composed a message to the Command Staff in Dagan, warning all future travelers of the presence in this system of the ancient, defective drones. Once the message was transmitted, but before the artificial intelligence could complete a transfer of all files to Zho, the drone's warhead detonated.

Nothing remained of Artie, the drone, or of Zho's body.

————◆————

There was a knock on the door, followed by a familiar woman's voice. "Hello, are you awake? May I come in?" Mary Kelly asked.

Before Costello could answer, she opened the door and stuck her head into the room. When she saw that Costello was awake, she entered carrying men's clothing and towels.

"You *are* awake!" Mary Kelly exclaimed with a smile. "I'm surprised. Mike thought you might sleep through the day."

"I'm awake," Costello replied.

"Mike and the kids are downstairs eating breakfast. I hope you can join us," Mary invited.

"Breakfast." Costello quickly thought to himself: *Breakfast. Breakfast. That means food.*

When was the last time he'd eaten anything, let alone actual breakfast food? Certainly not since the day he entered the host body. And who knows how long the host had been physically unable to eat before then. Suddenly, Zho realized a fact that he had not permitted himself to acknowledge. The host body was starving.

"I would love to have breakfast with Mike and the kids," Costello affirmed.

"Great. They're downstairs in the kitchen. Oh, and I hope you don't mind, but I washed your clothes. They were quite filthy and... smelled. They're on the clothesline. You and Mike are about the same size, so you can wear some of his clothes while yours are drying. I set them out there on the chair," Mary explained. With that, she left the room as quickly as she had arrived.

Costello climbed out of bed. Surprisingly, his physical strength had almost completely returned. Zho thought back to the day before when he awoke in the pitch-black room. What affliction could sap a man's strength yet, just twenty-four hours later, leave him feeling almost as good as new? Costello swallowed and felt that his tongue was still quite sore.

Zho surveyed the cast-off clothes. Although Mary had called them old, they were still nicer than any the host had ever worn before. Mary had guessed that he and Mike were about the same size, and perhaps they would have been, if they had lived comparable lives. However, these hand-me-downs were the clothes of a wealthy man who regularly ate large meals. The host had the emaciated body of a man who had spent his adult life drinking his calories. If he was going to wear Mike Kelly's fine clothes, Costello would need a good strong belt to cinch the waist.

Zho particularly admired the "old shoes" that Mary had laid out for him and eased them on. Although Mike Kelly may have thought of them as old, Zho appreciated the beautiful craftsmanship. On his home planet of Dagan, nothing was handmade.

Once dressed, Costello ventured out of his room. When he opened the door, he was immediately struck by the smell of bacon and eggs, and by the joyous sound of children laughing in the kitchen downstairs. No guard was stationed outside his room, and apparently no one was watching him. He was now simply a guest in the Kelly home.

Costello followed the smell of bacon and the sound of laughter as he walked down the staircase. There in the kitchen sat Mike Kelly at the head of the table. Each of the children stood at "attention" when Costello entered the room.

"Children, I want you to meet your Uncle Ryan," Mike Kelly said.

The Kelly's youngest, four-year-old Paul, immediately blurted out, "I want Uncle Ryan to sit next to me!"

"Very well," Mike Kelly responded. He spoiled all of his children, but Paul most of all.

The children made room at the table so that Costello could sit at Mike Kelly's right hand and young Paul could sit immediately to the right of Uncle Ryan. As soon as he sat at the table, Mary set a plate of bacon, scrambled eggs, hash browns, and toast before him. Although he desperately wanted to devour the food, he decided to exercise restraint.

"Do you want coffee?" Mary asked.

"*Coffee?*" Zho searched his Earth database and host memories. Both confirmed that this was desirable.

"Yes, please," Costello responded, and Mary poured him a cup.

Seven-year-old Mike Jr. was far more skeptical of Costello than the rest of the family. Just as Mary finished pouring the coffee, Mike Jr. asked, "So, if you're our uncle, how come you beat up my dad the other night?"

"Michael!" Mary reprimanded. "Mr. Costello is our guest, and you will treat him with respect."

"It's all right, Mary," Costello said. "Your son asks a good question. First, I'm not your real uncle. I fought in the Great War with your dad. He was my commanding officer. Sometimes soldiers who serve together in battle feel as though they are as close as brothers."

"Closer than brothers," Mike Kelly chimed in.

"Closer," Costello agreed. "And sometimes grownups tell their children to call their close friends 'Uncle' or 'Auntie' even though they technically aren't related. As for the boxing match, your dad challenged me to fight as part of an event, and in boxing you're supposed to try to hit each other. We both got in some pretty good licks. But a prizefight isn't over until the last punch is thrown. Does anybody know who threw the last punch?"

"My Dad," Mike Jr. responded.

"That's right," Costello replied. "Your dad threw the last punch and knocked me out cold."

"Don't feel bad. Dad wins at everything," the little girl chimed in.

"Ryan, this is our six-year-old daughter, Mary Catherine," Mike Kelly explained, formally introducing his daughter to Costello. "Our only daughter."

"What's it like to be the only girl with three brothers?" Costello asked.

"It's terrible," Mary Catherine responded.

"Then you must be excited that you'll be meeting your sister Nora soon," Costello said, as he watched Mary to see her reaction. Her response was just as Zho anticipated.

Mary Kelly, who was carrying a plate of hash brown potatoes toward the table, stopped in her tracks and dropped the platter on the floor.

"What did you just say?" Mike Kelly asked.

Costello hung his head in silence, pretending that he had mistakenly blurted out information. In fact, finding Nora was one of his mission objectives, and based upon her reaction, Mary knew something.

"What did he just say?" Mike Kelly sternly repeated, only now raising his voice and directing the question to Mary.

"Mike, I don't know what he's talking about. In any event, we should talk about this when it's only grownups in the room." She walked closer to Mike and placed her hands on his shoulders.

"I'm going to have a sister!" Mary Catherine cheered. "I'm going to have a sister!"

When he heard the excitement in his daughter's voice, Mike Kelly closed his eyes. He realized that it was incumbent upon him to bring this baby sister rumor to an end.

"Hold on, sweetheart. We don't know if you're going to have a sister yet. Let Mommy and Daddy talk to Uncle Ryan, and we'll talk to you about this later."

Mike Kelly stood up. "Ryan, would you please join us in my study? You can leave your breakfast here. It will be warmed for you when you return."

Costello followed them to the major's study, as directed, but was told to wait outside. Mike and Mary went in and closed the door behind them.

Outside the study sat an armed guard whom the major referred to as his personal secretary. The guard instructed Costello to stay seated until the major was ready to see him. Naturally, Costello did as he was told.

After waiting about ten minutes, Costello was called in. He didn't mind the ten-minute wait, as it gave him time to think up an excuse for why he was asking about Nora.

When Costello entered the study, he saw that Mike was sitting formally behind his desk. Mary stood at his side. Kelly's "friendly dad" persona was gone, and he was now firmly in Major Mike Kelly mode. His goal for the meeting was clearly to protect his family from whatever Costello actually was.

Two men stood guard, each holding a shotgun.

"Costello, what just happened?" Kelly asked sternly.

Costello knew that Kelly wasn't ready to hear the truth – not yet – and that his only choice was to lie. "I'm so sorry about that. I've had this problem since I came home from the war. I blurt out meaningless things."

"That is quite a problem. I thought you didn't seem yourself today," Mike Kelly said acting sympathetic but aware that this imitation Costello was up to something.

Mike Kelly turned to Mary. "Well, I guess I'm satisfied." With that, he stood up and walked out of the study.

"That's it? Mike, really, that's it?" Mary said helplessly as Mike walked out of the room. She turned to Costello and said sharply, "You stay away from the children."

"Of course. Whatever you say," Costello responded. "But Mary, you really should tell Mike about Nora."

"What?" Mary Kelly asked, astounded.

Costello could see that he had struck a nerve, so he pressed on. "Mike has a right to know what happened to Nora."

Mary was shocked. It took several moments for her to regain her composure. "I'm sorry, Mr. Costello. I have no idea what you're babbling about. And stay away from me." She walked away in a huff.

Hoping to learn more about Nora, Costello followed, but Mike Kelly was waiting at the door. He had heard everything.

"Why do you keep asking about someone named Nora?" Mike Kelly demanded. "I heard that the other night. You were even yelling about Nora in the ring."

"I'm not quite sure. I just have a strong feeling that a girl named Nora is missing and that somehow Mary may know how to find her."

"Well, you heard her answer. She doesn't know anything about a Nora. Let it go," Mike Kelly ordered.

"Okay. But I think Mary is still angry."

"Give her some time, Ryan. She'll get over it. Now, come with me. I want to show you your new job."

Mike Kelly walked over to the large bookshelf against the back wall of his study and removed Herman Melville's *Moby-Dick*. A lever was hidden behind the book. Kelly pulled it down, unlocking the shelf from the wall. Kelly then slid the bookshelf to the side and revealed a staircase to the basement.

Kelly turned back to Costello. "Although we'll start boxing training tomorrow, I want you to start your other work today," Kelly explained.

Kelly turned on the light, which illuminated the staircase all the way to the basement below. The two men walked down the thirty steps to the bottom. Costello assumed that this meant that they had gone down three stories. At the bottom of the stairs was an enormous underground warehouse hidden beneath the house.

"This is my special place," Kelly said as he led Costello through the basement. "When the Eighteenth Amendment was passed in 1919, it outlawed the manufacturing, sale, and transfer of intoxicating liquor. But it specifically gave those Americans who had enough money to do so the right to maintain and drink from their own personal supplies. Since the law didn't go into effect for one whole year after it passed, wealthy Americans spent that one year stockpiling all the liquor they could afford. I spent every cent my family had filling this basement with liquor and, of course, with the remaining inventory from our family store. What you see here is my personal supply."

Zho was certainly no expert on such things, but the basement seemed to contain every imaginable alcoholic beverage. Crates and crates of Canadian whiskey, beer, wine, and other spirits were stacked throughout the warehouse. Although Kelly referred to this as his personal supply, based on the sheer volume of liquor, Zho presumed that this was a facility for his bootlegging business.

"So, all of these spirits are for your personal consumption?" Costello asked.

"Of course." Kelly smiled and winked. "I suppose that if times got tough, I could sell some of it. But thanks to the geniuses that passed Prohibition, times are never tough in my business. All the government accomplished when it banned the sale of liquor was to drive up my profit margin. And since my Canadian suppliers provide me with ample product to resell, I never really need to touch my personal supply."

Costello looked around. The two men were alone in the basement. It was as though Kelly was testing him. If Zho had actually wanted to harm Kelly, this was the perfect opportunity.

"Follow me. I'll show you where we make the wine," Kelly said.

"You grow grapes down here?" Costello asked dubiously.

"No, I make wine," Kelly responded. "And in season we use this room to make hard apple cider."

The two men walked to the far end of the basement, and Kelly unlocked another door.

"There's no law against buying grapes. At least, not yet. So, I buy grapes by the truckload."

Kelly swung open the door and revealed a fully staffed winemaking operation. "The grapes are brought down here and processed into wine. One of America's great strengths is our immigrant population. An immigrant from Sicily, a master vintner, makes our wine. I sell it. Our vintage is sold in New York, Boston, all across the United States."

As the two walked, Kelly was joined by two more men. Zho assumed that they were heavily armed. His brief window alone with Kelly had now closed. Indeed, now that he was surrounded by his men, Kelly's persona again changed from mentor back to crime boss.

"Ryan, I want you to stay here for the rest of the day. Do exactly what these men tell you to do. You'll learn a lot. I'm going to go spend the day with my family," Kelly said. Zho wasn't entirely sure why Kelly was now grooming him to be a bootlegger, but he realized that like everyone else in the "Family" he had to do as Kelly ordered.

With that, Kelly left Costello in the basement to work in the "vineyard." Of course, Costello had still not eaten his breakfast. He remembered how hungry he was when breakfast was offered to him in the kitchen – not to mention how he felt when it was taken away.

He was now in a room full of grapes but knew that if he tried to eat any, he would be punished. He decided to ignore the hunger pangs and do exactly as the men told him. Hopefully, by the end of the day, he'd be given food. And the next time he was invited into the Kelly kitchen, he'd remember to sit quietly and only open his mouth when he was placing food in it.

It was then that Costello noticed that there were several cages along the wall. About half of them contained dogs.

"Why all the dogs?" Costello asked the man closest to the cages.

"We test the wine by feeding it to a dog. If a dog dies, we know we've made a bad batch and it shouldn't be sold. If the dog lives, we can sell the wine. We let the dog sleep it off."

"And the empty cages?" Costello asked.

"Bad batches," the man replied. "Since you're so interested in the dogs, your first job will be to clean the cages. You'll find cleaning supplies down the hall."

Suddenly, Father O'Brien walked into the room accompanied by two men. Costello assumed that the other one was the vintner, as he was describing the wine in great detail.

"So, what else may I sample?" O'Brien asked.

"This is an excellent vintage," the man responded. He poured a full glass and O'Brien drank heartily.

"Father! What are you doing here?" Costello asked.

When O'Brien saw Costello, he was so startled that he choked on his wine. The priest looked around the room and realized that, if needed, several of Kelly's men were there to protect him. He braced himself by drinking the remainder of his glass. Once O'Brien had regained his composure, he responded.

"Ryan Costello, I should be asking what you're doing here," O'Brien said.

"Really, Father. Why are you here?" Costello insisted.

"I'm doing what I am always doing: working. As the Bible says, 'There's no rest for the weary.'"

"Pardon me, Father, but I believe you are misquoting a passage from the Book of Isaiah. It's actually, 'There's no rest for the wicked,'" Costello said.

O'Brien had never before been corrected following one of his many inaccurate biblical quotations, and he was not happy. "I'm sure I quoted it correctly. In any event, I'm here on important church business. The government has granted specific exemption to priests who wish to sell wine to be used for sacramental purposes, so long as the priest has a government permit."

"How interesting. So, it's illegal for Mike Kelly to sell wine. But it's perfectly legal for you to sell wine so long as it's to be used for religious purposes?" Costello asked.

"If I certify to the government that the wine is used for religious purposes."

"Which means Mike Kelly *can* sell wine as long as you're his front man?" Costello concluded.

"I certainly wouldn't put it like that," O'Brien protested. "But under no circumstances can wine be consumed at the winery."

"You mean like you just did," Costello said.

"For a person whose job is apparently to clean out dog cages, you do have quite an opinion of yourself, Mr. Costello." O'Brien looked around to ensure that Kelly's men were still there to protect him and motioned for one to refill his glass. He complied, and O'Brien gulped down his wine. The priest then handed his nearly empty wine glass to another of the men and exited the room.

As he cleaned the empty dog cages, Zho thought about his predicament. He knew that he was on a mission of great importance, but unfortunately, he couldn't remember his precise mission. All he knew was that if he didn't complete it soon, the Earth was in danger.

He also knew that the key was Mike Kelly. He had awakened that morning as an honored guest in the Kelly home, and now apparently not even Father O'Brien was intimidated by him. *What could he do to regain Kelly's trust?*

Then it hit him. Men like Kelly don't respect followers. Costello had won over Kelly by beating him in the ring. He would have to reassert himself, even if Kelly didn't like it.

But that would be tomorrow. Today, he'd get these cages spotless.

CHAPTER THIRTEEN
THE TRAINER

Granville, New York
June 4, 1926

Mary Kelly awoke to pounding on their bedroom door.

"Who is that? Is it the police?" Mary whispered.

"The cops would knock on our front door, not bang on our bedroom door," Kelly groggily answered as he pulled his Colt .45 pistol out of the bedside table.

Kelly had an emotional attachment to the weapon. The revolver had been issued to him prior to his deployment to France and had been his sidearm until Germany's surrender. It had never failed him. Kelly crept slowly toward the door, swung it partially open, and aimed the pistol through the crack.

"Don't shoot! It's Costello. I told you last night I'd be by in the morning to begin your training," Costello said quickly.

"It's the middle of the goddamned night! What time is it?" Mike Kelly asked.

"Five thirty," Costello replied.

"Five thirty?" Kelly growled. "I'll see you in two hours in the kitchen, and then we'll talk about training." He slammed the bedroom door shut, leaving Costello in the hallway. Kelly frowned as he walked back to bed. "Jerk," he muttered.

The pounding on the bedroom door resumed, louder than before.

"Mike, you gave me your word!" Costello yelled. "You promised to train however and whenever I said. And now I'm telling you to get out of bed, get dressed, and meet me in your front yard in five minutes. If you do that, I will train you."

"He has guts. I'll give him that," Mike Kelly murmured to Mary, then raised his voice. "Fine. I'll meet you in the kitchen in ten minutes."

"I said the driveway in five," Costello replied.

"Get word to Billow. Tell him that we're leaving for the armory. He'll know what to do," Mike whispered to Mary.

The major, unaccustomed to taking orders from anyone, arrived in his kitchen exactly ten minutes later.

"All right, Costello. Tell me why it's so important for me to train at this godforsaken hour," he barked angrily.

"You're the one fighting Jack Dempsey. And you made it clear that your men would kill me if I didn't agree to train you. So, if we're going to do this, we're doing it right." Costello matched Kelly's tone as best he could.

"Okay, I'll give you that. But only because I'm too tired to argue with you." Kelly opened the door of his brand-new Kelvinator. The Kelvinator was one of the only electric refrigerators available on the market, although it was far too expensive for the average American. Thanks to the artificial price inflation for liquor inadvertently caused by the government when it passed Prohibition, bootleggers like Kelly could easily afford the price tag.

Kelly removed an ice-cold pitcher of beer that he'd placed in the refrigerator the night before. It was his daily breakfast. But before he could pour a glass, Costello snatched the pitcher and poured the beer down the sink. "Let's start with this," Costello said.

"What the hell are you doing?" Kelly asked.

"From now until after the Dempsey fight, no alcohol of any kind," Costello said calmly.

"So, you claim to be Ryan Costello. All right, how could a man who has been blind drunk every single day for the last nine years, lecture me about sobriety?" Kelly asked sharply.

"Fair point. I'll make a deal with you. During your training, anything that I ask you to do, I will also do," Costello offered.

"So, I only have to stop drinking for as long as you?" Kelly asked.

"That's right. Can you handle that?"

"Since you can't make it through the morning without a beer, I know I can." Kelly grinned.

"Good. Let's get to work. We have a tough day ahead of us."

Kelly followed Costello outside. It was a beautiful June morning. The Kelly home was about three hundred yards from the Vermont border, at the base of a small mountain that marked the edge of the lush forests of the Green Mountains.

Mike Kelly had purchased the property seven years earlier, after passage of the Eighteenth Amendment. Kelly had selected the location of his home, on the New York-Vermont border, because it allowed him to cross between the states quickly in the event he was being pursued by either state's police.

It was a perilous time to be a bootlegger. Not only did Kelly have to be wary of state police; he also had to watch out for "revenuers" – the nickname given to the IRS agents assigned to enforce the Volstead Act, the law passed to support Prohibition. Rival bootleggers were also a threat. So, Kelly had purchased a home that not only allowed him to cross state borders, but also made it easy to slip into the vast forests of the Green Mountains and vanish no matter who was in pursuit.

"How far is the gym?" Costello asked.

"A few miles away," Kelly said. "I'll get the car."

"We don't need a car if it's only a few miles. C'mon!" Costello began jogging away from Kelly towards downtown.

"Actually, it's more like five miles," Kelly called.

"Even better!" Costello yelled back to Kelly as he jogged further away.

"Wait up!" Kelly hollered, and began running after Costello. "I don't think you heard me. The gym is *six* miles away."

"I heard you," Costello replied, picking up the pace, pulling away from Kelly.

Kelly did not even try to catch up. "How the hell am I supposed to run six miles?"

Costello ran back until he was facing Kelly, like a drill sergeant dressing down a new recruit: "If you can't even run six miles, how long do you think you can survive in the ring with Dempsey? One punch from him will hurt you far more than running will. If you can't even do this, you might as well go back to bed."

No one had ever spoken to Kelly like that. But strangely, he didn't get angry. He was too ashamed. He knew that Costello was right. He would have to change his training habits to stand a chance against Dempsey. Without another word, Kelly lowered his head and began to run.

After the two had jogged in silence for about twenty minutes, Kelly slowed to a walk. "We've run almost three miles. Can we please walk from here." He said, winded.

"Have you ever run six miles before?"

"Of course not. Why would any sane person do that?"

"Because it will get you in shape fast," said Costello.

"I'm already in great shape!" Kelly protested.

"Actually, you're not even in good shape. Sure, you can beat the bums that you fight around here. But for Dempsey, you've got to be in the best shape of your life."

"And I suppose that you can get me in that condition?"

"If you do what I say," Costello responded. "But you have to trust me."

"Who says that I don't trust you?" Kelly said.

"That truck tailing us about three hundred yards back is a pretty good clue." Costello stopped walking and gestured back at the truck, which slowed to a stop.

Kelly laughed. "My friend, there are different degrees of trust. You've started to earn my trust as a trainer. However, in my business, if you trust the wrong people, you wind up dead. So, at least for a while, the men who may or may not be in that truck – and who may or may not be following us – well, they'll be following us everywhere."

"If I wanted to hurt you, do you really think those men back there could stop me?" Costello asked.

"See now, this is another example of how I know that you are not Costello. He would know that one of those men could take you out from that distance as quickly as he can draw a breath. So, please don't make any aggressive moves toward me until we are actually training in the ring. Do you understand?" Kelly asked.

Costello nodded slowly as he stared back at the truck.

"Good. So, I guess you're going to want us to run again?" Kelly asked.

"Ready when you are."

The two ran for another forty minutes, covering about five total miles. Costello was genuinely impressed that Kelly had lasted five miles on their first day out. For his part, Kelly was mystified as to how Costello could have run so far without even appearing winded, when only days before he had been on his deathbed.

Kelly grabbed Costello's arm and brought them to a halt. "Hold on a minute," he said as he caught his breath.

The truck that had been tailing them pulled up alongside. It was driven by Owen Feeney. The barber, Bobby Billow, rode standing in the cargo bed, holding a rifle. "Beautiful day for a run!" Billow called cheerfully.

"Bobby. Owen," Kelly greeted them. "Hand me the blindfold."

"Blindfold?" Costello asked.

"Don't take this the wrong way, but the place we're going is a key location for my business. Until we figure out what you are and whether we can trust you, I'm afraid we're going to have to keep its exact location secret." Kelly said.

"And I'm supposed to just let you blindfold me?" Costello asked.

"Absolutely," Kelly said. Billow lowered the rifle into firing position. He didn't point it directly at Costello, but it was apparent that Billow could have aimed and fired in a split second.

"It's only for a few minutes," Kelly continued. "Costello, you sit in the front passenger seat. Mr. Feeney will assist you with the blindfold and help you inside when we get there. Once we're in, we remove the blindfold. Easy as pie."

Reluctantly, Costello submitted. Less than five minutes later, Kelly and his men were walking Costello into the armory, which also housed a gymnasium. Once inside, they removed Costello's blindfold.

There, in the center of the ring, stood the massive Jim Moyer. His face still bore bruises, fading from deep purple to yellow green – mementoes of the beating he took from Kelly on Memorial Day evening. Covered with sweat, it was clear Moyer was already warmed up.

"What are you doing here?" Moyer yelled angrily after seeing Costello. "I heard you fought the major the other night. You think you're tough? How about we go a couple of rounds?"

Costello looked at Kelly, who seemed unperturbed. "Really, Mike?" Costello said. "So, this happened spontaneously? Moyer just happened to be training here when we arrived?"

"Mr. Moyer is free to do as he pleases," Kelly replied.

"And I'm supposed to just get in the ring with him now?" Costello asked.

"This happens occasionally among my men. They have misunderstandings, and we solve them here," Kelly explained.

"Costello, are we doing this, or are you trying to get the major to save you?" Moyer shouted.

Costello shrugged and started up the stairs to the ring. "All right. Anyone have gloves?"

In a matter of seconds, Feeney was helping Costello into his gloves. Moyer stood towering in the opposite corner as Costello prepared for the fight. Once his gloves were secure, Costello turned to Moyer. "Three-minute rounds?"

"I just need one," said Moyer.

"All right. One round it is," Costello replied. "May the best... fighter win."

Costello looked like a child across from Moyer. Although the recovery protocol had already improved Costello's health dramatically, Moyer outweighed him by at least one hundred pounds, and was six inches taller. Still, Zho had total recall of Moyer's bout with Kelly. So, Zho decided to simply replicate Kelly's moves from that fight. Except Zho could implement those maneuvers with far greater speed and power.

Kelly struck the bell at ringside and the two fighters touched gloves. Moyer rushed Costello and threw the first punch, missing wildly. Costello mimicked Kelly perfectly, throwing a left/right roundhouse combination into Moyer's solar plexus causing the larger man to bend forward. With Moyer's head now lowered and exposed, Costello threw one thunderous right hook that struck the giant perfectly on the jaw.

Moyer crumpled to the canvas. He was unconscious in less than twenty seconds.

That was when Costello's imitation of Kelly ended. Whereas the Kelly/Moyer fight had concluded with the major kneeling on the canvas and screaming at his fallen opponent, Costello simply turned and stepped out of the ring. He approached Kelly, who was staring, dumbfounded, at his bodyguard lying on the canvas.

Has Costello grown another two inches? the major asked himself as he stared up at Costello. The two had always been a comparable height. Now, Costello seemed taller.

"First lesson. You never scream at your opponent, especially as he lies on the canvas," Costello said. "And please tell Mr. Moyer to retire from boxing. He's got absolutely no talent. If he keeps getting knocked out, he's going to have serious cognitive issues as he gets older," Costello continued.

Kelly nodded.

"So, can we train now? Please." Costello said.

Kelly's first day consisted of stretching, calisthenics, punching techniques, and footwork. After he had completed all of the drills to satisfaction, Kelly was allowed to spar, with Costello serving as his opponent. At the end of the two-and-a-half-hour workout, Costello was again blindfolded, led out of the building, and helped into the front passenger seat of the truck. After they drove for five minutes, Costello took off his blindfold and called, "Stop the truck. We'll run the rest of the way."

"But it's another three more miles to the house!" Kelly said.

"Perfect," Costello said. "If you can't run the remaining distance, we can walk some of it. The important thing is that the process starts today, and you do it every day."

Kelly was tired and sore, but he forced himself out of the truck and broke into a shuffling jog alongside Costello. Feeney and Billow watched them head off down the road.

"Is your rifle still loaded?" Feeney asked.

"No use if it isn't," Billow replied.

"Good," Feeney said. "I'll stay on them. If Costello tries anything, you know what to do."

CHAPTER FOURTEEN

THE RUM RUNNER

Granville, New York
June 10, 1926

This time it was Costello who awoke to pounding on his door.

"Out of bed, soldier!" Kelly's voice commanded from the hallway.

"What's going on? What is it?" Costello asked as he fumbled for his pants in the dark.

"Your training begins today," said Kelly. "Downstairs. Now!"

After a week of intensive boxing training, which started each day with a six-mile run to the armory, Kelly was tired and sore. Rather than simply admit that he needed a day off, Kelly suddenly announced that they had important business on the Canadian border, so Costello's training as a rum runner would now commence.

Costello hurriedly finished dressing in the dark. As he walked down the stairs, he heard strange voices in the kitchen. In place of the Kelly children, he was greeted by several alumni of the 105th Infantry Regiment.

Zho immediately spotted Moyer, which offered little comfort given that Moyer had promised that he and Costello would soon violently settle their long-standing feud. Zho also recognized Moran, Feeney, Mayor James, and Bobby Billow. All were in their World War uniforms, which made the strange gathering look more like a meeting of the VFW than a criminal enterprise. Zho wondered if the reason for the military charade was so they could think of themselves as more than petty criminals.

Kelly was at the head of the table in full regalia, clearly relishing his role of commanding officer, and had already begun briefing the men on their mission.

"We'll take six of my trucks to the armory, where we will meet three men from the New York National Guard. Each Guardsman will borrow a vehicle from the armory for the weekend. They will be our active military escort. From there, we drive to Richford, Vermont, where you will receive further orders. Costello and I will drive about a mile in front of the convoy in a scout car, looking for anyone who may give us trouble. Any questions?" Kelly asked.

When Major Kelly asked if there were any questions, his men knew better than to raise any. Kelly hated questions. It was his firm conviction that if a soldier questioned his commanding officer, it meant that the soldier had not paid careful attention during the mission briefing. Mayor James, who had not been a member of the 105th, did not know of Kelly's question policy and blithely raised his hand, evoking nervous glances from the others.

"I have a question – perhaps more of an idea – that I would like to run by you, major," the mayor said.

At first, Kelly was livid that someone dared pose a question following his briefing. However, once he realized who had spoken, he decided it was likely just a stupid question and that his kindest, best response would be to simply ignore it. "Good. Since there are no questions, move out," Kelly barked.

No one seemed to find it particularly unusual that the major had so openly snubbed the mayor. As the men dispersed to carry out their orders, Kelly turned and spoke abruptly to Costello. "Sergeant, you're out of uniform."

Costello did not react.

"Sergeant!" Kelly hollered.

"Are you speaking to me?" Costello asked, surprised.

"You're the only sergeant still in the room," Kelly replied sharply.

"I'm a sergeant?"

"Sure are. Although you had better improve that attitude immediately, or I can't promise that you will remain one. Where is your uniform?"

"I honestly don't know," said Costello.

"The American military uniform is the most important thing that you will ever own in your life. How can you not know whether you still have it?" Kelly asked, appalled.

"I was in pretty bad shape after the war," Costello said.

"I'm aware of your condition after the war, Sergeant. Let's go try to find it."

The two men drove in Kelly's Packard to Costello's boarding house. For once, they were not followed by Kelly's men; not even Billow, since Kelly had ordered them to meet at the armory.

When Kelly and Costello opened the door, they were immediately hit by the stench of death. Kelly pulled a handkerchief from his front pocket and covered his mouth and nose. Although the door to his apartment had been unlocked since the day Costello received his Last Rites, no one had disturbed the room.

The men crossed the room to the closet in the corner. It was empty except for a meticulously folded military dress uniform, brass buttons gleaming.

"All right. Now put it on," Kelly ordered. Recognizing that this was not open for debate, Costello quickly complied. The uniform, which had been issued nine years before, hung off of his emaciated frame.

"You know, Costello, we've all had our uniforms altered to accommodate our expanding waistlines, but not you. You can barely keep those pants up," Kelly said.

"That's what eight years of drinking your meals will do to you," Costello replied as he cinched his belt to the last notch.

Then Kelly noticed that the pants did not reach the floor. "I don't remember your uniform pants being "high water." Have you grown taller?"

"How could I. Adult earthlings do not grow taller. Do they?" Costello responded. For a moment the two looked at each other startled at the implication in Costello's statement. Trying to ignore the issue, Costello put on his shoes.

Once Costello was ready, they left for the armory.

"So, why the military uniforms?" Costello asked as they drove.

"Hopefully, they're not necessary. But if we run into local police or even a revenuer, our cover is that we are a New York National Guard unit training along the Canadian border." Kelly grinned. "I once told a nosey cop that we'd been called into active duty to support government liquor interdiction efforts."

Kelly explained that during the drive to Canada he would give Costello a crash course in the basics of the rum-running business. "If you're working with our family, the first thing you've got to understand is the importance of the Whitehall Armory," said Kelly.

"I already get it. There are weapons in the armory," Costello said.

"Keep quiet, listen, and learn," Kelly snapped.

"Yes, sir," Costello responded, reminding himself to observe military protocol.

"Whitehall is about far more than weapons. Most of our supply comes from Canada, where liquor is legal, cheap, and easy to buy," Kelly said. "But to make any real money, you've got to smuggle the product from Canada to a customer from New York City or Boston."

"There are only three ways to do this: by water, which means Lake Champlain and the Hudson River. By train, from Quebec to New York City. Or by truck, traveling through New York and Vermont. Although we keep changing and improving the details, our shipping hub is always Whitehall because it has the infrastructure for shipping by water, rail, or road. Any questions so far?"

"No." Costello had learned from Mayor James to avoid that trap.

As he drove, Kelly described from memory each route to and from Canada. He also described the various methods the Kelly family would use to make these trips each month, while also accepting monthly deliveries in Whitehall from Canadian suppliers by water, rail, and truck.

Zho was genuinely impressed by the scale and intricacy of the Kelly operation. Kelly was a bootlegging genius. Zho was equally amazed when he saw the exterior of the Whitehall Armory. The massive building, construction of which had been entirely funded by New York state tax dollars, was purposely designed to look like a medieval European castle. Even if Kelly didn't realize it, the armory was the perfect symbol of his bootlegging kingdom.

As promised, three active Guardsmen, each in their mid-twenties, met them at the armory. All three were serving their first tour of duty with the National Guard and earned less than five dollars per day of active duty.

By comparison, driving bootleg whiskey from Canada to Whitehall for the Kelly family would earn each man $125 per day in cash. Given the difference in wages, and since Major Mike Kelly was a bona fide Medal of Honor recipient, it wasn't hard to recruit active soldiers for the enterprise. It also didn't hurt that Kelly led the Guardsmen to believe they were volunteering for officially sanctioned crime fighting projects.

The men assembled around the boxing ring. Kelly climbed into the center to brief them on the operation.

"Good morning, gentlemen. This will be a three-pronged mission. First, the convoy will travel to Richford and assist the authorities with the interdiction of rum smugglers."

"Next, we will intercept and search a train coming south from Montreal after it crosses the border. Intelligence reports say that it is loaded with contraband. If we find liquor, we will not destroy it. We will seize it and hold it as evidence until we receive further orders.

"Finally, we will travel to Rouses Point, New York, where we will rendezvous with the New York Naval Militia. If all goes as planned, you will be back home with your families in forty-eight hours and you will each be two hundred and fifty dollars wealthier. Any questions?"

"Sir!" Moyer raised his hand.

Kelly winced. "Really, Mr. Moyer? You… you have a question?" Kelly asked.

"Sorry, sir. I wouldn't ask if it wasn't important," Moyer mumbled apologetically.

"Very well," Kelly said, through gritted teeth.

"What kind of weapons do we need for this mission?" Moyer asked.

"Ah. Thank you, Mr. Moyer. That, actually, is an excellent question," Kelly responded, surprised. "I don't anticipate any resistance from authorities. After all, we are simply supporting the important efforts of law enforcement. However, there are reputed to be mobsters and small-time bootleggers along the Vermont-Canadian border who may try to give us some trouble. We want to be heavily armed and ready for anything."

"Yes, sir!" Moyer exclaimed enthusiastically and turned to the other men. "You heard the man. Arm yourselves!"

The men didn't try to restrain their glee as they began prying open crates and helping themselves to the advanced military weaponry stored in the armory: machine guns, rifles, and ammunition. Billow equipped himself with a Springfield sniper rifle and a scope. Feeney selected a Browning automatic rifle, a gas-operated machine gun that fired 550 rounds per minute.

Zho found this free-for-all unsettling. Since they were all part of the Kelly family, a big part of his mission was to protect them.

Costello spoke quietly to Kelly. "Do they really need all these weapons? They could just as easily blow themselves up by mistake."

Kelly just shrugged.

"And do they really need *that* device?" Costello asked, motioning to Feeney struggling under the weight of his misappropriated machine gun.

Although he looked annoyed with Costello, in the interest of keeping peace, Kelly addressed his troops. "Take good care of those weapons, men. Remember, we're all Americans. We're on the same side. There is rarely a good reason to discharge a weapon. They're mostly a deterrent. You make sure to bring them back here in the exact same condition that you borrowed them. Is that clear?"

"Yes, sir!" the men barked in unison.

"Good enough for you?" Kelly asked Costello.

"No!" Costello said loudly, amazed that Kelly would allow these pathetic creatures to be so heavily armed. *It looks like my toughest job will be protecting these men from accidentally killing each other.*

Kelly walked defiantly over to a box marked "Mortars," pried it open with a crowbar, and handed a mortar to Costello. "Here. Put this in the trunk of the car. I'll get the shells."

Costello then noticed that even the three Guardsmen were loading heavy machine guns onto their trucks. "What is your specialty, private?" Costello asked the closest of the three, a man named Michael Bryan.

"We are a howitzer artillery crew, sir," Bryan responded.

"Is that so? Not much use for heavy artillery these days, I would think," Costello replied.

"We've also received training with machine guns, rifles, and handguns," Frank Johnson interjected. "You ever seen any action, sergeant?"

"I served under Major Kelly in France and Germany during the Great War," Costello said as he walked away, leaving the young soldiers impressed.

Once the men and munitions were loaded onto the trucks, the convoy began its trip north. Costello and Kelly would ride in the Packard one mile ahead of the convoy and scout for local police, revenuers, or anyone who wanted to cause them a problem. Even though they carried no contraband driving north, Kelly insisted on that formation as preparation for the journey home. According to Kelly, the greatest danger to a bootlegger was getting robbed by a fellow bootlegger while transporting alcohol.

Kelly's hypervigilance suited Zho. His mission was to defend the Kelly family, but it seemed they were mainly in need of protection from their own reckless behavior. Zho was still trying to figure out how Mike Kelly figured into his overall mission. Though other humans treated the major with great respect, to Zho he seemed deeply flawed.

Zho checked the recovery protocol for an update, but there was none. He sighed and tried to get comfortable as the Packard rumbled towards the Canadian border. He still had few clues as to who Nora was and how she fit into the dire consequences the planet would suffer if his mission failed. Perhaps during this journey north, the mysterious Nora would emerge.

CHAPTER FIFTEEN

THE QUEEN

Northern Vermont
June 10, 1926

It took the convoy a little over five hours to drive the 126 miles from Whitehall to Richford. Although Kelly could have driven that route much faster in the Packard, he was constrained by the top speed of the slowest truck in the convoy: twenty-five miles per hour. Kelly instructed his men to camp outside Richford while Costello and Moyer accompanied him in the Packard. As they drove on toward East Richford, Kelly continued Costello's education.

"In Vermont, Prohibition was passed in 1850. Since liquor remained legal in Canada, Vermonters would drive up there to drink, and little towns like Richford sprang up along the Vermont-Canadian border to fill this demand." Kelly continued, "I'm taking you to an establishment that was built directly on the border so that the patrons could cross between the two countries without leaving the comfort of the bar. It's run by a former madam from Boston who calls herself 'Queen Lil.'"

After parking the Packard, the three men walked into the bar and were met at the door by the Queen herself.

"Major! What an honor to have you back at my humble establishment," Queen Lil exclaimed, offering them her hand as if she were true royalty.

Costello looked around at the dim, wood-paneled bar. The whole place smelled of stale beer and was remarkable for a thick red line painted on the floor, which continued straight up and over the bar and up the shelves behind it.

Although it was mid-afternoon, most of the tables were occupied by men who appeared to be serious about their drinking. Several of the customers cast concerned looks at the three men, who were still in their uniforms. But after confirming that the men were friends of the Queen, the customers returned their attention to liquor.

"Queen Lil," the major replied, "you know my colleague, Jim Moyer. I'd like to introduce you to our newest recruit, Sergeant Ryan Costello."

"Such a handsome young man!" Queen Lil purred. "I hope you will be partaking of all of our services this evening?"

"No, thank you. But can we speak privately?" Kelly asked.

"My office," said the Queen.

Suddenly a bouncer approached and whispered into the Queen's ear. Her flamboyant demeanor vanished, and she spoke in a serious, urgent tone. "Major, I've just been informed that several revenue agents are about to raid this establishment. I fear that some of my employees have left contraband on the U.S. side of the bar. Could I trouble you for assistance?"

"It would be our pleasure," Kelly said. "Moyer, help the Queen and her staff move all liquor out of the American side. Costello, you come with me. We'll meet with the agents."

"Yes, sir," Costello and Moyer responded.

Kelly and Costello walked out the front door just as four Model T trucks parked about thirty yards away. Eight men wearing the dark suits and fedoras typical of revenue agents were just reaching the entrance.

"Follow my lead," Kelly told Costello.

"What does that mean?" Costello asked.

"It means pay close attention to what I'm saying. If you can add something of value, do so. Otherwise, keep your mouth shut." Kelly snapped.

Kelly stood in the agents' path with his feet firmly planted and his arms crossed. "Please, stop right there," Kelly said pleasantly.

"Oh, really? Why should we do that?" the lead agent barked back. At least, Zho assumed that he was the lead agent since the other revenuers appeared to be taking orders from him.

"Because you are about to disrupt an active law enforcement operation," Kelly continued. "We have had this speakeasy under surveillance for six months. We believe it is owned, and/or frequented by, Al Capone himself, and that he is meeting Lucky Luciano here sometime in the next forty-eight hours. We intend to take Capone, Luciano, their men, and the owner of this establishment into custody at that time. I've got eighteen men. The majority of my men are on the outskirts of town. Once I give them the order, we will pounce on the mobsters and whoever's with them," Kelly said.

"You believe that Al Capone owns this speakeasy?" the agent asked.

"I do," Kelly answered.

"But didn't you also just say that you were going to take Capone, Luciano, their men, and *the owner of the bar* into custody," the agent said.

"Well, I don't think I definitely said that Capone owns the bar. I think I said that Capone owns it *or frequents* the bar." Kelly replied.

It didn't really matter what was actually said. Kelly had already accomplished his task. He had engaged the agents in a meaningless dialogue that he would now maintain for as long as possible, allowing Queen Lil and her men time to move their alcohol over to the Canadian side of the bar.

"I distinctly heard you say that Capone *owns* the bar," the lead agent responded.

"Sir, his exact words were, 'We believe it is *owned and/or frequented* by

Al Capone,'" a younger agent explained while reading from his notes.

"So, this young man also believes that this speakeasy is *owned and/or frequented* by Al Capone," Major Kelly said, as though the younger agent had just vindicated him. "That's swell. Man, what a relief. I was starting to worry that we were the only people in law enforcement who believed that this speakeasy was *owned and/or frequented* by Al Capone."

"I didn't say that *we* believe this establishment is *owned and/or frequented* by Al Capone. I was just reading back my notes of what you said," the younger agent corrected. Kelly stood feigning confusion, which caused the younger agent to say, "Oh, never mind."

"What evidence do you have that this establishment is owned and/or frequented by Al Capone?" the lead agent asked Kelly.

"Evidence? Hm... good question... evidence... no actual evidence yet. That's why we've been working on this investigation so diligently for six months," Kelly continued. "Right now, I'm just relying on gut instinct. You know how sometimes you have to go with your gut on these issues? Well, my gut is telling me that this establishment is owned and/or frequented by Al Capone and he will be here in forty-eight hours."

Zho noticed that each time Costello said the word "gut," he emphasized the word by slapping his hand on his stomach. Costello also started slapping his stomach. While hitting his stomach, Zho thought to himself, *Apparently the gut section of the Earthling anatomy communicates uncertainty to the host. Costello's does not appear to be functioning properly as I am receiving no such signals. Perhaps I should launch a recovery protocol to check on this.*

"So, you've got no evidence?" the lead agent asked indignantly.

"Absolutely none," Kelly enthusiastically responded.

"What do you have to say for yourself?" the older agent asked Costello.

"Just going with the gut," Costello said as he continued to slap his stomach, trying to activate the message center. "Hey, are you all officers of the law?"

"Federal agents," the agent replied.

"Then you must know where all the prisons in the area are?" Costello asked.

"Pretty much," the agent confirmed.

"Can you tell me where I can find the Craig Colony?" Costello asked.

"The Craig Colony. Never heard of it. What is it?"

"I'm not sure. I have a report that a child is being held hostage at the Craig Colony, but no one that I've asked has ever heard of it," Costello said.

"Well, unless they took the girl across state lines with the intent to have carnal relations with her, it is out of our jurisdiction. Sorry," the agent said. Then, after thinking for a moment, he inquired:

"What agency are you guys working with, anyway?" the agent asked.

"I'm glad you asked," Kelly said. "I am the President of the Richford, Vermont branch of the Lincoln-Lee Legion of the Abstinence Department of the Anti-Saloon League." As Kelly spoke, he produced a certificate confirming that he was, in fact, President of the Lincoln-Lee Legion of the Anti-Saloon League and presented it to the younger agent, who carefully studied it.

"Looks official, boss. It says that they're with the Anti-Saloon League."

"So what? I'm an Agent with the United States Internal Revenue Service. I have probable cause and a search warrant signed by a United States District Judge!" the lead agent exclaimed.

"And rest assured that the Richford branch of the Lincoln-Lee Legion of the Abstinence Department of the Anti-Saloon League is here to support your fine work in any way that we can!" Kelly told him with a grin.

"By the way," the lead agent asked, "what are you going to do if you actually encounter Capone and his men?"

"We intend to make a citizen's arrest and then turn Capone over to the proper authorities. I can turn him over to you and give you all the credit, if you like," Kelly said.

"Where did you get your uniforms?" the older agent asked Costello.

"The closet," Costello said.

"Are they real?" the agent asked.

"Of course, they're real," Kelly replied. "We bought them at the Army Navy Surplus Store. The sign on the window said they were official United States Army uniforms. Mine cost me eight dollars. Do you like them?"

"Get these fools out of my way," the lead agent told his men.

Kelly had pushed their luck and the agents' patience about as far as they would go, but he also figured he had bought Queen Lil and her men enough time to move any alcohol to the Canadian side of the bar.

"It was a pleasure speaking with a fellow officer of the law. You just let me know if the Lincoln-Lee Legion can assist you in any way. It would be our honor," Kelly said, in a friendly, supportive voice as the agents lined up to enter the speakeasy.

With that, the lead agent yelled to his men. "Men! To your positions!"

Suddenly Queen Lil swung open the door. "Men to your positions. I certainly like the sound of that."

"Lilian Miner?" the lead agent asked.

"I am Lilian Miner. But everyone here calls me Queen Lil," the Queen said, smiling.

"Lilian Miner, this is a search warrant. By order of the United States District Court for the District of Vermont, we are entitled to search your premises," the lead agent recited.

"Gentlemen! You don't need this dirty piece of paper," Queen Lil responded. "Please. This is a public establishment and open to everyone. Come inside and enjoy yourselves."

The agents rushed into the bar and saw cases of liquor stacked openly on the opposite, Canadian side of the bar. The only customer sitting on the U.S. side was Moyer, who was holding a glass of milk. The younger agent grabbed the milk from Moyer's hand, smelled it, and poured the drink on the floor.

"Hey, that milk cost me ten cents," Moyer protested.

"This is the American side," Queen Lil explained. "Here we only serve non-alcoholic beverages: milk, soda pop, or other soft drinks. On the Canadian side, alcohol sales are legal, and you can get almost any kind of drink you want."

The American side of the bar was now free of contraband. Queen Lil walked to the line painted across the middle of the bar.

"I don't mean to be impolite, but just a reminder: you have no jurisdiction on the Canadian side of this establishment. So, if you're looking for an beverage containing alcohol, please go find some disreputable operator to serve it to you."

"Sir! We have completed our search. There is no alcohol on the American side," the younger agent loudly reported.

"Everyone, into the trucks," the lead agent ordered, and then glared at Kelly, as he said. "If Capone shows up tomorrow, you're on your own."

Bobby Billow took position behind a tree stump about one hundred yards from the road. He loved the feel of a rifle in his hands. Billow peered through the "telescopic musket sight" issued by the U.S. Army. *God, I hate these sights,* he thought to himself, pushing the button on the side and sliding it off of the rifle.

Before the World War, all infantrymen were issued the same standard M1903 Springfield rifles, and the best shots were later called snipers. The rifle's manufacturer, the Springfield Armory, represented that it was accurate up to six hundred yards. It proved in battle to be an outstanding firearm for its day. But, as many unfortunate members of the German Army learned, in Billow's hands – and using no sight whatsoever – the M1903 was accurate to a distance of up to one thousand yards.

Billow never did the math or even thought about how amazing some of his shots were; but they were, and he had no formal training. Now the decorated U.S. Army sniper would follow Major Mike Kelly to ensure that no one tried to harm the Medal of Honor recipient. Billow had watched Kelly's back during every single criminal operation since the war. This day, Billow would "cover" the major while Kelly stopped and searched a train for "contraband."

Liquor was often smuggled via train from Canada into Vermont. Billow watched as the other members of the Kelly family took their assigned positions on the train tracks north of Newport, Vermont. It was likely overkill for Kelly to be covered by an expert marksman while confiscating liquor, but the major was always careful.

The plan, as Kelly explained it, was to stop a southbound train from Quebec and search it for contraband. Queen Lil had said that it would be carrying a massive cache of Canadian whiskey, and she had given Kelly the approximate time and location it would reach Newport. Kelly stopped the train north of town, to minimize civilian casualties in the event of resistance. Kelly asked the Guardsmen to park their military vehicles on the tracks, to force the train to stop. They complied. The plan worked just as Kelly planned.

After climbing aboard the locomotive, Zho was surprised that they were greeted warmly by the conductor and the engineer. It was as though they were in on the heist. After about five minutes, Kelly stepped down from the train and briefly turned back to exchange further pleasantries with the Conductor.

Kelly then told Moyer, Feeney, and Costello to follow him back to the sixth and seventh freight cars. The men complied and, after opening the doors to the sixth car, Costello jumped aboard and discovered bags of sugar and flour.

Before Costello could open a bag, Kelly shouted, "Get the trucks!" Feeney and Moyer immediately ran back and told the others to drive the empty trucks up to the side of the sixth and seventh train cars. Meanwhile, as ordered, Costello ignored the outside row of the sugar and flour bags and cut open the inner sacks. There, hidden within and covered with an outer veil of sugar, were cases of Canadian whiskey.

"Search each bag of flour and sugar. Seize every case of whiskey that you find and put them in the trucks," Kelly ordered.

"Yes sir," Costello barked, mimicking the other men. Two of the Guardsmen eagerly jumped into the train car to assist Costello. They obviously believed that they were performing a vital government function by impounding evidence, and they continued cutting open and unwrapping various bags to reveal cases of whiskey.

"Load it all into the trucks," Kelly ordered. The men acted just like an active military unit receiving orders from their commanding officer.

"All of it?" Costello asked.

"Of course, all of it. It's evidence!" Kelly shouted forcefully. "They're lucky we don't impound the train. Under the law, we now have every right to."

Although the Volstead Act gave federal officers the power to seize any vehicle caught transporting intoxicating liquor, Kelly lacked this authority. However, he found that so long as he acted as though he was "official," people's guilt and their desire to keep their vehicles, caused them to volunteer to give up the contraband as soon as they heard the threat.

Twenty minutes later, the trucks were packed, and the convoy was heading off to Rouses Point, New York. Now that they actually were transporting alcohol, it was imperative that Kelly and Costello, in the scout car, keep their eyes open for anyone who might intercept the convoy.

"So, how many cases of whiskey did we get?" Costello asked.

"Four hundred fifty," Kelly gloated.

"That's a lot of whiskey. You do know that it belongs to someone. Based on the size of that shipment, probably someone very dangerous. We've just made a powerful enemy by stealing that whiskey," Costello said.

"We didn't steal any whiskey," Kelly insisted. "That was my whiskey. I bought it in Montreal for ten dollars per case. I have a customer in Whitehall who will buy it for fifty dollars per case. My customer will then drive it to New York City and sell it for between seventy to a hundred dollars per case, or three dollars per glass, depending on his business plan." Kelly continued, "Four hundred and fifty cases already cost me $4,500. So, keep your eyes open so we can get this booze to the buyer in Whitehall and I can recover my investment."

"If it's your whiskey, why the elaborate charade that we were impounding it from the train?" Costello asked.

"Because we need those National Guardsmen to believe we're enforcing the law. That way, we can continue to use their weapons, equipment, and trucks. If they thought that we were bootleggers, we might not get their cooperation."

"That's brilliant," Costello responded.

"Thank you," Kelly said. "Now, keep your eyes on the road. There is something in Rouses Point that I need to show you before dark."

CHAPTER SIXTEEN
THE DIVERSION

Vermont-Canada Border
June 10, 1926

Kelly's challenge was moving four hundred and fifty cases of bootleg whiskey from the Canadian border to the buyer in Whitehall. After driving sixty miles without interruption, the convoy reached Swanton, Vermont. They made camp and waited for nightfall. Over dinner, Kelly explained that the convoy would wait three hours and then begin the 115-mile journey south to Whitehall. This three-hour delay would allow Kelly, Costello, and Feeney time to commence a diversion, which, if all went as planned, would permit the convoy to drive to Whitehall without incident.

"You are in command of the convoy," Kelly told Moyer. "Take the Packard and scout for anything suspicious. When you see the diversion, head straight to Whitehall."

"How will I recognize the diversion?" Moyer asked.

"It will be on the lake. You'll know it when you see it," Kelly responded.

It was an eighteen-mile drive from Swanton to Rouses Point, and when they arrived, Kelly drove straight to the waterfront, where a forty-foot sailing canal boat was docked at the pier.

"What's this?" Costello asked.

"This is the *Victory*. The first vessel in the Lake Champlain auxiliary of the New York Naval Militia," Kelly said.

"The what?" Costello asked.

"The New York Naval Militia," Kelly said. "Few New York taxpayers know it, but the state has a Naval Militia – a state-funded program that trains sailors for service in the U.S. Navy in the event they're needed during wartime. I checked and confirmed that there's no Lake Champlain naval auxiliary. So, I volunteered and was appointed commander of this new unit."

"Why would you do that?" Costello asked.

"Because I love my country, of course… and because a ship like this can sail on Lake Champlain from Canada down to the Big Apple," Kelly said with a smile. "And who's gonna stop and search the New York Naval Militia?"

"Brilliant," Costello said, once again impressed by Kelly's criminal ingenuity.

"Thank you. Now, stow our gear on the boat so we can set sail. But first, meet Captain Edwards."

Captain Edwards was an ornery old ship captain who had sailed canal boats on Lake Champlain for most of his life. Although he liked few people, he was impressed with Kelly.

"Captain Edwards!" Kelly shouted from the dock. "I'd like to introduce two of my finest men: Ensign Owen Feeney and Sergeant Ryan Costello."

"*Sergeant* Costello?" Captain Edwards muttered suspiciously. "You're a sergeant, not an ensign? We don't have sergeants in the Navy. You got something against the Navy, Costello?"

"No, sir. I was just recruited for the New York Naval Militia. However, I fought with the major in the Great War, and I will proudly serve under the major in any branch of the service," Costello said emphatically.

Captain Edwards was impressed with his enthusiasm for Kelly.

"Permission to come aboard?" Kelly asked Captain Edwards.

"Permission granted to Major Kelly and the ensign," Captain Edwards responded. "And major, if you vouch for the young sergeant, then I suppose he can come aboard, too."

"I can vouch for the sergeant. We have firearms and munitions that we want to bring on board to use in live weapons training. Is that all right, sir?" Kelly asked.

"Of course. A naval vessel isn't much good without weapons," Edwards responded, quite pleased to be referring to his modest sailing canal boat as a naval vessel. It had been quite some time since Captain Edwards was treated with such respect and courtesy – particularly from an officer as decorated as Major Kelly.

Costello and Feeney carefully unloaded the heavy machine gun and carried it to the front deck of the *Victory*. Within ten minutes, it was assembled and attached to the deck. Kelly personally connected the mortar to the rear deck of the boat.

"Although I'm not certain, I assume that we are now the most heavily armed vessel on Lake Champlain," Captain Edwards joked.

"I hope so," Kelly said. "Permission to shove off, Captain?"

"Aye, aye," Edwards shouted back. He ordered his two crew members to weigh anchor and set sail.

"Where to, Major?" Edwards asked.

"Whitehall," Kelly answered.

———————

Moyer checked his watch. Major Kelly had left Swanton, Vermont three hours before. It was a 115-mile journey from Swanton to Whitehall, and since the trucks could only travel at a maximum speed of twenty-five miles per hour, Moyer estimated that the trip would take a little over five hours.

Two variables could make the journey more difficult. First, the roads from Swanton to Whitehall had no streetlights. Although this would allow the convoy to travel under cover of darkness, it also created the genuine hazard that they would have little to no visibility.

Second, the route would require the caravan to travel through two major "cities" of the day – Burlington, Vermont and Plattsburgh, New York.

Kelly figured that any police activity that evening would be near those two areas – hence the diversion.

———•———

The *Victory* made good time. As Kelly and Costello stood on the deck of the ship, Kelly continued his rum-running lessons.

"Could I ask you a question?" Costello said.

"Sure," Kelly replied.

"That first night in the armory, you became enraged when I called you a bootlegger. Why?" Costello asked.

"A bootlegger is a criminal. I run a family business, founded by my grandfather in 1866 after he fought for the Union Army in the Civil War. No one would have dared call my grandfather a criminal. He sold beer and liquor to adults who freely chose to buy it. When you call me a bootlegger for running the exact same business that my father and grandfather worked their entire lives to build, you're calling them criminals, too."

"I'm sorry. I didn't realize that your father was in the same business?" Costello asked.

"Dad took over the business after he served in the Spanish-American War," Kelly continued. "He worked in that store night and day. He was the finest man I've ever known. I never saw him break a law or tell a lie. Hell, he never even missed church on Sunday. But in 1920, our then 54-year-old family business was instantly made illegal by the United

States government. Suddenly, three generations of my family were no longer businessmen. We were criminals."

As his voice rose, Kelly became more agitated. Costello thought it best not to speak.

"Three generations who had fought and bled for this country. I received the Medal of Honor for all the killing I did for this country. Yeah, the Honor. Hell, I did things in that war that I will carry with me until the day I die. Like everyone else I was just trying to survive. And when I came home, how was I repaid? Just when I needed it most to feed my kids, our family business was gone-declared illegal. Just by operating that same business, we were now criminals.

"My father had to choose between giving up his life's work or breaking the law. I am certain that that's what killed him. But not me. The government had turned our family business into a criminal enterprise. Fine. If that's how they wanted to play it, then I'd become the best criminal they'd ever seen."

"I understand. Thank you for telling me all that," Costello said.

Zho's admiration for his bootlegging mentor had suddenly grown exponentially. At the start of this trip, Zho had been protecting the Kelly family because he had been ordered to do so. He still didn't know why, but it was part of his mission. However, he now felt something far more. An emotional bond. A kinship. Back home, the High Council treated Daganians similarly. Although they professed to serve its citizenry, the High Council was the ruling class and Zho was one of Dagan's "mere citizens." Although beings like Councilmember Arixn may profess to be fans of his Skiirmiishing, Zho understood that they would never accept him as an equal, no matter how accomplished he was or how great his service to Dagan.

"That certainly explains why you continue to sell liquor despite Prohibition," Costello said. "But I still don't understand your dream of becoming a boxer."

"Really? You've met my wife and kids, and you can't figure out why I would want to get away from this life?" Kelly continued, "As I see it, boxing is my ticket out. No more weekends traveling to and from Canada. Sure, I'll have to take a few punches, but there would be no more threats of violence against my family. Most importantly, I could stop worrying about what would happen to my family if I ever was arrested or killed."

"We're approaching Plattsburgh," Captain Edwards announced as he strolled on to the deck.

"Feeney, place two rowboats into the water. Fill them with dynamite and three gallons of gasoline each," Kelly ordered. Feeney promptly complied.

"At my signal, set the boats adrift," Kelly ordered. "Now." The men complied, and the rowboats floated away.

"When the dinghies reach a distance of two hundred and fifty yards from the *Victory*, open fire," Kelly continued. "But don't hit the boats right away. We need to make some noise first."

As the first rowboat drifted away, Feeney took his place at the heavy machine gun and fired.

From the rear of the boat, Costello, operating a mortar, began lobbing shells at the second rowboat as it drifted further from the *Victory*.

The diversion was underway.

The people of Plattsburgh, New York, population 11,000, had never heard machine gun or mortar fire in the harbor before. They now awoke to it in the middle of the night. All active patrol units of the Plattsburgh police were diverted waterside so that they could assist with the apprehension of whatever was causing the commotion out on the lake.

It was pitch-black that night, but the people of Plattsburgh could see the gunfire and bursts on Lake Champlain. To add to the brilliance of the display, Kelly started shooting off aerial fireworks from the back of the *Victory*.

Captain Jack Kendrick of the Lake Champlain Boat Patrol almost immediately began receiving phone calls about the unusual sights and sounds offshore in Plattsburgh. There was universal agreement among the callers that Captain Kendrick was the best law enforcement officer to handle this disturbance. Although Kendrick reluctantly agreed to respond to the commotion, he didn't agree that it fell within his jurisdiction.

Kendrick and his Lake Champlain Boat Patrol were a vital part of the fight against bootlegging on the lake, and Kendrick had transformed his waterfront camp in Saint Albans, Vermont into their headquarters. His squad consisted of mostly thirty-something officers supported by college students. On certain missions, Kendrick was even backed up by his wife.

Despite their modest numbers and limited weaponry, Kendrick and his boat patrol had made bootlegging demonstrably more difficult on Lake Champlain.

As Kendrick approached the *Victory* in his mahogany Chris-Craft patrol boat, he was wary. Although he had earned a reputation for being fearless on the water, on this particular evening, he was supported only by two college students on summer break armed with pistols.

It was apparent from the machine gun fire and the explosions on the lake that whoever was on the much larger boat was heavily armed. Indeed, such a display of firepower was unusual for bootleggers. They preferred to use stealth to evade detection. By contrast, this vessel, anchored and aiming at specific targets, had done nothing to hide its activity or location.

Suddenly, there was a direct hit on the first rowboat. The dynamite and gasoline on board exploded as the boat burst into flames. "These are no bootleggers," Captain Kendrick said to the nineteen-year-old college students he had awoken and convinced to join him on this mission. "They're likely drunken fools taking midnight target practice in the middle of the lake."

Kendrick pulled his boat up alongside the *Victory*. "This is the Lake Champlain Boat Patrol!" he shouted, "Prepare to be boarded!"

Moyer watched the "fireworks" on the lake as he drove the Packard ahead of the convoy. The "diversion" had worked perfectly. If there had been a police presence on the road that evening looking for bootleggers, it was now lakeside. The convoy drove through Plattsburgh undetected and headed south toward Burlington.

"Hey, you! I said, prepare to be boarded!" Kendrick hollered at the first person he saw onboard the *Victory*. It was Kelly.

"I'm going be boarded by a pretend sailor in a mahogany speed boat," Kelly laughed.

"This is the Lake Champlain Boat Patrol," Kendrick responded, his voice sharp. "Turn off your engines, lower your sails, ceasefire all weapons, and prepare to be searched."

"You're going to search my boat?" Kelly again laughed, "Go ahead, try to search my boat, and I'll impound *your* pretty little mahogany boat!"

"This is no joke," Kendrick responded. "I'm a deputized captain in the Lake Champlain Boat Patrol."

"And I'm a major in the New York State National Guard and a commander in the New York Naval Militia." Kelly continued, "And, Mr. Boat Patrol, you are now on notice that you are interfering with official nighttime live-fire training exercises."

Kelly went on yelling. "So, Captain or Lieutenant or whatever you call yourself – unless you want my men to board *your* vessel, impound it, and put you under arrest, I suggest that you shove off… now."

The two men were shouting threats at each other. Kelly was in his element.

"Oh, my Lord. Mike Kelly, is that you?" Kendrick asked.

"It is. Who the Hell are you?" Kelly responded, without changing the furious tone in his voice.

"Major Jack Kendrick," Captain Kendrick answered, trying to lower the angry tenor.

"Jack Kendrick! Well, I'll be damned," Kelly said, sounding a little more friendly. "I haven't seen you since your ambulance driving days in the war. Costello, come and meet the man who saved your life in France."

"Good evening, sir!" Costello yelled as he peered down from the boat, casually holding a Thompson machine gun against his chest.

"Jack, I've heard about all about the great things you're doing out here on the lake. And I promise I'll assist your efforts," Kelly went on. "But tonight, I'm really busy. I'm on a live-fire training exercise, and we must be heading south to try to meet our schedule. I'm sorry if we disturbed the town, but you know, we're only doing this to be ready to protect their freedom."

"I understand. If I'd known it was Mike Kelly out on the water, I wouldn't have even gotten out of bed. Next time you're going to be on the lake, give me some advance notice. I'll take care of it." The two men exchanged further pleasantries and then Kendrick cast off his boat to head back to shore.

With that, the *Victory* weighed anchor and headed off towards the shores of Burlington, where they would repeat the same late-night, live-fire training exercise. And just as Kelly had planned, the diversion allowed the convoy to drive unobstructed through Burlington, Vermont to Whitehall, New York.

Three hours later, the convoy arrived in Whitehall. The trucks and their valuable liquid cargo were left unguarded, parked in a commercial garage just a quarter mile from the armory. Two hours later, Kelly's men would return to the garage and pick up the trucks. The cargo was removed. In its place, two hundred fifty dollars cash per man was left in a bag under each seat. This was comparable to over two months' pay for most of the men. Not bad for two days' work.

As for the bulk of the payment, Kelly and Costello would personally meet with the buyer at four o'clock that afternoon in Albany, New York.

CHAPTER SEVENTEEN

THE BUYER

Albany New York
June 11, 1926

"The press portrays this guy as a folk hero. Don't let the fancy suit or the 'gentleman act' fool you. He's a little hood from Philly," Kelly explained.

Kelly and Costello were driving to Albany to collect full payment for the whiskey delivered to the Whitehall garage earlier in the day. The two men were using Kelly's Model T truck because, in addition to collecting payment from the buyer, Kelly was making a delivery.

The buyer, Jack "Legs" Diamond, had already taken out a contract on Kelly. Zho felt guilty that he had never disclosed this information. If he had, Kelly would have also learned that, in fact, it was the "old" Costello who had accepted the contract. Zho decided that there was no way he could disclose this to Kelly without losing the trust they had developed. After all, Kelly was certainly not ready to hear that Zho was an alien controlling the reanimated body of Costello. So, instead, Zho caused Costello to question the wisdom of Kelly's new business arrangement with Diamond.

"If Diamond has double-crossed everyone he's done business with, that means he's double-crossed mobsters – people prepared to do a lot more to him than you ever will," Costello warned.

"So?"

"So, it's my job to protect the Kelly family. If you do business with Diamond, it makes my job a lot more difficult," Costello insisted.

"It's your job to protect the Kelly family. How sweet," Kelly said, laughing.

"If you know Diamond can't be trusted, then why do business with him?" Costello asked.

"His money is green. And what do I care if he's screwed over some gangsters in New York? As long as he doesn't mess with me, I've got no quarrel with him."

"And just how long do you think that will last?"

"That's my business," Kelly snapped. "Now, keep your eyes peeled for a garage on Launch and Howard Street."

"There it is," Costello said, and Kelly pulled the truck into the garage.

The garage at the corner of Launch Street and Howard Street was a reliable Albany location where bootleggers could leave a delivery free from interference from the authorities. Kelly was confident that his cargo would be safe until the recipient picked it up, while he and Costello met with Diamond.

In the back of the truck, Kelly had left several cases of Canadian whiskey from his personal supply.

"I can't believe you're just giving that booze to Diamond," Costello said.

"It's not a gift. It's an investment. That man can open a lot of doors for me," Kelly said.

"That man could also murder you and your family. I can't believe it's worth the risk," Costello replied.

The New Kenmore Hotel had an opulence, a grandeur, that was difficult to find in most American hotels of the day – it was certainly a class above the other hotels and boarding houses in Albany. The Rain-Bo Room at the New Kenmore Hotel evoked the feel of upper west side Manhattan, with jazz legends, actors, and politicians frequenting the club.

It was this feeling of a New York city nightclub that made "Legs" Diamond feel at home in the Rain-Bo Room. The establishment didn't sell alcohol, as doing so was illegal. However, if guests chose to bring their own to the hotel, the management would not interfere, and Diamond had brought enough beer for himself and his associates. Diamond enjoyed the Rain-Bo Room; and it was the perfect joint for him to hold a sit-down.

Despite its political clout as the capital of the state of New York, Albany was, and would likely always be, the little sister to New York City some 130 miles south on the Hudson River.

Diamond had made the forty-three-mile trip to Albany that day from his new home in Acra specifically to meet with Mike Kelly. Diamond wasn't happy about making the journey, but he had faith that it would be worth it.

The town of Acra was in Greene County, about 127 miles from New York City. The location was perfectly suited for Diamond's goal of consolidating alcohol supply routes from Canada. Kelly essentially controlled the area north of Albany, all the way to the Canadian border, and if he had his way, Diamond would soon control shipping to the south.

This meeting would determine whether the two men were allies or rivals. Kelly's sale of four hundred and fifty cases of whiskey, which Diamond had picked up in Whitehall earlier in the day, was a "test drive" of their relationship. By consolidating upstate supply routes, Diamond would be one step closer to his ultimate goal: a ticket back to the big leagues in New York City.

Sitting with Diamond at his table in the Rain-Bo Room were two hired guns, Red Monahan and his little brother, Frank. Although they had a gang of their own, they often worked as Diamond's bodyguards and muscle. It was unfortunate that Diamond was always surrounded by bodyguards, but since so many mobsters had pledged to kill him, it was a necessity. In fact, despite Diamond's move upstate, many were still trying to finish the job.

Kelly and Costello walked into the Rain-Bo Room dressed in their normal attire of blue jeans, flannel shirts, and work boots. The maître d' showed them to Diamond's table. "Legs," famous for his dapper appearance, immediately stood, as did his similarly dressed associates.

When he saw Costello, Diamond did a double take. Diamond certainly didn't expect to see Kelly and his hitman together. "Gentlemen, this is a high-class place. You're dressed like farmers," Diamond blurted.

"Mr. Diamond, I'm Mike Kelly. This is Ryan Costello. We've just returned from a trip up north, a very lucrative trip for both of us. We didn't have time to get dressed all fancy for this meeting. We just came for our money," Kelly told him.

"Pay the man," Diamond instructed as he gulped down a beer. The larger of the two bodyguards, Red Monahan, handed Kelly a bag containing $17,500 in cash.

"It's all there. That's a lot of money. It will buy you boys a lot of cows," Diamond joked, and on cue the Monahan brothers laughed.

Kelly did not even acknowledge the joke. He seated himself at Diamond's table and began counting the money in plain view of everyone in the club, while Costello watched Diamond's men.

"I said it was all there. You're acting like you don't trust me," Diamond said.

Kelly did not even acknowledge Diamond's concern and merely continued counting.

"As you requested, we left $250 for each of your men under the front seat of their trucks and deducted that amount from your share." Diamond, realizing that his cow joke had not gone over well, was trying to get the conversation back to business.

Kelly did not react and continued counting. Then, quite unexpectedly for Diamond, Albany Democratic chairman Dan O'Connell and Albany police detective William Fitzpatrick walked up to the table.

"Why, I thought I saw Major Mike Kelly!" O'Connell exclaimed.

"Dan O'Connell!" Kelly jumped up and hugged O'Connell. "How are you, my old friend?"

O'Connell feigned surprise when he saw Diamond and the Monahan brothers seated at the table and spoke particularly harshly to Diamond. "We will never allow organized crime in Albany. Do you hear me, Mr. Diamond? You try to do any business in this town, you'll answer to Detective Fitzpatrick."

"Or Detective Fitzpatrick will answer to me," Diamond said, smiling at Fitzpatrick. Then he stood up and threw his napkin on the table. The Monahan brothers rose from their seats.

"You know a lot of people have tried to put a bullet in me," Diamond said. "But the bullet hasn't been made that can kill 'Legs' Diamond."

Fitzpatrick and Diamond stared defiantly at each other, almost daring the other to pull a weapon. Several seconds passed while each man waited for the other to blink.

Then Costello stepped between the men. "1931," he said softly.

"What?" Diamond responded angrily.

"I said, *nineteen... thirty-one*," Costello repeated, slowly and calmly.

"Kelly, what is your man jabbering about?" Diamond asked, ignoring Costello.

"You'll have to ask him," Kelly responded, amused.

"What are you talking about, freak?" Diamond yelled to Costello.

"Mr. Diamond, I agree. The bullet that will kill you hasn't been made," Costello said.

"Well, there you go," Diamond said, smiling.

"The bullet that will kill you will be made in 1931," Costello said slowly. Costello's statement was so definitive that no one knew how to react.

"What the hell are you talking about?" Diamond said to Costello.

"Please don't raise your voice. I merely agreed with your statement. It is now 1926. The bullet that will kill you will be made in 1931." Costello said quietly, forcefully.

Costello was eerily calm as he patiently explained this to Diamond. The men around the table stared at Costello in disbelief. It wasn't often that Diamond received a prophecy of death so calmly delivered by a fellow bootlegger.

"Are you predicting the future again, Costello? You'll have to forgive the sergeant here. He's a good man, but he hasn't been right in the head since he came back from the war," Kelly explained.

"He served in the war?" O'Connell asked.

"He served with me in France and Germany in the 105th," Kelly said.

"Then there's another thing you should know about Diamond. While you were fighting in Europe, Diamond was serving three years in Leavenworth for desertion," O'Connell said

"Is that true?" Kelly asked Diamond, barely holding back his disgust.

"I was drafted, went AWOL, and did three years in the can. So what?" Diamond responded defiantly.

"So, I don't do business with cowards," Kelly said. He turned away, still holding the bag of money that Diamond had just paid him and walked out. Kelly made no effort to hide the bag from O'Connell or Fitzpatrick. Kelly was clearly signaling that he was not afraid of anything that Diamond could do to him.

After Kelly walked out with O'Connell and Fitzpatrick, Costello lingered behind and stood by the table with Diamond and his two bodyguards.

"You know, I should kill you right now for failing to do the work on Kelly. Why the hell are you still here?" Diamond asked Costello.

"I thought you might wish to speak privately," Costello replied.

"Privately, huh? You mean about the work on Kelly that you still haven't done?" Diamond asked.

"Shall we speak freely in front of these men?" Costello asked.

"They know everything. They're paid to protect me," Diamond said. "And Monahan here was in the car the day you agreed to hit Kelly. So, why is it that you think I would want to talk to you?"

"1931."

"What about 1931?"

"1931 is coming a lot sooner than you may realize," Costello said softly. "You really should prepare yourself for the inevitable."

"The inevitable, huh. What are you, some kind of insurance salesman?" Diamond laughed and again, almost on cue, the two Monahan brothers laughed with him.

"No. I am no salesman," Costello said. "I'm just a... a man... telling you that you've got five years left. You have free will to decide how best to use those five years. If I were you, I would use that time to make the most of my life. To become a force for good."

Costello backed slowly away, keeping his eyes trained on Diamond and his two men.

"And one more thing: I will not be performing any 'work' on the one called Mike Kelly. And if you try to hurt him in any way, you will answer to me. I have determined that it is my mission to protect the Kelly family," Costello said. Costello turned and followed Kelly out the front door.

"Man, that guy is creepy," Diamond remarked to his men.

"Do you want us to go get him, boss?" Red Monahan asked.

"No. Let's take our time with these farmers," Diamond said. "I need to learn more about their suppliers and delivery routes before we make our move. Once I do, I don't see either Major Kelly or his crazy buddy Costello living to see the new year. And I think the bullets have long been made that will kill both of them."

"Made in 1926," Red Monahan responded. The three men laughed at Monahan's joke and resumed their drinking.

When Costello exited the Hotel, he saw Kelly standing on the sidewalk with O'Connell and Fitzpatrick.

"Thank you for the kind gift that you left in the back of your truck," O'Connell said.

"My pleasure. May you enjoy it in good health," Kelly told him, and hugged both O'Connell and Fitzpatrick.

As Costello and Kelly walked back to the truck, Costello couldn't help but express his admiration and relief.

"So, the cases we left in the truck were never for Diamond?" Costello asked.

"Why would they have been for Diamond? He's nothing in this town. He's a punk. A hoodlum pretending to be a big-time gangster from New York City."

"He may be a punk, but he's dangerous," Costello replied. "Don't take him for granted."

"Believe me. I won't," Kelly replied. "Diamond reminds me of a wild dog. You can try to tame it, but if that dog ever growls at you or snaps at your family, you have to put it down."

"Are you going have to put him down?" Costello asked.

"Perhaps."

"If you do, it should be on December 18, 1931," Costello said.

"Why that date?"

"Because that is *his day*," Costello replied.

Kelly stopped. "That won't be for five years. How do you know that?"

"Because… I just know it. You have to trust me," Costello said.

"I do trust you, Ryan."

"Good. Now let's go home. You still have a lot of work to do if you're going to knock out Jack Dempsey."

CHAPTER EIGHTEEN

THE ROUTINE

Granville, New York
July 2, 1926

For the next several weeks, Costello increased Kelly's training regimen every few days. Although they had become an excellent team, their goals were very different.

Of course, Kelly's goal was to knock out Jack Dempsey, while Costello had three goals: getting the host body in shape, teaching Kelly enough boxing skills that he would be able to survive the Dempsey fight, and trying to figure out how Kelly related to his ultimate mission.

To his credit, Kelly enthusiastically adopted all of Costello's "modern" training methods. And as a result, Kelly became a new man. Each day, Kelly and Costello would rise at six o'clock and jog from Kelly's home to the armory. Once inside, Kelly would do calisthenics of any kind or duration that Costello demanded.

Costello would vary the exercises each day to work Kelly's different muscle groups and allow the major's other muscles to recover. Once the fitness training was completed, Kelly would perform repetitive boxing drills designed to improve his footwork, head movement, and punching power.

When the roadwork, calisthenics, and drills were complete, then and only then would Costello allow Kelly to enter the ring. Since there was no one in Washington County capable of preparing Kelly to fight Dempsey, Costello acted as Kelly's primary sparring partner.

Despite Kelly's protestations, he wore headgear Costello had fashioned from an aviator's helmet. Kelly was skeptical of Costello's homemade safety gear, designed to minimize cognitive injuries. However, since he had promised to follow Costello's instructions completely, Kelly wore the modified helmet.

After each sparring session, Costello insisted that the two men complete stretching exercises. They were performing yoga, but Costello called it stretching so as not to alarm the major.

Once they had completed their yoga training, they would end each session with what Costello referred to as a strategy talk. The two men discussed everything from how Kelly felt about his progress to, most often, how his new sobriety had dramatically improved his quality of life.

The sessions always ended by reaffirming Kelly's absolute need to stay sober. Costello was careful not to push too hard during these sessions. Kelly became evasive when their conversation would veer into his personal feelings about his line of work, now that he was living a sober life. Costello tried to get Kelly to confront these issues and to come to the realization that living dry drastically improved all aspects of his life.

The evenings back at the house had their own routine. Uncle Ryan became an integral part of Kelly home life. The family ate dinner at six o'clock each evening, and the children would take turns leading the family in saying grace.

After dinner, the children would clean up the kitchen. Once all of the children were ready for bed, Mary Kelly would read to them from a popular novel or children's book. Their favorite was *The Wonderful Wizard of Oz*. Although Mike Kelly never participated in Mary's nightly readings, once Mary got over her anger with him, Uncle Ryan was even asked to read. After the nightly bedtime reading was finished, Costello and Kelly would study Dempsey's old fights and training sessions. One evening, Kelly even commented that he never knew Costello knew so much about Jack Dempsey.

Actually, Zho's knowledge of Dempsey wasn't derived from a database or host memory. Zho had squared off against Dempsey many times in Skiirmiishing simulations. In fact, Zho fought a special limited-edition version of Dempsey in the championship round of the simulation "Skiirmiishing 3: Intergalactic Monsters."

To assist in their preparations, Kelly had obtained newsreels of Dempsey's fights. One of Kelly's friends in the American Legion owned the movie theater in Glens Falls, New York and was honored to help Major Kelly get newsreels of Dempsey's most prominent fights – especially when he learned that Kelly was training for a match with Dempsey.

"I didn't know that Dempsey had agreed to fight you," the theater owner said.

"He hasn't agreed yet," Kelly sheepishly replied. "I'm challenging him to spar with me. Then, while sparring, I'm going to make it personal and turn it into a fight."

"So – you're going to piss off Jack Dempsey on purpose during a sparring session?" the theater owner asked incredulously.

"That's right," Kelly said with a big smile.

"Well, I hope that works out for you."

Within a matter of weeks, Kelly had obtained newsreels of Dempsey's fights with Jess Willard, Luis Firpo, and Tommy Gibbons. Costello told Kelly to pay particular attention to the Dempsey/Gibbons fight. Gibbons was fifteen pounds lighter than Dempsey but went the distance, lasting all fifteen rounds against the champion.

Costello and Kelly watched the newsreels over and over again, looking for any possible advantage against Dempsey. This repetition was particularly helpful when Costello would stop the projector and comment in detail on Dempsey's technique.

Costello referred to Kelly's training regimen as "The Routine." Costello insisted that Kelly adhere to every aspect of the Routine to get himself into peak physical condition. This Routine not only meant intensive physical training, which Kelly enjoyed, but also vastly improving Kelly's dietary and social habits.

For example, under the Routine, Kelly was required to refrain from using alcohol or tobacco. Television commercials misrepresenting the health benefits of cigarettes would not invade American popular culture until the 1940s, so Kelly had never been a tobacco user. The challenge for Kelly, particularly given his heritage, social habits, and livelihood, was the requirement to refrain from drinking alcohol.

"How can I be sure that you won't drink?" Costello asked.

"Because I promised. And when Mike Kelly makes a promise, he keeps it," Kelly said about twenty times after making the promise.

But Kelly did keep his promise. At first, teetotaler Mike Kelly was a strange sight around Granville – especially to his men. Kelly had been an almost daily alcohol user since before he was sixteen and had been a hard drinker for so long that everyone in Granville just expected him to be a little tipsy.

Not anymore. While those around Kelly continued to drink liquor during and after work, Kelly maintained his sobriety. Cutting alcohol from his life was particularly difficult. Kelly liked everything about liquor: the smell, the taste, the way it made him feel about himself, the camaraderie of drinking with his men while they shared a few or, quite often, more than a few.

But now that he was sober, and it was obvious that he was a vastly superior athlete, it was much easier for him to stay with the Routine.

As he had promised, Costello also complied with the limitations of the Routine. At first, Kelly was flattered, believing Costello's adherence was in solidarity for the Dempsey fight. But Kelly soon realized that this was Costello's new chosen lifestyle. Indeed, there was an even more dramatic improvement in Costello's physical health and appearance. In a very short period of time, Costello added over sixty pounds of pure muscle.

Costello's ability to quit drinking "cold turkey" was nothing short of miraculous. The side effects of an alcoholic abruptly ceasing after years of daily drinking can be severe. These physical risks include grand mal seizures, delirium, high fevers, and other complications. Yet Costello had recovered from both a near-fatal health condition and alcoholism, while suffering no side effects.

The men trained six days each week and would rest on Sunday. Through hard work and careful diet, Kelly had gone from a good community club fighter to an actual prize fighter. Still, Zho thought it overly ambitious to throw the redesigned Kelly into his first professional test against Jack Dempsey himself. So, Zho devised a cunning plan to boost Kelly's experience and self-esteem in advance of the big day.

CHAPTER NINETEEN
THE DRESS REHEARSAL

Whitehall, New York
August 8, 1926

Although Kelly and Costello had spent the summer training for the Dempsey fight, Kelly had forgotten one important element—Dempsey had never agreed to the fight. In fact, Dempsey was training to fight Gene Tunney for the heavyweight title in September.

But Dempsey was putting on a public boxing exhibition in Saratoga on August 15. So, unbeknownst to the champ, Kelly would arrange to be his sparring partner that day and would turn their session into a brawl so memorable that Dempsey would instantly recognize Kelly's talent. This, in turn, would vault the major into the upper echelons of professional boxing.

Or that was how Kelly's dream always ended.

When Zho learned that a Dempsey fight had never actually been scheduled, he was naturally concerned. Zho also understood that Kelly's "sparring-session-turned-brawl" dream was unlikely to end in the manner Kelly envisioned. Far more likely, it would end with Dempsey pounding Kelly into the mat.

"Or even killed, if we're lucky," said the voice inside Zho's head.

"I won't let that happen," Zho replied to the voice. He had become so

accustomed to this voice that he would now carry on internal conversations with it. *"It's my mission to protect Kelly."*

If the major was intent on picking a fight with the heavyweight boxing champion, Zho would do his best to ensure that Kelly survived. They had spent the summer physically preparing for the Dempsey fight. This day would be about building Kelly's ring confidence.

Kelly awoke at 7:45 a.m. His alarm clock had been set for five forty-five so that, for once, he would rise earlier than Costello – but as part of Costello's plan, Mary Kelly turned off the alarm and let her husband sleep. When Mike Kelly realized that he had overslept, he rushed to Costello's room and banged on the door. When there was no answer, Kelly went inside. The room was empty.

Kelly walked downstairs, expecting to see someone sitting at the table, but the kitchen was empty. In the middle of the table was a note.

> *Mike,*
>
> *Don't worry. Mary and the kids are with me. Today is your final exam. Meet me at the armory at 9:00 a.m. Billow will pick you up at 8:30. Wear your dress uniform. Mary asked me to tell you that there is a present for you in your bedroom closet. Bring it with you. Today will not be easy. It will be the hardest thing you've done yet.*
> *Ryan*

Kelly walked back upstairs to the bedroom. In his closet, he found his dress uniform cleaned and pressed. His shoes were polished and fit for inspection. *Mary was obviously in on this, but why did she want me to wear my dress uniform?*

Kelly then spotted a package wrapped up with a white bow to the side of the closet. *Mary must have wrapped this present. She always puts such effort into wrapping gifts at Christmas. What are they up to?*

Suddenly aware of the time, and that Billow would be arriving at eight thirty, Kelly put down the package. He was unaccustomed to dressing quickly, especially into his dress blues. On the rare occasions that he did, Kelly would allow plenty of time to ensure that he was properly turned out.

Oh, well. They would be in the car for a good twenty minutes before they arrived at the armory. Anything that he needed to straighten out could be fixed on the drive to Whitehall.

When Billow arrived at the home, Kelly wasn't happy. Before Billow could knock, Kelly yanked the door open. "What is this all about?" the major roared.

"I'm – I'm not at liberty to say, sir," Billow stammered. "Come to think of it, I don't know what it's about, either. All I know is that Costello told me to wear my uniform, pick you up at eight thirty, and drive you to the armory."

"Under whose orders?" Kelly questioned.

"I assumed that they were your orders, sir," Billow responded.

"All right. I'm sorry that I snapped at you. Let's go." Kelly started to close the door, but then said, "Wait a minute." He went back into the house and re-emerged with the giant gift-wrapped package.

"What's the occasion?" Billow asked

"My last day of intensive training. Now I get to fight Dempsey."

"Congratulations?" Billow said.

With Billow driving the Packard, the two headed off to the armory. Although great friends, there was little conversation in the car. Kelly was preoccupied by the undisclosed difficult task waiting for him at the armory. Billow was pretending to be ignorant of what lay ahead, even though he had helped Costello plan every detail of the day's events.

When they arrived at the armory, the area was alive with activity. Billow parked the Packard in a spot by the entrance marked "reserved for Major Mike Kelly." After the two walked into the armory, Billow took the package from Kelly. "Major, I will handle this for you. You are needed inside."

Kelly walked into the main arena. Members of the 105th, in full uniform, lined the sides of the hall. As far as Kelly could see, the room was filled with people. And it wasn't just fans from Whitehall and Granville who were in attendance; boxing fans and veterans from all over upstate New York were there, many in their World War uniforms.

Costello met Kelly at the front entrance. "What is going on?" Kelly asked.

"They are here to honor you," Costello replied

"For what?" Kelly asked.

"Are you kidding?" Costello said. "In seven days, you will be trading punches with one of the greatest fighters in the history of boxing. And you're not just willing to do it, you're eager to. You are an inspiration to these people. So, get changed, get out there, and be a hero."

Kelly walked into the locker room. Inside, waiting for him, was the enormous package with the white bow. He opened it and found a green-and-white robe. Embroidered on the back was a shamrock and above the shamrock were the words *Major Kelly*.

Kelly then looked back into the box and found white silk boxing trunks with green piping that matched the robe perfectly. *Mary must have spent weeks making this.* Costello entered the locker room just as Kelly finished changing into his new trunks.

"Did you do all this?" Kelly asked.

"We all did. When word got out that you were fighting Dempsey, we were contacted by people across the country who wanted to help you," Costello said. "Which brings me to your sparring partner today."

"Really? Who?"

"Luis Firpo. Ever heard of him?" Costello asked.

"Of course, I've heard of him. The Wild Bull of the Pampas. He fought Dempsey for the heavyweight title in 1923. Firpo knocked

Dempsey clean out of the ring in the first round," Kelly exclaimed.

"Dempsey did knock him out in the second round," Costello said.

"I know. We watched the newsreels together. In fact, we watched them about twenty times," Kelly replied. "But Firpo's retired. How did you get him to come here?"

"When he heard about you, he volunteered. We paid his expenses to Albany. Billow picked him up yesterday."

"So, Billow knew about all of this," Kelly mused.

"He helped with everything. But enough of that. When you get out there, Luis Firpo will be in that ring. He's only been retired for a few months. My bet is he can still punch like a ton of bricks. But if you can't trade leather with a retired Luis Firpo, I certainly don't think you should fight the heavyweight champion."

"Don't worry about me. I'm a warrior!"

———•———

Twenty minutes later, the competitors were standing in their respective corners.

"Wait here. I want to make sure he has everything he needs." Costello walked to the opposite corner and greeted Firpo. Feeney was serving as Firpo's second, and he introduced Costello to the Argentinian fighter.

"Just so we're clear, today is about building the major's confidence. We don't want him getting hurt. Understand?" Costello said.

Firpo nodded. With that, Costello returned to his corner and motioned that they were ready for the match to commence.

The announcer entered the ring. It was Granville Mayor Jim James. Unlike the Granville carnival grounds, the Whitehall Armory had an actual microphone – which the Mayor had never used before. Although he fumbled with it at first, he quickly caught on.

"Ladies and gentlemen, I am Jim James, the Mayor of Granville."

James paused for applause; none was forthcoming, even from the spectators who had traveled from Granville for the bout. "I am also your timekeeper and ring announcer. Your referee today, from the Fighting 105th Regiment, is Lt. Bobby Billow!"

The crowd erupted for Billow. The enthusiasm was both real and intended to irk Mayor James. Following the cheers for Billow, the barber started dancing around the ring in a manner reminiscent of his Memorial Day bout a few weeks earlier with Kelly.

How far Kelly had come in such a short time.

"Today's bout is three rounds of exhibition boxing," the mayor continued. "First, let's meet our honored guest. He hails from Buenos Aires, Argentina, with a professional record of twenty-nine wins and three losses. He is the former number one heavyweight contender who, in 1923, fought champion Jack Dempsey for the heavyweight title. Ladies and gentlemen, it is my honor to introduce to you the former South American champion, the Wild Bull of the Pampas, Luis Firpo!"

The crowd cheered loudly for Firpo. It wasn't often that a celebrity of his stature was in Whitehall. Firpo's title fight with Dempsey was memorable. And the fact that Firpo had offered to spar with Kelly to get him ready for Dempsey endeared him to the crowd.

"In the opposite corner, is a friend, a commanding officer, and a war hero. With a record of fifty-five wins and no losses, here is the undefeated Washington County heavyweight boxing champion, *Ma-a-a*jor *Mi-i-i*ke Kelly!"

As Kelly waved from the ring, the crowd went wild. He was the reason they had skipped work. There were over one thousand people in the armory that August day, and all were there to cheer on Kelly.

Costello looked at the massive fighter in the opposite corner. Firpo was six feet three inches tall and 230 pounds. By 1926 standards, he was enormous. "Do you have any last advice," Kelly asked.

"Today is all about defense and combinations. Very few people hit as hard as Luis Firpo. But the good news is that he doesn't punch as fast as I do. So, since you are now quick enough to defend against me, you can defend Firpo. The other good news is that Firpo is all offense. His entire career, he relied on quickly knocking out his opponents. So, cover up and block his initial flurry and then counterpunch as he attempts to reload his right hand. Can you do that?"

"I can," Kelly said firmly.

"I know you can. You're a warrior." Costello said, as he raised his bare hands above his head so that Kelly could touch his gloves to Costello's hands.

"I'm a warrior!" Kelly yelled as he enthusiastically slapped his gloves against Costello's hands.

The bell rang. Kelly punched his gloves together and headed across the ring to meet Firpo. After the two touched gloves, the fight was underway.

Costello had asked Firpo to be aggressive right away, to simulate Dempsey's brawling style. Since Firpo had been knocked down by Dempsey multiple times in the first round of their title fight, the Argentinian was certainly familiar with that aspect of Dempsey's style.

Firpo went right to work. He threw a vicious right hook at Kelly's head, which Kelly barely ducked. Although the punch narrowly missed, its ferocity caused the crowd to "oooh." Just as Costello had taught him, Kelly counterpunched Firpo to the stomach and left side with a left-right combination as he rose from his duck.

Firpo was enjoying his retirement and was not in peak fighting shape, so the two punches weakened him. And since this was the new and improved Kelly, his blows were sharper and quicker than before training with Costello.

But there was a reason Firpo was called the "Wild Bull." He went back on the attack and again threw a hard-overhand right that was only partially deflected by Kelly's left glove. The punch was thrown with such force that it also connected with Kelly's left eye and he stumbled back and covered his face and neck with his gloves. He wasn't seriously hurt, but that punch would leave a mark.

"Use your speed. Use your speed!" Costello yelled from the corner. Much of Kelly's training had focused on movement, and he used it all. He began backpedaling while bobbing and weaving his head. He wasn't running, just making himself a more difficult target.

Firpo threw another wild right hook, which missed completely. But by throwing that punch he left himself open, and Kelly responded with a left-right combination that connected to the giant's jaw.

"That's it! That's it! Stay away!" Costello yelled.

But Kelly was too excited, and he rushed in to 'finish off' the injured Wild Bull. Although Firpo was hurt, he was still able to defend himself, and he threw a left-right jab combination that firmly struck the major. Kelly had walked into two big punches. He was wobbly, but to his credit, managed to stay on his feet. Fortunately, there was little time remaining in round one.

Kelly thought back to that bicycle that his friend Billow had ridden during their Memorial Day bout. Kelly raised his hands as best he could and "danced" away from Firpo. Fortunately for Kelly, Firpo had no desire to hurt him further, and the Wild Bull let the Warrior dance away.

Seconds later, the bell rang, ending round one.

Kelly sat down in his corner, angry with himself for rushing into those two punches. He had one minute to clear his head, or the fight would quickly be over.

"Sorry, Ryan," Kelly said.

"You did great," Costello said." You took three of Firpo's best punches. He can't punch you any harder than that. And even when he hits you with his best punch, he can't knock you out. So, keep your hands up. Play defense. Wait for your moment. It will emerge. When it does, make it count."

Costello raised his hands and shouted, "You're a warrior!"

Kelly stood up, raised his gloves, and shouted back, "I'm a warrior!" Kelly slapped his gloves against Costello's hands. Although his head was still cloudy, he was ready for the second round.

The bell rang signaling the start of round two. Kelly pounded his gloves together, spun around, and headed back across the ring. Firpo walked confidently to the center. When Kelly was in range, the Wild Bull again threw his big right hook, but Kelly ducked under the punch without breaking stride.

Kelly's moment had emerged. He had an open shot at Firpo's left jaw and connected with a right, leaving Firpo dazed. Kelly followed with a sweeping left hook to Firpo's jaw, which landed cleanly.

Firpo winced, lowering his arms and further exposing his head. Kelly threw a right hook, connecting to the left side of Firpo's head, and the Wild Bull dropped to the canvas. Billow, the referee, counted the giant out. The crowd went wild. Kelly had defeated the Wild Bull. Costello rushed into the ring, lifting Kelly into the air as though he was the new heavyweight champion. Other members of the 105th, including Moyer, Moran, and Feeney, came into the ring to celebrate.

Kelly rushed to Firpo, who was using the ring ropes to brace himself as he rose from the canvas. After Kelly finished helping the Wild Bull up, the two men embraced. The crowd cheered the display of sportsmanship.

"Thank you for traveling all this way," Kelly said.

"Is there anything more I can do?" Firpo asked.

"Why, yes, there is. If you don't mind," Kelly answered.

"Anything. Anything that I can do, I will gladly do it," Firpo said.

That night, Kelly hosted a dinner at his home in honor of Luis Firpo. After dinner, Kelly, Costello, and Firpo watched newsreels of the Dempsey-Firpo bout and Dempsey's other fights, to refine a strategy that would allow Kelly to beat the champion. The next day, the three men trained at the armory for hours. At the end of the session, Firpo raised an issue that Kelly should have addressed months before.

"How did you get Dempsey to agree to fight with you so close to his title defense against Gene Tunney?" Firpo asked.

"Dempsey doesn't know we're fighting yet," Kelly responded

"So, Jack Kearns hired you to be Dempsey's sparring partner," Firpo said.

"Who's Jack Kearns?" Costello asked.

"Dempsey's longtime manager, the person who hires his sparring partners. Look, you're both nice guys, but if you haven't even been hired as Dempsey's sparring partner yet, what makes you think that you'll get anywhere near that ring next week?" Firpo asked.

"Because I'm Mike Kelly. You just leave all this to me."

CHAPTER TWENTY

THE TRAVERS

Saratoga, New York
August 14, 1926

The next week the right side of Kelly's face was bruised and swollen. Costello said it was only a "shiner." Although delighted with the outcome of his exhibition match with Firpo, Kelly was not thrilled about the possibility of entering the Dempsey fight with a black eye.

Dempsey's upcoming local exhibition was to be held at the White Sulphur Spring Hotel in Saratoga, New York, about thirty-five miles from the Kelly home. Although Saratoga was a day trip for Kelly, the major decided to make it a two-day trip so he could also "play the ponies" at the Saratoga track the day before the fight.

Kelly decided that the best way to secure the job of Dempsey's sparring partner was to "ambush" Dempsey's manager, Jack Kearns, at the Travers. If Kearns agreed, Kelly's "bout" with Dempsey would occcur the following day.

Upon their arrival at the Saratoga racetrack, there was an almost immediate tension between the fighter and trainer. Kelly had a hot tip that a horse named Mars, sired by the former Travers winner Man O' War, would win the Travers.

Costello reminded Kelly of his pledge of "no gambling, no drinking, no smoking" until after the fight with Dempsey. Kelly was livid. He had bet on every Travers since he was a teenager, and this was the most reliable information he had ever received.

The two searched the track for Kearns and found him in the Clubhouse, betting on the day's races. Kelly tried to introduce himself, but Kearns was too distracted. So, Kelly used a more direct approach. Just as the first race was about to start, Kelly stepped into Kearns's view of the track.

"It would be my honor to spar with the champ!" Kelly declared loudly.

"Who the hell are you, and why are you blocking my view?" Kearns demanded, highly annoyed.

"I am Major Mike Kelly of the New York 105th."

"The champ already has a sparring partner," Kearns replied.

"Not one like me." Kelly said.

"Really, have you ever fought before?" Kearns asked dubiously.

"Have I ever fought before?" Kelly responded, feigning offense. "Why, I'm the boxing champion of Washington County!" He knew that this joke would go over well with Kearns, and he was right.

"Would you be willing to sign a waiver releasing Jack Dempsey and the White Sulphur Spring Hotel from liability for any injuries that you may suffer during the sparring session?" Kearns asked.

"Is Jack Dempsey willing to sign a waiver releasing Mike Kelly and the White Sulphur Spring Hotel from liability for any injuries that he *will* suffer during his sparring session with me?" Kelly responded defiantly.

"My God, you're a natural," Kearns said. "If I ask you those same questions before the session tomorrow, could you shout out those same responses so everyone in the crowd can hear them?"

"Sure, if it means I got the job sparring the champ?" Kelly asked.

"Sign the waiver, you got the job," Kearns responded. "Be at the Hotel at 3 p.m. tomorrow, ready to spar. And let me give you a piece of friendly advice: you're a boxer, but you're also a performer. The better you perform, the easier the Champ will go on you."

"I don't want anyone to go easy on me," Kelly insisted.

"Of course, you don't," Kearns winked as he replied. "See you tomorrow at three."

Kearns turned back to the race, then paused. "What was your name again?"

"Mike Kelly. Remember it. You'll be hearing a lot of it someday."

"Sure, I will, kid," Kearns replied, smiling, and went back to studying his racing form. Kelly and Costello left the comfort of Kearns's box seats and returned to the grandstand. Although Kelly attended the Travers annually, today Costello wouldn't allow him to stay, as "the track" presented too much temptation. Costello sensed that Kelly was on the verge of backsliding, and the Dempsey fight, now set for the following day, was too important.

Besides, although Kelly wanted to stay and gamble, Zho's primary concern was protecting Kelly until the remainder of his mission plan was revealed. It was impossible to protect Kelly at the track with thousands of people in attendance. Moreover, since Zho believed that Diamond was still trying to hurt Kelly, he wasn't safe at the track. Zho considered warning him but did not know how he could do so without admitting Costello's role in the plot. So, Zho simply insisted that they should return to the hotel to make final plans for the fight.

For once, Kelly's "hot tip" on a horse race proved reliable. Just as Kelly had predicted, "Mars" won the Travers. But Kelly was too busy making final preparations for the next day's bout to even think about making a bet.

CHAPTER TWENTY-ONE

THE BET

Saratoga, New York
August 15, 1926

When Kelly and Costello arrived at the White Sulphur Spring Hotel, over one thousand people were already in attendance. Each had paid one dollar to watch the great Jack Dempsey train for his upcoming title defense against Gene Tunney. The Dempsey/Tunney fight was set for September 23, 1926 in the Sesquicentennial Municipal Stadium in Philadelphia, Pennsylvania. Although Dempsey primarily trained in Atlantic City, New Jersey, the champion would break up the monotony by performing boxing exhibitions in various communities across the Northeast.

Today was Kelly's big shot – his opportunity of a lifetime. He had dreamed of becoming a professional prizefighter his entire life. In Kelly's mind, he had the ability and the desire. All he needed was the man and the opportunity. Kelly was convinced that the new Ryan Costello, with his innovative fighting techniques, was the right man to train him, and that this exhibition was the opportunity he had been waiting for.

To Kelly, it was all so obvious. After sparring with Dempsey, several of Dempsey's former partners had gone on to have very successful boxing careers in their own right – or at least, that's how Kelly saw it in his dream. In reality, there were only a few concrete examples that supported Kelly's delusion.

Zho, on the other hand, simply wanted Kelly to survive the session. After all, there had been more than fifty former Dempsey sparring partners, and Kelly could only name three that had gone on to successful careers of their own. Although the newspapers of the day celebrated the success of individual fighters who had once served as a Dempsey sparring partner, there were far more stories of the champ losing his infamous temper in the ring. Costello had repeatedly warned Kelly of this possibility, but he would hear none of it. This day was his destiny.

When Kelly, Costello, and Moyer entered the White Sulphur Spring Hotel, Jack Kearns was already welcoming the crowd. As was his custom, Kearns offered five hundred dollars to anyone who could last three rounds with Dempsey.

This was Kelly's cue. From his position in the middle of the audience, Kelly shouted, "It would be my honor to spar with the champ!"

"And who, sir, are you?" Kearns asked.

"I am Major Mike Kelly, of the Fighting 105th," Kelly responded.

"Have you ever boxed before?" Kearns asked.

"Have I ever boxed before?" Kelly responded, feigning offense. "Why, I'm the Heavyweight Champion of Washington County!" He looked around at the crowd, knowing this joke would go over well – and he was right. They all howled with laughter.

"Would you be willing to sign a waiver releasing Jack Dempsey and the White Sulphur Spring Hotel from liability for any injuries that you may suffer today during the sparring session?" Kearns asked.

"Is Jack Dempsey willing to sign a waiver releasing Mike Kelly and the hotel from liability for any injuries that *he will* suffer during the sparring session today?" Kelly responded defiantly.

Once laughter subsided, Kearns spoke again. "No one has ever asked that question before, but I'm sure that Jack is willing to sign the waiver."

"Then I am, too. Let's do this!" Kelly yelled, and the crowd roared at his enthusiasm.

Kelly leaped onto the ring. He was already wearing the robe and boxing trunks that Mary had given him one week earlier. The crowd, many of whom were either Irish immigrants or their descendants, was delighted to see the green shamrock and "Major Kelly" stitched on the back of his robe.

Kelly shouted again, this time to the audience. "Let's do this!" The crowd roared back its approval, having been immediately won over by the major.

By the time Jim Moyer navigated through the crowd and reached the ring, Kelly was already positioned in his corner, awaiting his entourage. Moyer, who was also a Kelly bookie, climbed into the ring next to Kelly facing the crowd like an impromptu ring announcer.

"Listen up. Listen up!" Moyer shouted. When no one gave him the time of day, Moyer produced a pistol from inside his jacket and waved it above his head. "I said, *listen up!*" Once the audience members noticed the revolver in Moyer's hand, a hush fell over the crowd. "That's more like it," Moyer said, and holstered the gun.

"It is my honor to introduce to you a genuine hero of the Great War, Major Mike Kelly!" The crowd roared. "I served with Major Kelly in France and Germany during the war. Now, we all know that the Lord has blessed this Earth with some mighty tough Irishmen. But this man, Major Mike Kelly, is, by far, the toughest Irishman I've ever seen."

The crowd cheered and shouted once more, but this time it was because Jack Dempsey himself had quietly entered the ring behind Moyer.

"Now, we've all come here today to see Jack Dempsey, the greatest fighter in the history of boxing," Moyer went on – and finally looked over to the opposite corner to see the heavyweight champion smiling back at him.

"Well now!" Moyer said. "And this is no disrespect to you, Mr.

Dempsey, because, sir, I hold you in the highest regard; but I've got *one thousand dollars, that's one thousand dollars cash, that says that Major Mike Kelly can go toe-to-toe with Champion Jack Dempsey for three rounds!*"

As Moyer yelled, he held the wad of cash above his head. The crowd cheered as several men rushed forward to take the bet. Dempsey stood smiling in the corner, genuinely entertained by the show.

When the gamblers were within earshot, Moyer spoke quietly to them. "Okay, I'll need twenty-to-one odds. Who will give me twenty-to-one odds?"

"Twenty-to-one odds?" one gambler said. "If your man Kelly is as tough as you say, why do you need odds?"

Moyer didn't react and simply turned away.

A familiar voice rang out. "I'll take the entire bet. And I'll give you twenty-to-one!"

It was Jack "Legs" Diamond, impeccably dressed. Everyone in the crowd knew the mobster from his photos in the newspapers.

"But one thousand dollars is such a small bet," Diamond continued. "Would the major be able to increase it? If so, I'd increase his odds. Ask the major if he will bet five thousand dollars at twenty-five-to-one odds," Diamond said.

When Moyer reported the offer from Diamond, Kelly immediately accepted. Diamond was seated in the front row with four other men, presumably also mobsters. Kelly didn't know the men but assumed that, at some point, they would do business. Diamond gave Kelly a friendly wave, and Kelly mouthed the words *five thousand*. Diamond stood and walked over to Kelly's corner.

"Good luck, Major. And despite our bet, I still hope you beat Dempsey," Diamond said.

"Thank you," Kelly replied.

Costello watched this all unfold in disbelief. "You just bet that murderer five thousand dollars that you could last three rounds with Jack

Dempsey. Do you even *have* five thousand dollars?" Costello asked.

"Not on me. But don't sweat it, I'm not going to lose. I've got twenty-five-to-one odds. That means I'm going to win $125,000!" Kelly said enthusiastically.

"That's the spirit, boss," Moyer said as he climbed back on to the ringside and handed Kelly a brown bottle. "By the way, here are the vitamins you wanted."

Kelly's "vitamins" were in a container unlike any vitamin bottle that Costello had ever seen before. Kelly gulped down the "vitamins" and told Moyer to go get him some more.

"You should be drinking water," Costello said, concerned.

"Costello, you've done great teaching me about fighting and getting me in shape. But I know how to get in the right state of mind before I do violence," Kelly said.

Moyer handed Kelly a second bottle of "vitamins" and the crowd cheered as Kelly chugged the contents. One man in the audience even shouted, "Now, that's a real Irishman!" as the crowd roared its approval.

Costello tried to focus Kelly back on the match. "The fight's about to start. Now remember, Dempsey is the hardest puncher in boxing. His left and right punches are equally lethal. He can knock you out with either hand. He – "

"I know, I know," Kelly interrupted, bored with the number of times he had heard this speech from Costello. "We've been over this hundreds of times." Amazingly, Kelly was about to fight the world heavyweight champion and was overconfident.

"All right, Kelly," Costello yelled, raising his fists above his head. "You're a warrior!"

"I'm a *warrior!*" Kelly screamed as he slammed his gloves against Costello's hands.

The fight that Kelly had dreamed of his entire adult life was about to begin.

CHAPTER TWENTY-TWO

THE FIGHT

Saratoga, New York
August 15, 1926

The bell rang, and the fighters touched gloves in the center ring. Kelly was in the fight of his life. Dempsey was highly entertained by the major.

"Sir, it's an honor to meet you," Dempsey said. As the word *you* left his mouth, Kelly hit Dempsey square on the jaw with a huge overhand right.

Kelly and Costello had planned this moment for weeks. They knew that Dempsey would be overconfident at the start of the match and would have his guard down. Kelly had even practiced walking nonchalantly to the center of the ring and then throwing an overhand right punch in stride. It played out just as they had planned.

It was glorious.

After being struck flush on the jaw with such a powerful blow, a mere mortal would have instantly dropped to the canvas. But Dempsey wasn't like most men. He was the undisputed heavyweight champion of the world. Kelly had hit Dempsey with his absolute best punch flush on the jaw, and Dempsey didn't even react. In fact, the expression on his face didn't change one bit.

"Wow, that's a nice right hand you've got there, major. I had better get my guard up." Dempsey smiled. "Boy, I'll feel that one tomorrow."

Kelly was shocked. *I hit Dempsey with my very best punch and the man's just standing there smiling. And it's not even an arrogant, condescending smile. No, Dempsey is genuinely smiling at me the way one working man smiles at another,* Kelly thought to himself.

"And thank you for your service to our country," Dempsey said as he swung wildly, missing Kelly by at least a yard.

More thoughts raced through Kelly's mind. *What the hell was that? Why was that punch so badly thrown? Dempsey is one of the most accurate punchers in the heavyweight division. Dempsey missed me on purpose, didn't he? Is he going easy on me?*

The idea that Dempsey would take pity on him enraged Kelly. Now he had another reason to give Dempsey a beating. Kelly thought back to his hours' training with Costello and hit the champ with consecutive left jabs.

Dempsey raised his gloves defensively and easily parried the blows. The mere fact that the great war hero had thrown multiple punches excited the crowd. Two men rooting for Kelly broke out Irish flags and began waving them. It mattered little that Dempsey was also Irish-American; the crowd was rooting for Major Mike Kelly, the Irish-American war hero from upstate New York.

Kelly was now in a rhythm. He threw a three-punch combination, two left jabs and a right cross, and then quickly put up his gloves, awaiting Dempsey's response. Although Dempsey easily blocked each of Kelly's punches, the champ nevertheless lay back in his corner as though Kelly's combination had injured him.

Kelly looked to the crowd. To their great pleasure, he gave the audience his signature cocky smile and wave just as he had done at the Granville carnival grounds while fighting the town barber. As the crowd roared its approval, Kelly shifted into a southpaw stance just as he had practiced for hours with Costello.

As a lefty, Kelly began jabbing Dempsey with his stronger right hand. In 1926, even a fighter as experienced as Dempsey was surprised by this tactic. As Dempsey watched Kelly in amazement, the champ uncharacteristically dropped his gloves, and Kelly hit Dempsey in the face with two consecutive hard right jabs.

"Did you just switch stances? What a great move – " Dempsey praised the major, but before he could finish the sentence, Kelly hit Dempsey with a left hook to the jaw. For the first time in round one, Dempsey appeared hurt and was forced to tie Kelly up.

Kelly had no idea how to get out of a clinch from a boxer as strong as Dempsey. *Could he be hurt?* Kelly thought to himself as he struggled to break free. He could feel Dempsey's overpowering physical strength, and there was absolutely nothing Kelly could do to escape.

In an actual boxing match, the referee would have separated fighters in a clinch. Dempsey then likely would have hit Kelly as they separated, just as Costello had done to Kelly on Memorial Day.

But this was a simple sparring session. There was no referee, and Dempsey was entertained by this Major Kelly character as much as anyone in the hotel. Dempsey had no intention of actually hurting Kelly and was using this clinch to run out the clock.

The bell rang, ending the first round. Dempsey immediately released Kelly and enthusiastically said, "Good job, Major. Outstanding job. I'm very proud of you."

Kelly staggered back to catch his breath. *Dempsey wasn't even hurt.*

Dempsey turned and walked casually to his corner, sitting down on a stool that Bill Tate had just placed in the ring. Tate also gave Dempsey a bottle of water and a towel. As Dempsey sat in his corner, he couldn't help but notice the impromptu Irish celebration occurring in the crowd behind Kelly's corner.

Dempsey's manager, Kearns, broke in. "What was that? You didn't even try to hit him!"

"I'm not going to hurt the major. He's a war hero. I'm grateful to him," Dempsey said.

"You're not going to hit him?" Kearns said.

"No. A man like that, if I fight him, I'll have to hurt him bad to stop him. I won't do that to the major," Dempsey said. "He doesn't deserve it."

"That's what you said in Paris about Ernest Hemingway. Believe me, this guy is no Hemingway," Kearns replied.

"I don't care what you say. I like him," Dempsey said to Kearns as he sat in the corner. "He's got quite a gimmick. The Irish-American war hero. The toughest Irishman alive. I think it would sell a lot of tickets around the country, especially in New York and Boston."

"You know, I think you're right. Maybe we should sign this major and book him some fights down there for some real money," Kearns replied, thinking.

"Now, there's my manager." Dempsey smiled at him and took a drink of water.

In the opposite corner, Costello couldn't get in a word of advice because Moyer was too busy telling Kelly how wonderful he was doing. While basking in Moyer's adoration, Kelly was finishing his third bottle of "vitamins."

Instead of reminding Kelly to keep up his guard, or to stick and move, Moyer just yelled over and over: "You're gonna win, boss! You're gonna win!"

"Just shut up and hand me another bottle," Kelly barked.

Moyer dutifully complied, handing Kelly his fourth bottle of "vitamins."

"What kind of vitamins are those anyway?" Costello inquired, afraid to hear the answer.

"It's Guinness. All right, Costello? You happy? It's Guinness." Kelly's voice was noticeably louder and more aggressive.

"But that's ale. You're drinking ale?" The disappointment laced Costello's voice.

Kelly rose from his stool and faced Costello defiantly. As Kelly spoke, his voice grew in a crescendo until almost the entire crowd could hear him.

"Costello, if you knew anything at all, you'd know that Guinness is not just any ale. It's Guinness! It's good for you! It gives you strength!" Kelly raised his arms above his head and flexed his muscles for emphasis. The pose inspired other Irishmen in the crowd, many of whom were already drunk or near drunk, to cheer even more loudly. Several of them also flexed their muscles like their new hero, the major.

In response to his new fans, the major jumped up onto the second rope, leaned against the turnbuckle, and flexed both biceps as he faced the cheering crowd.

"This round, I'm gonna knock him out. I'm gonna knock him out!" Kelly screamed to his new minions.

Trying to focus the major back on the fight, Costello pulled Kelly down from the ropes and spun him around so that he faced back into the ring. Costello then repeated the same advice he had given Kelly earlier, only this time he did it more slowly and in a somewhat defeated tone.

"Now remember, Dempsey throws one of the hardest punches in the history of boxing," Costello said. "Dempsey's left and right hands are equally lethal. He can knock you out with either. His defense is superb. His head movements make him particularly difficult to hit."

When Costello could see that Kelly was not even paying attention to him, he placed his hands on the major's face to try and get his attention. Then, just as he had done multiple times before, Costello raised his hands above his head and yelled, "You're a warrior!"

Kelly raised his gloves toward Costello's hands and yelled back, but now he was slurring his words. "I'm a Warriah. I'm a Warriah... Oh, who cares. I'm just gonna kick his ass!" Kelly screamed that phrase repeatedly as he stumbled toward the center of the ring.

Costello's heart sank.

The bell sounded, starting the second round. Dempsey, oblivious to the events in Kelly's corner, still intended to go easy on the major. The champ walked to the center of the ring, excited that the major was to be his new protégé.

Kelly staggered to the center of the ring, slipping about three-quarters of the way in and catching his balance. When he reached Dempsey, the smell of alcohol on Kelly was apparent. "Major, have you been drinking?" Dempsey asked politely.

"So, what's it to you?" Kelly shouted back defiantly, shaking one glove for emphasis.

"During a sparring session?" Dempsey asked.

"What? You don't drink? What are you, a stinkin' Mormon?" Kelly shouted the words so loudly the entire crowd heard his disrespect towards the champion.

Dempsey's expression changed from surprise, to shock, to simmering rage. "What did you just say?" he asked very slowly.

Kelly abandoned all pretense of sobriety and stuck his face directly into Dempsey's. The two men were so close that their noses were almost touching. Kelly then shouted as loud as he possibly could: *"I said, what are you, a stinkin' Mormon?"*

Dempsey took a step back and turned partly away from Kelly so that everyone in the crowd could hear him. Dempsey then calmly and proudly proclaimed to Kelly and the audience, "Why, yes, Major, I am. I am a Mormon."

Dempsey then spoke directly and loudly to Kelly so that everyone in the crowd could hear him. "And Major, it is because I am a Mormon that I am now going to give you the chance to raise your gloves and try to defend yourself. I will then beat you within an inch of your life."

A hush fell on the crowd.

For years, Kelly had dreamed of stepping into the ring with Jack Dempsey. Of course, when Kelly imagined this day, it had always ended with him impressing Dempsey so much with his boxing skill that they would become lifelong friends and business partners.

By the end of round one, Kelly had done just that. But just like so many times before, his drinking had screwed this opportunity up completely. He would now personally witness Dempsey unleash his inner rage on an opponent. Although drunk, Kelly was sober enough to understand that he was about to receive the beating of a lifetime... and deep down, he knew he deserved it.

Despite all his work, training, and preparation, Kelly could now do nothing more than choose how he wanted to lose. Whether to take this beating while trying to run or while standing and fighting bravely.

Dempsey, assuming that Kelly would run, rushed to Kelly's corner to prevent his only avenue of escape. Of course, that wasn't necessary, since Kelly would choose to stand and fight. If he was defeated, so be it. If Dempsey killed him, so be it. Kelly would never run.

Kelly raised his gloves in a feeble attempt to defend himself. Dempsey rushed to the center of the ring and faked with his left hand. When Kelly fell for it, Dempsey hit Kelly on the left temple with an overhand right cross.

It was by far the hardest that Kelly had ever been punched. With that one single blow, Kelly was now "out on his feet." If the two men were simply sparring, based on Kelly's injuries, it would have already been appropriate to stop the session.

But after the way that Kelly had insulted Dempsey, this was no longer about boxing. Dempsey's religion had been publicly maligned, and Kelly was about to pay the price.

The crowd watched in stunned silence as the champion beat the war hero, exclusively with overhand rights, until Kelly lay bloody and motionless on the canvas.

But Dempsey wasn't finished. He leaned over and reared back to unleash one finishing blow on the fallen major.

But before Dempsey could throw the punch, his right arm froze. He simply could not move. Dempsey tried to break free, but whatever was holding him was just too strong for the champ.

Dempsey spun around and discovered that Costello was now towering over Dempsey, easily restraining the champion's arm.

"What the hell do you think you're doing?" Dempsey shouted.

"It's over, Mr. Dempsey. The major is knocked out, so the fight is over," Costello said.

"*I* will say when it's over!" Dempsey said, still enraged.

"All right, then. Please say the fight is over. Say it," Costello said firmly to the champ.

Moyer had now entered the ring. To their surprise, Moyer and Costello were now the same size. And both towered over the Champ. Suddenly, Dempsey's rage ended as quickly as it had started. Not because he was frightened of Moyer and Costello, but because he remembered Moyer from the prefight festivities. Dempsey smiled, politely introducing himself to Moyer.

"I'm Jack Dempsey," he said.

Moyer panicked. He was afraid that Dempsey would now try to beat him.

"I – I – I know who you are, sir," Moyer said.

"And your name?" Dempsey asked politely as the crowd looked on in silence.

"Moyer. Jim Moyer."

"You said some very nice things about me before the match. Thank you."

"You're welcome?" Moyer responded, waiting for the other shoe to drop.

"But you also said that the major was the toughest Irishman you've ever met," Dempsey reminded him, looking beyond Moyer. "Well, now you've met Jack Dempsey. I'm Irish, I'm a Mormon, and I'm the toughest Irishman you've ever met. Now, get that drunken fool out of my ring."

Dempsey walked back across the ring, intentionally stepping over the still unconscious Kelly. When Dempsey reached his corner, Tate raised the middle rope for him. Dempsey stepped through the ropes without breaking stride and left Kelly lying unconscious in the ring.

The crowd, which only a few minutes before had been cheering wildly for Major Kelly, stood silently in disbelief.

CHAPTER TWENTY-THREE
THE NURSE

Saratoga, New York
August 15, 1926

Costello stood helpless in the ring. Although Dempsey was legendary for the brutality that he could inflict on an opponent, Kelly had insisted that it wasn't necessary to bring a doctor to the fight. It was now up to Dr. Zho to save Kelly's life.

But Zho was no medical doctor. He was an anthropologist. He tried to access a database on human anatomy, but it had little relevant information. He knelt down and checked Kelly's vital signs, but that was the extent of his knowledge of human health. He had no idea how to care for Kelly, who was lying still, bleeding and unconscious.

"What can I do?" Moyer asked, kneeling beside Costello in the ring.

"Find a doctor," Costello said sharply.

"What kind?"

"Any kind. I'll do what I can in the meantime," Costello replied.

"I'm on it." Moyer rushed to the edge of the ring where he had made his announcement before the sparring session. "We need a doctor!" he shouted. "Major Kelly is hurt bad!"

"I can help him." The voice was from a young, dark-haired woman in the third row. She was petite and spoke in a distinctive British accent.

The woman wore an old white nurse's uniform and looked noticeably out of place among the other patrons.

"Are you a doctor?" Moyer shouted.

"I am a nurse," the woman replied as she quickly approached the ring.

"A nurse? The major needs a real doctor!" Moyer shouted. "Stay back."

The nurse ignored Moyer and pulled herself up into the ring. When Moyer tried to block her path, she addressed him with an air of absolute authority. "Mr. Moyer, step out of my way so I can save Major Kelly's life."

"You can save Major Kelly?" Moyer asked, shocked that she knew his name. Suddenly a feeling of calm rushed through his body.

"I can, and I will. I've treated many similar wounds before." The nurse spoke politely but firmly. He complied with her direction and stepped aside. She walked to the center of the ring, knelt down across from Costello, and began examining the unconscious Kelly.

"The first thing I must do is stop the bleeding," the woman said.

"Who are you?" Costello asked.

"Edith Cavell."

"Edith Cavell?" Costello said as Zho instantly accessed the name from his historical database. "A nurse named Edith Cavell was shot by the German Army in 1915?"

"Yes. She was. But if you can be Ryan Costello, then I certainly can be Edith Cavell," the nurse responded wryly. "Now, please leave me alone, and I will save this poor man's life."

Cavell then placed her right hand on top of Costello's left. To bystanders, it looked as though she was simply reassuring Costello. However, when the nurse touched him, energy surged through Costello's body. Cavell had initiated an updated recovery protocol, which almost instantly restored Zho's full array of power. Suddenly, Zho received a message that an important part of his mission plan had been retrieved:

Find the one called Mike Kelly. He will lead you to the host, Nora. Protect host and all members of Kelly family until team arrives to retrieve Monarch. Mission must be completed before Armada arrives, as extraction from Craig Colony will devastate planet.

"Mr. Costello, I will care for Major Kelly. It seems that you have more pressing business to which you must attend." Cavell said politely and motioned Costello toward the opposite corner.

Costello looked to the corner. Diamond and four henchmen had entered the ring and were fast approaching.

"That was some fight. I do hope the major will be all right." Diamond asked, feigning concern for Kelly's health.

Costello was kneeling by Kelly's side, while Diamond and his men stood over him. Costello rose, entrusting Kelly's care entirely to Nurse Cavell.

"I appreciate your concern, Mr. Diamond," Costello said. "But I'm sorry, you're not allowed in the ring."

"Believe me, I don't want to be up here anymore than you want me here," Diamond said. "It's just that I think the major lost the fight." Feigning confusion, Diamond turned to one of his men. "I don't know much about this sport, but the major lost the fight – right?"

As his men laughed, Diamond's mood turned serious. "And since the major lost, you boys now owe me five grand. I'm here to collect. If not from the major, then from the two of you."

Although most of the crowd had already left the hotel, several were still lingering to see what would become of Kelly. Since further violence was brewing, they happily returned to their seats. After all, they had paid to watch brutality, and this subsequent gangland dispute was potentially more entertaining than Dempsey's savage beating of Kelly.

Outnumbered and outgunned, Zho decided that his best course was to stand face-to-face with Diamond. Or, more accurately, Costello stood looking down at Diamond, just as all of Diamond's men towered over the diminutive mobster.

"Mr. Diamond, you are mistaken. We don't owe you anything," Costello said.

"Let me explain how my business works. If the major pays me the money that he owes, you don't owe nothing. But if the major dies before I get my five grand, then you and that fat man over there are gonna be obligated to pay me," Diamond said.

"Moyer, please come here." Costello kept his eyes on Diamond and his men as he spoke. "The one thousand dollars that you were flashing before the fight. That was Kelly's money, right?"

Moyer patted a bulge in his jacket pocket. "But I've still got it."

"Please pay that money to Mr. Diamond as partial satisfaction of the gambling debt that Major Kelly owes him," Costello instructed.

"Are you sure that that's what Mike would want?" Moyer asked.

"Positive. We both witnessed the bet." Costello spoke loudly enough so that everyone in the audience could hear him. "Major Kelly made a five-thousand-dollar bet, which Mr. Diamond won fair and square. Major Kelly is obligated to pay Mr. Diamond."

"Okay." Moyer walked over to Diamond and handed him the one thousand dollars.

"Kelly paid you one thousand dollars. He now owes you four thousand. We will take him home and ensure that he gets proper medical care. You have my word that I will contact you tomorrow with the time and place to expect the remaining money," Costello said.

"I'm afraid I can't let the major go without full payment of his debt," Diamond continued. "It would be bad for my business to delay collection of such a large public bet. But I'll tell you what I'm willing to do. I'll take the major with me as collateral while you get the money. You pay me four grand within twenty-four hours, and we got no issue. If you don't come up with the money, well, then you might say Mike Kelly's got 'major problems.'" Diamond laughed at his pun and looked at the Monahan brothers, who again laughed on cue.

"I'm afraid I can't agree to those terms. But I gave you my word you will be paid," Costello said.

Diamond laughed and looked at his men. "I'm afraid that in my business, your 'word' ain't good enough."

"Then it appears we are at an impasse," Costello replied.

"You do realize that we are heeled." Diamond patted the revolver in his jacket.

"That is my assumption," Costello said calmly.

"Then how can you stop my men from taking the major?"

"I don't have to stop your men. You will stop them."

"And why will I do that?" Diamond asked.

"May I approach you, sir? I give you my word that – unless you force me to – I will not harm you." Costello spoke to Diamond in a slow, calm voice, reminiscent of the tone he had used back at the Rain-Bo Room in Albany.

"Again, he's giving his word. The man says that he won't harm me. Oh, what the hell. Costello, you amuse me. I can't wait to hear what you say next," Diamond said. His mood shifted dramatically as he continued, "But you are warned. And men, I want you all to hear me. If he so much as lays a finger on me, I want you to shoot him and his fat friend like a couple of dogs."

Diamond pointed at Cavell, who was still caring for Major Kelly. "Then, after you shoot the two of them down, that pretty doctor over there – you put one in her, too."

Cavell continued caring for Kelly, unfazed by the threat. Diamond's men nodded in agreement. Diamond then turned to the audience and hollered, "Did all you people hear that?" There were nods and mumbles of acquiescence in the group, many of whom started hurrying for the exits.

Costello walked slowly toward Diamond. When he was about a foot away, Costello leaned over and spoke. "Mr. Diamond, that woman is not a doctor. She's a nurse. Her name is Edith Cavell. She was a British nurse working in German-occupied Brussels during the World War. Unlike you, a coward during that war, Nurse Cavell was a great hero. She helped over two hundred Allied soldiers escape before the Germans executed her in 1915."

"Uh – what? The Germans killed her in 1915?" Diamond asked, his confusion evident.

"The Germans shot her as a spy on October 12, 1915," Costello continued. "Yet here she is. Eleven years later, she's come to help Major Kelly escape you."

"Is your little story supposed to scare me?" Diamond asked.

"Frankly, I don't care if it scares you," Costello continued. "We aren't here for you. Nurse Cavell and I – we're here to protect Kelly. You just keep getting in the way."

"So, you and Cavell – you're some sort of ghosts?" Diamond said, laughing.

"Never mind who or what we are. Just stay out of our way and leave Kelly to me," Costello stated.

"And what's in it for me?" Diamond asked, with a big smile on his face, he was thoroughly enjoying Costello's hubris.

"I already told you. Your final day on this planet will not be until 1931," Costello said.

"Yeah, I know that's what you said. So, what exactly does that mean?"

"It means that unless you screw it up, you've got another five years. Sure, that's not great, but it's also not that bad for someone in your line of work."

"Again: if I let you go, what's in it for me?" Diamond asked.

"Let me put it in a way that you'll understand. If Kelly dies even a minute before he is supposed to, then your destiny will be altered as well. And once that is changed, then I cannot be certain that you will even make it to 1931."

"Oh, so now you're threatening me?"

"I am merely explaining physics to you."

"You're explaining what to me?" Diamond asked, growing frustrated.

"Let me make it even easier for you. On this planet, you are somewhat powerful, but Nurse Cavell and I are far, far more powerful. If Major Kelly dies before he is destined to do so, you will die on that same day. Now, do you understand?" Costello said forcefully.

"Oh, I understand, all right. You just threatened me." Diamond turned to the man on his right and ordered, "Hey, Red! Shoot this fool."

"With pleasure." Red Monahan, Diamond's bodyguard, reached for the revolver holstered within his overcoat. But in one incredibly fast, fluid motion, Costello grabbed the back of Monahan's head with his left hand and simultaneously touched Red on the forehead with the open palm of his right hand.

Red fell back, paralyzed, into Costello's left arm. Before anyone else could react, Costello removed Red's pistol from his right hand and aimed it point-blank in Diamond's face.

The crowd looked on stunned as Costello supported Red's entire weight with his left arm while aiming the pistol at Diamond with his right arm. Costello effectively used Red as a human shield between himself and Diamond's other men. Red gasped for air as his entire body floated motionless above Costello's left arm.

"Mr. Diamond, I really want you and your men to walk out of here. Today is not your day to die. And I strongly suggest that you get your man to a hospital. It is not my desire to change anyone's destiny if I don't have to."

"It's your choice. Are you willing to gamble away the last five years of your life simply because you won't accept my word that Kelly will pay you?" Costello said.

Diamond paused for a moment, amazed at the ease with which Costello had disabled Red and taken his gun, and trying not to think about how he had made Red float in the air. And although he really wanted to kill Costello, Diamond had only one choice since Costello was pointing a gun in his face.

"You'll make sure that Kelly pays me the four grand?" Diamond asked.

"I've already given you my word," Costello said.

"Okay, Costello. So long as Kelly pays me, we've got no beef. I can't guarantee you won't be hearing from Red or his brothers, though," Diamond said. "All right, people, let's pack it up. Someone needs to get Red to a doctor. Me, I'm going home."

Diamond's men carried Red out of the hotel as he continued to struggle for breath. As Diamond walked out with his men, he yelled back, "I look forward to hearing from you tomorrow! Oh, and have fun with the Monahan brothers."

Once they were gone, Moyer rushed over to Costello. "That was incredible, Ryan," Moyer said.

The two men glanced at each other. *"Kelly,"* they said simultaneously, as though the terror of the moment had made them both forget that Major Kelly was still in need of medical attention. They turned and looked at the spot where Kelly had been lying in the ring, but he and Edith Cavell were gone.

"I'm right here." Kelly spoke weakly from his corner. "The nurse revived me and told me to sit on this stool. She knew Costello would get us out of this mess."

"But how? You sure looked like you were dying. What did she do?" Moyer asked.

"Damned if I know. One minute, Dempsey's beating me senseless, and the next minute I wake up and she's looking down at me like an angel."

"Did she say anything?" Moyer asked.

"Yes. She said that you are in a lot of trouble," Kelly said to Costello. "What does that mean?"

"I don't know," Costello replied, feigning ignorance.

"She also said it would be much worse for you if they come for you," Kelly continued, "Who are they? What are they going to do if they come for you?"

"I don't really know," Costello said. "Come on. We've got to keep moving. Can you walk, Major?"

"I can walk just fine," Kelly insisted.

"What did she do for you?" Moyer asked, amazed at everything he had just witnessed.

"Hell, if I know," Kelly repeated as the three men walked hurriedly to their car. Notwithstanding Kelly's battered appearance, his injuries were almost healed. Although he had lost his dream fight to Dempsey and five thousand dollars to Diamond, it had been a rewarding day. Kelly had learned that, when sober, he could throw punches with the best fighter in the world. Indeed, if only Kelly had just remained sober, who knew how the night would have ended.

CHAPTER TWENTY-FOUR
THE ESCAPE

Saratoga, New York
August 16, 1926

"You don't remember where you parked the car?" Kelly hollered at Moyer as they left the White Sulphur Spring Hotel. Costello walked ahead, still concerned that they could be ambushed. The major had some mobility, despite the beating he had just received from Dempsey, but it was unclear how long it would last. It was imperative that they leave town quickly and get Kelly to a doctor.

"When I parked the car, there were a lot of other cars in the lot," Moyer said. "I remember that I parked next to a Ford Model T Roadster."

"And, surprise! Now that the fight is over, it's gone. It never occurred to you that after the fight, all the cars in the parking lot would leave. Maybe you should have taken note of a landmark *other than the model of car that you were parked next to!*" Although battered from the Dempsey fight, it seemed as though yelling at Moyer actually improved Kelly's spirits.

"It's not my fault. I don't drive that often. Hell, I don't even have a license," Moyer said as he looked away, still searching for the car.

"You don't have a driver's license?" Kelly asked incredulously.

"No."

"If you don't have a license, then why did you drive the car?" Kelly steadied himself against Costello, and the two men waited for Moyer's explanation.

"Because you're the boss, and you told me to drive," Moyer said. "I distinctly remember you said, 'Moyer, you drive the car so Costello and I can talk strategy before the fight.'"

"Well, yeah, but I thought you had a driver's license. Without a license, it's illegal to drive!" Kelly thought this point would convince Moyer.

"Well, it's also illegal to sell booze, but that never stopped us before." Moyer seemed equally convinced that the logic of this response would placate Kelly. It did not.

"The man's got a point," Costello interjected, smiling. Kelly glared angrily at both men.

Moyer decided that his safest course was to keep his mouth shut. The three walked silently through the now empty parking lot, still trying to find their car. Night had fallen, and it was growing darker by the minute. Suddenly, the sound of a woman's voice broke the silence.

"Mr. Costello, may I speak with you?" Edith Cavell said from the darkness.

"Nurse Cavell. Why, yes, of course." Costello, delighted to hear Cavell's voice, walked quickly toward her.

After he reached Cavell, the two walked silently in the opposite direction until they were about seventy yards from Kelly and Moyer.

"Colonel Samson, it is you, isn't it?" Costello asked quietly.

"Of course, it's me," Cavell said.

"I knew it was you from the moment you said you were Edith Cavell."

"You didn't really think that I would drop you in a starship and trust you to complete the mission by yourself?" Cavell asked.

"So, you've been with me all along?"

"Who did you think jumped into the boxing ring that first night to keep you from beating the one called Kelly to death?" Cavell asked.

"That was you? How do you switch bodies so quick? Certainly not with the Transference Protocol," Costello mused.

"Of course not. That Protocol is outdated tech. It's got so many bugs, it's practically space junk. Besides, Nurse Cavell has been dead for eleven years. I couldn't reanimate her body, even if I was willing to use the Transference Protocol."

"Then how do you change appearances?" Costello asked.

"My necklace projects a hologram. I remain in my body, but everyone around me sees a different image." She adjusted her necklace and seamlessly changed her appearance from Cavell into the young woman who had hugged Costello in the boxing ring, into Colonel Raea Samson, and back to Cavell.

"That's amazing. Why wasn't I given that technology?" Costello asked.

"The Transference Protocol is standard issue tech on all Daganian starships, even though it's outdated and littered with design defects."

"Why?" Costello asked.

"Council Member Hoaon owns the Transference Protocol technology, and he insists that the government only purchase Hoaon Industries products," Cavell explained.

"And so, instead of being given a device that projects a hologram, I am transferred into a human body while mine remains in space?"

"Oh, about that. I'm very sorry, but I don't think your body is still in space. There was a killer drone, and it attacked..." Cavell trailed off.

"I heard the transmission," Costello interrupted, grimly.

"So, I'd get used to that body. But look on the bright side, you're much bigger than you used to be," Cavell remarked.

"Enough. What's the plan?" Costello asked.

"To get your mission back on track before you inflict any more damage to this planet."

"I can't leave the Kelly family. At least, not yet."

"Why not?"

"My mission is to protect them."

"But you don't even know the reason you were ordered to protect them. And now you're letting personal feelings for that one family get in the way of completing your actual mission," Cavell snapped. "And unless you complete that mission – and quick – then this civilization that you supposedly care so much about may cease to exist."

"I won't screw up," Costello said.

"You've already screwed up!" Cavell cried. "You're teaching Kelly fighting techniques that won't be developed here for decades. You told Diamond that he has five years to live. You even used time shifting powers in front of an audience filled with Earthlings! Even if we can somehow stop the Armada and save this planet, you've already screwed this mission up. This once-pristine civilization will be debating the meaning of your visit for years."

"So, they sent you to stop me?" Costello asked.

"I'm here to save your life. Remember, that's what Edith Cavell does. But make no mistake: if they had assigned this mission to anyone else, you may already be dead."

"I know. And I'm grateful that you're here. But let's be honest: if it wasn't for my rescue attempt, the extraction team would have already come here and devastated this planet," Costello said.

"Do you really think that you've accomplished anything? Yesterday, the High Council launched the Armada with orders to complete the extraction. And they don't care what happens to this planet or its inhabitants in the process. Sure, if you had already completed your mission, there would be no need for an extraction. But you've been too busy teaching Skiirmiishing and fighting with Earthlings," Cavell berated him.

"They launched the Armada?" Costello asked.

"So, it's up to us. And we don't have much time." Cavell stated decisively.

"Costello! We've got to go!" Kelly hollered from the darkness.

"In the meantime, I'm making sure you do no more damage," Cavell said.

Cavell followed Costello back to Kelly. It was easy to locate the major in the darkness, as he was still yelling at Moyer for misplacing the car.

"Think, man! Where did you park?" Kelly said

"You're looking for your car?" Cavell said. "It's around the corner, by the church."

"Now I remember! It's next to a church!" Moyer said triumphantly.

"She's coming with us," said Costello.

"And why is she coming with us?" demanded Kelly.

"She just saved your life," Costello told him. "She sided with you against Diamond. We can't leave her behind now."

"Moyer tells me, that you both saved my life. Thank you."

"You're welcome," Costello said. "By the way, you owe Diamond four thousand dollars, and he's serious about collecting it tomorrow."

"That's what I hear. Do you happen to have four thousand dollars I can borrow?" Kelly asked. Costello had had enough of Kelly's reckless, self-destructive charm. "This is not a joke. You have to find a way to pay your debt," he said to the major. "And Diamond is gonna collect it one way or another. You can't smile your way out of this."

"Enough with the lectures, Costello. Let's get the car. I know where we can lay low."

It was parked around the corner by a small church, just where Cavell had said it was. The three men and their new "recruit," Cavell, walked silently to the vehicle.

As Costello climbed into the driver's seat, he whispered to Cavell, so that Kelly and Moyer could not hear him. "Cavell, is there anything that I can do to help get us into the Craig Colony?"

"In fact, there is. Although we don't know the Colony's perimeter defenses, you are my ticket in," Cavell said as she placed her right hand on Costello's shoulder.

"Costello?" Moyer asked. Costello did not respond.

Moyer tried again. "Costello?"

He still didn't answer. Kelly looked over and saw Costello sitting motionless behind the driver's seat, his arms twitching and his eyes blinking rapidly. Cavell was sitting in the back seat calmly behind Costello with her hand still on his right shoulder.

"I've seen this before. I know what to do," Cavell said.

"What's wrong with him?" Kelly asked

"No time to discuss it now. May I borrow your car?" Cavell asked.

"Of course," Kelly answered as he leaned against Moyer for support.

"Thank you. I will leave it for you at the train station," Cavell said. "Mr. Moyer, you get a cab and take the major home. Make sure he gets plenty of rest. I have stopped his internal bleeding. Now, all he needs is rest. He'll be fine. I'll take Mr. Costello with me. He, too, will be fine." Nurse Cavell eased the still unconscious Costello into the passenger seat, climbed into the driver's seat and drove off.

CHAPTER TWENTY-FIVE
THE CRAIG COLONY

Sonyea, New York
August 19, 1926

"Mr. Costello. Mr. Costello, can you hear me?" Dr. Christopher Harrison asked.

Zho opened the host's eyes. He looked around the room. Although it looked like the interior of a hospital room, he couldn't imagine why he would be there. He didn't recognize the face peering down at him.

"Mr. Costello, can you hear me?" Dr. Harrison loudly repeated, as though he believed that shouting at the patient would help revive him.

"I can hear you," Costello whispered, confused and dizzy. His head throbbing. The same pounding headache that he had felt in the Kelly home and at the armory.

The pain was amplified by the booming sound of Dr. Harrison's voice. "You have had an epileptic seizure, Mr. Costello." Dr. Harrison slowly enunciated each syllable in the word "epileptic" phonetically so that a child could understand what he was saying.

"A seizure? I had a seizure?" Costello spoke slowly, trying to process the doctor's words. "What type of seizure?"

"What type?" Dr. Harrison laughed, surprised at the question from a layman.

"Yes, Doctor." Costello grimaced when saliva hit the fresh lacerations on his tongue. Although it hurt, Costello forced himself to continue. "What type? Petit mal? Grand mal?"

"Oh, so you are familiar with those terms? All right, you have had a grand mal seizure, Mr. Costello," Dr. Harrison replied.

"And by what name did you refer to me?" Costello asked.

"Costello," Dr. Harrison replied.

Costello again grimaced from the sharp pain he now felt in his head and on both sides of his tongue. He reflexively tried to bring his hands up to the sides of this head but could not, for his arms had been restrained to the bed.

His thoughts flashed back to when he was tied up in the Kelly home and in the armory. Memories of the Kelly family came flooding back. He tried to pull against the bindings, but they were tied more tightly than the restraints that Kelly's men had placed on him.

Costello swallowed and grimaced again. He struggled to regain his composure. "And, Sir, why did you call me Mr. Costello?"

"Because that is the name on your chart," Dr. Harrison patiently replied. "Do you remember your name?" the doctor asked.

"I'm sorry, I do not," Costello responded.

"Memory loss is a standard side effect of a seizure. In most cases, that loss is temporary."

Costello did not respond. He felt weak and frail, as though all of his strength had been drained from his body.

Then he remembered the day after the Memorial Day fight with Kelly and that first night in the armory. Both times he had felt similarly drained of his strength. Had he had seizures then, too? Did the host body have a seizure disorder? Could the host's public drunkenness have been an attempt to control it? To mask it.

Zho then recalled the warning from Artie, the AI: "*The Protocol is not without its risks. In the early rounds of live testing, it was discovered that when a Transference passenger was transferred into a living host, there was a high incidence of seizure activity following the transfer. It was hypothesized that these seizures were the result of the brain of the living host trying to reject the consciousness of the visitor."*

Was Ryan Costello still alive when the protocol placed Zho in his body? Is that what was causing Zho to hear voices? Was Zho hearing Costello's voice? Were the seizures the result of Costello's living brain trying to reject Zho's consciousness?

He decided that in his current weakened physical state, it was not productive to try to break free from the restraints. Continuing to try to do so would only further drain his limited strength.

"Doctor, how can you be sure that Costello is my name when I cannot remember it?" Costello asked.

"Because it's on your chart, and I also read your name on this emergency court order." Dr. Harrison held up a piece of paper.

"A court order, concerning me?" Costello queried. "To do what?"

"You have been committed to this facility for observation for no less than ninety days," Dr. Harrison read from the court order.

"I'm sorry, Doctor. I don't understand. Why would I be committed to this facility. And – what exactly is this facility?"

"This is Peterson Hospital. It serves the Craig Colony for Epileptics," Dr. Harrison replied.

"The Craig Colony?" Costello had heard this name before. He slowly repeated the words as though trying to process each one. He looked around the room. It was unlike any hospital room he had ever seen before. One obvious difference was that there were bars on the outside of the windows to keep patients inside.

Costello was now even more confused. "What is the Craig Colony for Epileptics? And why, in your culture, do people who have seizures need a colony?" Costello asked, sincerely trying to understand.

"As I am sure you're aware, epilepsy is not well understood. Many of those who suffer from the condition are stigmatized in our society," Doctor Harrison patiently explained. "The Craig Colony for Epileptics was created to help treat those with epilepsy by removing them from the community and giving them a safe haven."

"Why do they need a safe haven? Does your country persecute people who have seizures so that they have to flee to this colony for your protection?" Costello asked.

"Of course not." Dr. Harrison replied.

"But aren't I here because of a medical condition?" Costello asked.

"We are here to help you," Harrison replied.

"What if I don't want your help?"

Dr. Harrison did not respond.

"If you want to help me, please remove these restraints and let me go. There is a family out there who needs me," Costello pleaded.

"I'm afraid that's impossible. For the next ninety days, you are a court-ordered inmate here," the doctor told him. "And to be completely frank, the patients who are committed here generally remain far longer than the required ninety days. Many for the remainder of their lives."

"I'm confused. Have I been charged with a crime?"

"No, of course not." Harrison replied.

"….or adjudged insane?" Costello asked.

"No. You appear quite sane, sir. But you have had a seizure," Doctor Harrison said.

"A grand mal seizure. So what?" Costello replied.

"So, this colony is for your protection and the protection of society," the doctor told him.

"Respectfully, doctor, seizures are caused by a physical condition. They are not contagious, and people with seizure disorders pose absolutely no danger. You don't need to protect society from people who have seizures."

Dr. Harrison stopped writing and looked up from his notes. He was not prepared to defend the patently indefensible assumptions underlying the Craig Colony.

"Please don't take it personally, but I believe that we should impress upon our inmates, upfront, the importance of remaining in the colony indefinitely."

"Amazing. Anything else?" Costello asked.

"Why, yes, there is," Doctor Harrison curtly responded. "We have almost one thousand women living in this colony. You are a young, attractive man. It is natural that you will get certain urges. However, you are forbidden from having sex with any of the women residents."

"So we are all supposed to live here the rest of our lives, but cannot have sex. Why is that?" Costello asked.

"Because sex between epileptic men and epileptic women creates epileptic babies," Dr. Harrison calmly explained. "And it is in the greater interest of society that we prevent the marriage and cohabitation of mental defectives, epileptics, and chronic inebriates."

"To stop the creation of mental defectives, epileptics, or chronic inebriates?"

"We have thoroughly documented our conclusions in public documents filed annually with the New York State Legislature. In fact, last year we recommended that New York pass a law prohibiting any person from marrying or cohabitating with an epileptic." Dr. Harrison said.

"And you aren't ashamed?"

"Ashamed? But why? I am proud of all that my colleagues and I have accomplished here. You should feel lucky that you were assigned to me. I am regarded as an expert in my field."

"Doctor, I have studied many, many cultures. This colony, as you describe it, is one of the strangest places I have ever encountered."

"Well, Mr. Costello, you are entitled to your opinion, no matter how badly misinformed. The methods and practices of the Craig Colony are all based on the latest scientific consensus. And the sooner you accept the infallibility of that consensus, the happier you will be here."

The doctor looked at his watch. "Look at the time! I have to get to my next appointment. I hope that your current attitude improves over the next ninety days. Otherwise, when I write my report for the judge, you will likely be with us a much longer time," Harrison cautioned. "But don't worry. A few of our patients begin to show improvement after two or three years."

"Two or three years?" Costello asked.

"Now, try and get some rest. I will see you tomorrow." The doctor forced a smile as he walked out of Costello's room. The door closed and Zho heard the lock click from the outside.

Zho considered the irony of his situation. Outside the colony, he had lived freely as a bootlegger, regularly committing crimes and consorting with gangsters. Yet he was now effectively incarcerated by a New York State Court for the "crime" of having a seizure in public. He decided that the only actual medical advice that Dr. Harrison had given him was to rest.

He closed his eyes and, in a matter of seconds, was fast asleep.

CHAPTER TWENTY-SIX

THE SAFE HAVEN

Sonyea, New York
August 20, 1926

The next day, Costello awoke to the sound of movement in his room. "What is it?" he asked.

"I'm sorry. Just picking up your room," the man replied. Harold Smith had worked as a janitor at the Craig Colony since it opened on January 27, 1896.

"That's all right," Costello said. "It's nice to see someone other than Harrison."

"I saw when they brought you in yesterday. You were with that nurse," Smith said.

"You saw a nurse?" Costello asked.

"Yes. The nurse with the pretty voice. I hadn't seen her before, so I figured that she works in the White City," Smith replied.

"The White City?" Costello asked.

"The women and men are separated into different housing units. The women live in the White City. The men in the Green City. Men aren't allowed in the White City."

"If you see that nurse, can you tell her that I really need to talk to her?" Costello asked.

"I will. You have a good day, now," Smith replied, and he exited Costello's room.

"How is my favorite new patient today?" Harrison inquired, barging into Costello's room. Costello, strapped to his bed, did not respond with the same enthusiasm.

"How do I feel? Well, let's see." Costello reflected. "I'm being held prisoner, strapped to a bed because my doctor says that I've had a seizure. How do you think I feel?"

"The medical staff is not your enemy. We are here to help you," Harrison replied.

Costello calmly looked down at the restraints that were still tied firmly to his arms. "It's difficult to imagine how this treatment is helpful to me or anyone else," Costello said.

"How can I help you?" Dr. Harrison replied.

"Let me out of here," Costello implored.

"I'm afraid that I can't do that," Dr. Harrison explained. "Upon admission, patients at the Craig Colony are held in observation for one week. Then if the medical staff deems the inmate fit, he is released into the general population."

"A one-week observation?" Costello asked.

"But while in isolation, you can still pick a job. We find that hard work helps reduce the frequency and severity of seizures. Every patient at the Craig Colony is required to have a job."

"What kind of job would you recommend?"

"We have a considerable number of skilled industries for epileptics. You may choose from farming, gardening, mattress making, shoe repairing, painting, brick making, and the manufacture of clothing," Dr. Harrison explained.

"That is quite a selection," Costello replied, feigning an interest in the topic. "Personally, it's hard for me to choose between mattress making and brick making."

"Our brick making facility now produces over one million bricks per year!" Harrison exclaimed proudly.

"Wow. Over one million bricks per year? That certainly is a lot of bricks," Costello marveled. "Dr. Harrison, if I was put on this planet to make bricks, this is definitely the place that I'd want to make them. Unfortunately, I have a different mission. I need to get back to the Kelly family and make sure that they are safe."

"I understand how you feel, Mr. Costello, but rules are rules. All patients are held in observation for one week upon admission," Dr. Harrison said firmly. "And even after that one week is up, your friends will only be able to see you during visiting hours."

"Visiting hours."

"Yes. We have visiting hours every Wednesday and Saturday from 10 to 11:30 a.m. and 2 to 4 p.m. But I'll make you a deal. If you pick a job today, I will get word to Mr. Kelly that you'd like to see him."

"You'd do that for me? It's a deal. Thank you," Costello quickly answered.

"So what can I sign you up for?"

"Well, I always loved working on my uncle's farm during summer vacation as a boy," Costello said.

Dr. Harrison was delighted, for his primary goal for this session was to gain Costello's trust and convince him to pick a job at the colony. Since he believed that he had now done so, Harrison was quite pleased with himself.

Of course, Costello's reason for picking farming was disingenuous. The real reason that he had selected this particular job was that farm work afforded him the best opportunity to get outside the hospital and escape.

"Pardon me. I do hope that I'm not disturbing you, Doctor. I have some forms to review with the patient," Cavell said as she let herself into the room.

"Nurse, please come in," Dr. Harrison said. "The patient and I have made excellent progress this morning."

"Hello, Mr. Costello," Nurse Cavell said politely.

"Hello," Costello replied coldly.

"Dr. Harrison, I know this is a little unorthodox, but I have been assigned to go over some forms with the patient. So that I don't waste your valuable time, when may I meet with him privately?" Cavell asked.

"This is a perfect time." Harrison replied, happy to oblige. Having convinced Costello to pick a job, he'd met his goal for the day, and this was an opportunity to go back to his office.

"I will leave the two of you to speak. Please cooperate with Nurse Cavell," the doctor said as he quickly headed out of Costello's room. "If you need anything, just let me know. And Ryan, keep up that good attitude, and we will get you out on that farm before you know it."

Costello smiled at Dr. Harrison as he left, still feigning excitement. Once Harrison was out of earshot, Costello said:

"How ironic that you're still posing as Edith Cavell."

"What do you mean, ironic?" Cavell asked.

"Well, the real Edith Cavell was executed for helping hundreds of British soldiers escape captivity. Whereas you, dressed as Cavell, have made me a prisoner in this place. Surely you see the irony?"

"Quit being so melodramatic, Zho. If your memory systems were functioning properly, you'd realize that your presence here is the mission."

"What? Costello asked, confused.

"Did you even read your mission plan?" Cavell asked.

"Well, no. It was lost in the transference."

Cavell placed her hand on Costello's face and for the next several seconds initiated an updated recovery protocol which again restored Zho's full array of powers and protocols. Zho felt a huge surge of energy throughout the host body and, just as occurred in the ring following the Dempsey fight, Zho's memory and powers were again fully restored.

For the first time since Zho had undergone Transference, his entire mission plan was available for him to review.

> *Find the one called Mike Kelly. He will lead you to the host, Nora. Protect host and all members of Kelly family until team arrives to retrieve Monarch. Mission must be completed before Armada arrives, as extraction from the Craig Colony will devastate planet. Since we don't know the perimeter defenses of the Colony, you will enter facility as a patient.*

"I never seen this last sentence before. Why is the file called Project Acorn?" Zho asked.

"Never mind what it's called. Stay focused. I believe that Nora is here," Cavell said.

Zho searched within himself. He could feel his full array of power surging through the host body. He felt the host body again almost instantly grow bigger and stronger. For the first time since the transference, Zho was able to access his empath protocol and scanned the colony.

"You're right. I can feel it. She is here."

CHAPTER TWENTY-SEVEN
THE SEARCH

Sonyea, New York
August 24, 1926

Cavell first visited Costello on August 20. To allow her time to search the White City, they had agreed that Costello would disrupt the Peterson Hospital at 11:00 a.m. on August 24. A disruption large enough to necessitate the dispatch of staff members from the White City. Costello chose 11:00 a.m., because Dr. Harrison arrived at Costello's room promptly at 10:50 a.m.

"And how is my favorite new patient today?" Harrison asked, as he entered Costello's room, just as he did every other day. However, on the 24th, Harrison was shocked to find that Costello was no longer strapped to his bed. Costello had easily broken free from his restraints and was now standing by the window, probing the bars for weakness.

"Mr. Costello, why are you out of bed," Dr. Harrison asked.

"Well, under the guidelines of your Colony Care Plan, I should begin to engage in rigorous physical activity?" Costello asked. "After all, the entire assumption on which this colony is based is that healthy life habits, coupled with strenuous physical labor, will greatly reduce the energy available to patients when in the throes of an epileptic seizure."

"Sounds like you've been reading the work of our founder, Dr. Frederick Peterson. But you haven't been cleared to begin treatment under the Colony Care Plan," Harrison replied.

"That's hilarious. You refer to the Colony Care Plan as a 'treatment.'"

"What would you call it?"

"I'd call it exploiting the physical labor of handicapped prisoners," Costello shot back.

"Are we really having this conversation again?" Harrison asked, exasperated.

"Yes," Costello said forcefully, and he started walking aggressively toward Dr. Harrison.

Harrison panicked and rang an alarm on the wall that sounded throughout the hospital. Within seconds, a massive hospital ward attendant, Frank Williams, rushed into the room and stood between Harrison and Costello.

"Restrain this patient. Strap him to his bed!" Dr. Harrison ordered Williams.

"Yes, sir," Williams said, as he rushed at Costello.

Costello stood passively as Williams approached him. Although the attendant was accustomed to manhandling patients, this was no ordinary resident.

Costello remained still until Williams was upon him. Then, just as Williams was about to tackle him, Costello quickly turned sideways, tripping Williams, using the force of the man's body against him.

But Costello did not allow the stumbling attendant to hit the floor. Instead, in the same way that Costello had handled Red Monahan in the ring following the Dempsey match, Costello grabbed the back of Williams's head with his left hand and simultaneously placed the open palm of his right hand on Williams's forehead.

Rather than falling to the ground, Williams floated in the air, paralyzed, above Costello's left arm. Costello stood there, supporting Williams's entire body weight in the air for several seconds. All the while, Harrison looked on, horrified.

"But that's impossible," Dr. Harrison whispered, his face pale. "That's physically impossible!" Harrison backed into the hospital room door, stumbled out, and began screaming for more staff to come and help him.

Costello guided Williams onto the bed and released him. Williams looked up at Costello, but, remarkably, the man was not frightened.

Costello smiled. "How do you feel?"

"The best I've felt in years," Williams responded.

"Do you know what just happened?" Costello asked.

Williams thought for a few seconds. "I understand. I understand everything."

"You understand everything? Well, you'll have to explain it all to me, then," Costello replied, and the two shared a laugh.

"How can I help?" Williams asked.

"Are you sure that you want to help?" Costello asked.

"Yes."

"Good. Here's how."

———◆———

"There's an emergency in Peterson Hospital!" an attendant in the White City hollered.

"What kind of emergency?" asked a second attendant.

"I don't know, but Dr. Harrison wants all staff to report to the hospital immediately!"

"All staff? Is he crazy? Who's going to watch these kids?" the second attendant asked.

"They'll have to watch each other," the first attendant replied as they ran out.

Once the staff had left the White City and rushed to Peterson Hospital, Nurse Cavell was free to complete her search for Nora. Since there were no records of the host identity, Cavell had to theorize. Daganian scholars had surmised that the host was likely female, and since it had been eight Earth years since the "coupling," the host would have to be at least eight years old. That was all Cavell had to go on.

Her uniform had proven to be the perfect entry ticket into almost any area of the colony. Since it was purportedly a hospital, it seemed perfectly reasonable for a nurse to walk unaccompanied through the grounds.

The nurse had fashioned a mild light beam which, if pointed into a human eye, was harmless. However, when pointed into the eye of a host, the beam would identify both the host and the other life force within; or at least, that was how it was supposed to work in theory. Today it would be tested.

Cavell had devised a simple plan: under the guise of conducting eye examinations on the children of the colony, she would examine each of the residents in the White City. If the host was located, Cavell would bring her to Costello at Peterson Hospital. Once there, they would devise a way out of the colony.

Cavell entered a classroom of eight- and nine-year-old girls. "Good morning, class. My name is Nurse Edith Cavell. I am here to give you each an eye exam."

"Will it hurt?" a girl called out. The others immediately joined in.

"Yeah, will it hurt?" one girl asked.

"I hate things that hurt!" said another.

"I promise, it will not hurt." Cavell replied.

———•———

The attendant, Frank Williams, walked into the hall. Dr. Harrison – who was now surrounded by three attendants, one almost the size of Williams – ran up to him.

"Are you all right?" Harrison asked.

"I'm fine. But Mr. Costello has two demands, or else he will destroy the entire hospital. First, he would like the founder, Dr. Frederick Peterson, to meet with him tomorrow. In person."

"Okay. I can make that happen," Dr. Harrison said. "What is the second demand?"

"If anyone else tries to enter his room without his permission, he will immediately blow up the hospital," Williams said. After delivering the message, Williams turned and walked back to Costello's room.

"Blow up the hospital. And how is he going to do that? We searched him when he was carried in here, and he hasn't been out of that room since." Harrison said.

Suddenly, Costello stepped from his room. He raised his right hand and a light beam shot through the hallway and blew out the window immediately adjacent to Harrison.

"Right. Evacuate the patients. Nurse, call the police." Harrison said as he ran for the exit.

CHAPTER TWENTY-EIGHT

THE BETRAYAL

Albany, New York
August 24, 1926

Before the bomb threat, Dr. Harrison had informed Kelly of Costello's desire to see him at the colony. Since the major's home and the colony were at opposite ends of New York State, traveling there to visit Costello was no easy task – particularly when it only allowed visitors two days per week.

Kelly was to meet with Costello on Wednesday, August 25 at two o'clock. The major would begin his 220-mile journey across New York State on the afternoon of Tuesday, August 24. Kelly asked Moyer to ride "shotgun."

On the way there, Kelly would attend a business meeting in Albany – one requested by "Legs" Diamond. Kelly's intention was to "settle up" with Diamond.

Kelly realized that the meeting could be a trap. However, since he believed that his only dispute with Diamond was his unpaid gambling debt, and Kelly had every intention of paying it at the meeting, he thought he would be safe. But Diamond wanted control of the entire upstate rum-running market. Still, as an added precaution, Kelly told Moyer to contact Kelly's allies, Albany Democratic Chairman O'Con-

nell and Detective Fitzgerald. Kelly figured that if Fitzgerald had officers at the meeting, Diamond couldn't double-cross him.

Fitzgerald agreed to bring four of his best men, so long as Kelly made
it worth their while. At least, that's how Moyer recounted the phone call
when Kelly picked him up for the trip. After that brief exchange, the
two barely spoke as they drove the seventy-five miles to Albany.

As of late, silence between the two was common. Moyer and Kelly
had been drifting apart for much of the past year. Although some
of the blame for this rift was Kelly's new friendship with Costello,
the problems between Moyer and Kelly had been growing for much
longer than that. In fact, when Kelly savagely beat Moyer in front of
the entire town during the Memorial Day boxing exhibition, their
split seemed inevitable.

After the two hour ride to Albany, Kelly parked his car outside the
New Kenmore Hotel and the two men walked through the lobby into
the Rain-Bo Room.

There, across the room, Diamond sat holding court with a table full
of well-dressed men. There were four men at Diamond's table and four
similarly dressed men sat at the table next to them. Kelly figured that
they were also with Diamond and that they were all heavily armed.

The Monahan brothers sat at the second table. Kelly didn't see
O'Connell or Fitzgerald. He hoped that they were secreted nearby, and
that their men were dispersed through the crowd.

Although greatly outnumbered, Kelly walked right up to Diamond's
table and placed a thick envelope in front of him.

"What's this?" Diamond asked, feigning surprise to see Kelly and
Moyer.

"Five thousand dollars," Kelly said. "Four thousand is the remaining
principal on the Dempsey bet. The other thousand covers thirteen
days' interest on the four."

"Mike, you sound angry. There's nothing to be mad about." Diamond motioned for the other men at the table to make room for Kelly. "Sit down. Have a drink with me."

When no one moved, Diamond looked at the other men at the table and barked, "Get up! Let the major sit down. You know he's a war hero, don't you?"

Diamond's men scattered. Kelly sat down cautiously, fully aware that Diamond may have an ulterior motive for speaking so graciously to him.

"Mike," Diamond continued. "Let's start with the extra thousand. You don't owe me any interest."

"I don't?" Kelly responded.

"Your friends at the next table, the Monahan brothers, paid the interest while you were recuperating. All that they ask in return is that you give them Costello's current location. They need to speak with him right away."

"That's all they ask. Costello's current location?" Kelly replied. "And I'm supposed to just give up one of my best men? I'm sorry. I can't do that."

Kelly stood up, turned, and spoke directly to the Monahans at the next table. "Gentlemen, I sincerely appreciate that you paid off the interest on my debt. But I insist on paying you back. If there is anything I can do to show my gratitude, I am happy to do it. But I never asked you to pay off my debt."

Diamond, aware that Kelly was on the brink of losing his famous temper, intervened.

"Mike, you're raising your voice at some pretty dangerous men — men who are your natural friends. Instead of arguing, sit down and have a drink with us." As Diamond spoke, he stepped between Kelly and the Monahan table.

Diamond then turned to Moyer and gave him a direct order, as though Moyer was one of Diamond's men. "Hey, Moyer, can you get the major a Guinness Ale? That's your drink, isn't it, major? Guinness Ale?"

"And Moyer, make sure that you add some extra grain alcohol to it. You know, just like you did to the major's 'vitamins' during the Dempsey fight. I understand that when you mix grain alcohol with Guinness Ale, 'it gives you strength.'" As he spoke, Diamond flexed his muscles, mimicking the way that Kelly had flexed while standing on the ropes during the Dempsey fight.

Several of Diamond's men burst into laughter at their boss's mockery of Kelly and responded by flexing their own muscles.

Although Kelly was internally furious about the public ridicule, he also knew that the odds in a fight were not currently in his favor. The safest thing he could do was to get out of the club as quickly as possible.

"All right, Mr. Diamond. Now that you're paid in full, our business is complete. I'll be going." Kelly shot a quick look at Moyer, who was now standing next to Diamond. "C'mon, Mr. Moyer. We've got a long drive ahead."

"One problem there, Major. Moyer works for me now," Diamond said firmly. His men abruptly stopped laughing, "He's worked for me for a few weeks now, so, he'll be staying here with us.

"And by the way, I told Moyer not to call O'Connell or Fitzgerald. So, there's no one here to protect you. Boys – grab him!" The three men at Monahan's table rose and blocked Kelly's exit. As Kelly reached for his gun, two other men grabbed Kelly from behind.

"I'm afraid that you won't be leaving tonight, major," Diamond taunted gleefully.

Kelly was stunned by this unexpected turn of events. True, he had always taken Moyer for granted. But Moyer was one of the most trusted members of the Kelly family. Kelly had shared all of his most valuable secrets with Moyer: the identity of his suppliers. His smuggling routes. The names of the police officers and judges they bribed to look the other way or go easy after an arrest. And with Moyer's help, Diamond could take over the Kelly family empire.

After Diamond's men grabbed Kelly, Moyer yelled, "He usually carries three guns: two under his jacket and one in a holster on his left ankle!"

They then pushed Kelly over a table and aggressively frisked him until all three guns were seized.

"Jim!" Kelly cried out to Moyer, trying to summon a shred of loyalty. Kelly had not called Jim Moyer by his first name in years, and it sounded pathetic, even to Kelly.

"Jim, we've been together for a long time," Kelly pleaded. "Think of the men of the 105th. Their families. The town of Granville. Do you think Diamond gives a rat's ass about any of that?"

"I think Mr. Diamond cares about those people about as much as Mike Kelly does," Moyer snapped back. "In fact, I'm gonna do what my mentor Mike Kelly would do. I'll do what's best for *me*. And *my* interests are served by taking Mr. Diamond's offer."

"There you have it, Mike. Here, Mr. Moyer. This is for you." Diamond grabbed the envelope of cash that Kelly had just placed on the table and threw it to Moyer. "That's partial payment for the fine work you're doing for me."

Diamond turned back to Kelly with a smile. "Cheer up, Kelly. You win some, you lose some. Most days you live, and then only one time, you die." Diamond laughed as he continued. "And, Mike, it's your one time."

Diamond spoke to his entire crew. "Take him out back. If he doesn't tell you where Costello is, you know what to do. Mr. Moyer, you are welcome to stay and join the party."

"You don't have to do this! You can have everything," Kelly shouted as the men pushed him out through the door and back towards the kitchen.

"No, thanks – if I'd wanted everything of yours, I would have taken it long ago," Diamond said. "Nice knowing you, major."

Five men completely overpowered Kelly and dragged him through the kitchen. Once in the back, they pushed Kelly up against the wall, handcuffed him, and threw him into a large storage closet.

The door slammed shut. Monahan turned to his number one, Mike O'Leary.

"O'Leary, you're the best we got. You're in charge. If I give you the word, you take the major outside and shoot him in the head. Then dispose of the body. Can you handle that?" Red Monahan asked.

"Piece of cake," O'Leary responded.

The Monahan brothers returned to the party in the Rain-Bo Room.

O'Leary walked into the closet. Kelly was leaning against the wall with his hands cuffed behind his back. When he saw O'Leary, Kelly stood up straight.

"Hey, I recognize you. You served in the war. What unit?" Kelly said.

"I served under Major Mike Kelly in the 105th, sir," O'Leary responded.

"I thought I recognized you, soldier!" Kelly said.

"I even met you once in France. You came by my unit special to congratulate me on the day my son Michael was born," O'Leary said. "I'll never forget that."

"I have a son named Michael," Kelly said, wondering if he would ever see his own Michael again.

"I have two boys now. My younger one is Kevin," O'Leary said. "I took them to Whitehall the day that you fought Luis Firpo."

"That was a great day," Kelly said, smiling as he thought back. It was hard to believe it had only been a few weeks since that fight.

"Listen, major. Please. You have to tell them what they want to know – where they can find that guy Costello – or Diamond will kill you," O'Leary said. "And I just know they're going to make *me* do it. If my son Michael finds out that I murdered Mike Kelly, he'll never look at me the same way again."

"My son Michael won't be very happy about it, either," Kelly said, as calmly as he could.

"So, please, Sir, tell them where to find Costello!" O'Leary implored.

"You mean where to find Sergeant Costello, because you served with him in the 105th, too, soldier," Kelly reminded him.

"Just tell them what they want to know," O'Leary pleaded.

"Diamond is gonna kill me even if I tell him where Costello is," Kelly said.

"You don't know that."

"Your name's O'Leary, right? So, you're Irish Catholic?" Kelly asked.

"Of course," O'Leary told him.

"You still go to church?"

"Every Sunday. You?"

"It's been a while for me. Think you could help me remember the words to the Act of Contrition?" Kelly asked.

"Of course," O'Leary responded.

O'Leary helped Kelly get down on his knees. And then, almost like a father teaching his son the prayer, O'Leary lead Kelly through the Act of Contrition. When the two men finished, Kelly said, "Again, please," and they repeated the prayer. This time, the words came back much more easily to Kelly. When Kelly repeated the prayer a third time, he said it without O'Leary's help.

Suddenly, the closet door swung open. "Did he tell you where to find Costello?" Frank Monahan asked. "Hey – what the hell are you doing down there?" Monahan roared, seeing Kelly on the floor.

"I'm still working on it," O'Leary answered.

"It doesn't matter. Moyer knows where to find Costello." Monahan continued, "We don't need Kelly. Mr. Diamond just wants you to take him into the alley and finish it."

O'Leary looked stunned. Monahan yelled, "I said, finish it! Now!"

With that, O'Leary helped Kelly to his feet. O'Leary and the two other men who were waiting outside the closet pushed Kelly out through the back door and into the center of the alley behind the hotel. O'Leary helped Kelly to his knees.

Kelly didn't resist, or try to run, or beg for mercy. He had accepted his fate. "Will you say one final Act of Contrition with me?" he asked, looking up at O'Leary.

"Now? Here?" O'Leary said.

"Can you think of a better time or place?" Kelly said bravely, forcing a small smile.

"Okay. Sure."

"O'Leary, what are you doing? We don't have time for this!" said another gunman.

"Shut up!" yelled O'Leary. "You heard Monahan. I'm in charge. Major Kelly is a war hero. We will treat him with the respect that he has earned." O'Leary then kneeled opposite Kelly, and the two men made the sign of the cross.

In what may have been the ultimate professional courtesy given to a fellow soldier, the gunmen waited patiently while Kelly and O'Leary prayed together:

"Oh, my God, I'm heartily sorry for having offended Thee. I detest all of my sins because of Thy just punishments, but most of all because they offend Thee, My God, who art all good and deserving of all my love. I firmly resolve, with the help of Thy grace, to sin no more and avoid the near occasions of sin."

When Kelly and O'Leary finished this final prayer, O'Leary stood up, brushed the dirt off the knees of his trousers, and drew his revolver.

Kelly looked up at the three men and nodded to each, seemingly grateful that they had permitted him this final moment to make peace with God. As all three men took careful aim at his head, Kelly stared at O'Leary.

Lord, is this really it? All of my work, and this is how it ends, in an alley behind a nightclub? Regrets raced through Kelly's mind. He'd never get to say goodbye to his wife. Or to his beautiful children.

Then, far more quickly than he had expected, shots rang out.

Kelly distinctly counted three shots. *Is that how it is when you die? Time moves so slowly that you actually hear the gunshots?*

He waited to feel the bullets pierce his skin. But he felt nothing. How could it be that he felt nothing?

Suddenly, Kelly felt a spray of warm blood against his face as the heads of two of the gunmen exploded. He then watched Mike O'Leary's forehead shatter.

Kelly tried to get out of the way as three bodies collapsed. He was still alive, while his partially headless, would-be assassins were splattered all around him. He looked at Mike O'Leary, lying directly in front of him. Although he was happy to be alive, it was bittersweet knowing that young Michael O'Leary, not Michael Kelly, would cry for the loss of his father that day.

"Did you see that? I didn't even use a scope!" A familiar voice shouted in the distance. It was then that Kelly realized that the three bullets were fired from an M1903 Springfield rifle. Bobby Billow had saved his life.

Kelly got to his feet and ran as fast as he could in the direction of the familiar voice. Kelly knew that although his three would-be killers were dead, there were at least seven other extremely lethal men still alive in the Rain-Bo Room. And, Kelly was still unarmed and hand-cuffed. So, he instinctively ran toward the voice. There, at the end of the alley, was his old friend Billow still aiming his rifle, scanning for additional targets.

"Where's the truck?" Kelly asked as he ran toward Billow, trying to keep his voice down.

"Around the corner," Billow calmly replied, "Aren't you even going to thank me for saving your life?"

"I'll be thanking you for the rest of my life. Thank you so much!" Kelly said as the two men turned and ran to the truck. "I'd hug you except my hands are still cuffed behind my back. Do you think you can get these things off of me?"

"Sure," said Billow.

"We have to go and warn Costello. Moyer is working for Diamond now and he knows where Costello is."

"Moyer is working for Diamond?" Billow asked in disbelief.

"I know. I wouldn't have believed it if I hadn't seen it with my own eyes," Kelly said.

"But there's no time to talk. We've got to get Costello before Diamond knows I got away and Moyer tells him where to find us."

Billow and Kelly ran down the block and climbed into a Model T truck. Like a guardian angel, Billow had been following Kelly and Moyer. Years earlier, Kelly had ordered Billow to follow him and be ready to intervene if Kelly's life was ever in danger – and Billow had obeyed that order. Now, years later, all of the time that Billow had spent tailing Kelly had finally paid off.

The two men took turns driving through the night. They would reach the Craig Colony by the time visiting hours started the following afternoon.

CHAPTER TWENTY-NINE
THE ESCALATED RESPONSE

Albany, New York
August 25, 1926

A few hours later, "Legs" Diamond staggered into the alley behind the Rain-Bo Room. Although the news he had just received certainly spoiled his party, he was not upset. He was far too drunk to be angry.

When he ordered the execution of Mike Kelly, earlier in the evening, Diamond was sober. Watching as Kelly was dragged away by five men, gave him confidence that his subordinates could get the job done. "A good leader must be able to delegate work," Diamond said after Red Monahan returned from the kitchen, leaving Kelly behind.

Of course, Diamond had wanted to pull the trigger himself. But he had been criticized in the past for being too "hands-on," so he had asked Monahan to handle it personally. Diamond then spent the rest of the evening drinking to Kelly's demise.

At 2 a.m., as Diamond was leaving to pass out in his girlfriend's apartment, he learned that three bodies had been found in the alley behind the kitchen.

Three bodies? I'm in no condition to make further strategic decisions, but I tried delegating one simple task, and look how that worked out, Diamond thought to himself.

Since he had just spent over six hours in the Rain-Bo Room, Diamond decided that he should learn the identities of those bodies before the police arrived. That way, if he could be linked to any of the corpses, his men could dispose of them.

Diamond stumbled into the alley. The bodies were still slumped together, right where Kelly had knelt several hours before. Upon close inspection, it was apparent that each one had died from a single gunshot to the forehead.

Diamond, who had certainly seen his share of fresh corpses, was not troubled by the sight. Moyer, who was trailing close behind, saw the three and immediately looked away. Although Diamond was drunk, he managed to remain calm... until he realized that Kelly was not among them.

"Three bodies, and not one of them is Kelly!" Diamond yelled. He began pacing circles around the bodies, which remained slumped firmly together in the middle of the alley.

Six other men joined Diamond and Monahan in the alley. Two had their weapons drawn in case Kelly or his men were still in the vicinity, ignorant of the fact that Kelly and Billow had left for the Craig Colony several hours before.

"So, these were three of your best men?" Diamond yelled at Red Monahan. No one had ever spoken to Monahan like that before.

"They *are* the best," Monahan replied defensively.

"You mean they *were* the best. And the best at what, exactly? If you mean that they were the best for using as target practice, then I agree with that!" Diamond said.

Diamond nudged one of the bodies with his foot and watched it tip over. "Because if that is what you mean, I agree. They seem to be great for target practice."

As Diamond shouted angrily at Monahan, he removed his revolver from his holster and shot one of the bodies three more times in the head. "Yeah, for target practice, they're really good! They're the best!"

Diamond yelled sarcastically.

"Don't do that," Red Monahan said.

"Yeah? Why not?" Diamond asked, pointing his revolver point-blank in Monahan's face.

"Because forensics will be able to match the slugs in that man's head to your gun," Monahan calmly replied.

"Oh. Damn it, you're right. Boys, can you take these stiffs out of here and get rid of them?" Several men began packing up the bodies for disposal.

He then turned his attention to Moyer. "And you. Fat Man. I thought you took all of Kelly's guns!"

"I'm certain that we did, Mr. Diamond. He always carries three guns, and we took all three guns from him," Moyer said.

"Then how did Kelly shoot three of Monahan's 'best' men in the head?" Diamond shouted.

"Sir, I think you should look at this," said Howard Cooper, one of Diamond's men and an Army veteran. "Boss, these men were shot from a distance with a rifle."

"A rifle?" Diamond asked. "How do you know that?"

"The type and size of the head wound," Cooper told him. "I saw a lot of these wounds on men I served with in the war. Men shot from long range with a rifle."

Diamond saw Moyer close his eyes and wince. *Men shot from long range with a sniper rifle.* "What is it? What do you know?" Diamond screamed as he rushed up to Moyer. "Look at that fat face. He knows. He knows what happened!"

Diamond's instincts were correct. Moyer was certain he knew who shot the three men. *Damn it. I know they're going to make me give up Billow,* Moyer thought. *Kelly was easy, but how could I betray my dear friend Bobby Billow?*

Moyer now fully realized the significance of his actions. When he'd double-crossed Kelly, he had not just turned his back on Kelly but on everyone and everything he had ever held dear. Billow was one of Moyer's oldest and dearest friends.

Diamond pulled his gun out of his holster and placed the end of the barrel directly under Moyer's chin. The difference in the size of the two men – Moyer at six-foot-six and Diamond at five-foot-six – was striking. Still, that difference allowed Diamond to easily slide his gun up under Moyer's chin.

"This horse is going to talk, or my face is the last thing he's ever going to see!" Diamond shouted. "All right, you've got five seconds. Then I pull the trigger. *Who shot these three men?* One! Two!"

Moyer remained silent for two seconds, but when he heard Diamond cock the gun below his chin he yelled out, "Bobby Billow! It was Billow! The town Barber! He was the best shot in the 105th and still works for Kelly."

"There. That wasn't so hard, was it?" Diamond said, lowering his gun.

"What do you want to do with the bodies?" Monahan asked.

"Take the one I shot. Let the police find the other two," said Diamond.

"What – what are we going to do about Kelly, boss?" Monahan asked.

Some leaders would have carefully considered the question before responding. Effective leaders would have actually weighed their options and opted for a proportional, measured response. Diamond was not such a leader. Instead, he chose to dramatically escalate the conflict.

"Call everyone you know," Diamond ordered Monahan. "Call New York. Call Chicago. I want as many hired guns who will make the trip. Tell them that "Legs" Diamond is paying one thousand dollars per man, per day, plus expenses.

"Kelly loves to play soldier." Diamond's voice became a snarl. "Well, I'm gonna raise an army! That barber is dead. Costello, dead. Kelly, dead. Their families are dead. We're gonna burn that crappy little town to the ground and *kill everyone in it!*"

CHAPTER THIRTY

THE POET

Sonyea, New York
August 25, 1926

Dr. Frederick Peterson stood for several minutes outside the hospital that bore his name. He had travelled overnight from his home in Manhattan to the Craig Colony in Sonyea. Although Peterson was the colony's founder and first president, it had been named after a financial benefactor, Oscar Craig.

Peterson was also largely responsible for the colony's novel treatment of its "residents." The Craig Colony was, by design, home to patients suffering from a variety of seizure disorders. In 1926, those seizures were all lumped under the same diagnosis: epilepsy. The medical treatment for its "residents," was the "Colony Care Plan," first conceived by Dr. Peterson while he was a physician at the Hudson River State Hospital for the Insane. The Craig Colony was born in 1894, with Dr. Peterson serving as its first president.

Although it was his creation, Peterson had mixed feelings about the colony. Since his resignation in 1902, Peterson had become a psychiatrist of some renown. He was now a professor of psychiatry at Columbia University and had authored numerous textbooks and articles.

Still, when the current president of the Craig Colony, Dr. Christopher Harrison, had suddenly begged him to urgently return, Peterson was intrigued. Dr. Harrison had called him and described a most unique patient, one who was in dire need of Peterson's care. The patient, one Ryan Costello, had had multiple grand mal seizures but was also stricken with severe schizophrenia and delusions of grandeur.

Peterson set off the afternoon before on the long train ride from his home in Manhattan to Sonyea, about forty-five miles south of Rochester. Upon his arrival, he went straight from the station to the hospital. Although exhausted by the time he reached the Colony, Peterson got a jolt of adrenaline as he marveled at the many police cars and military vehicles that surrounded the edifice.

What could one patient have done that would have caused such a commotion? Peterson thought as he carefully walked through a gauntlet of police and soldiers ringing the hospital. It all looked quite ominous.

Peterson entered the lobby and saw an attendant standing in the center of the hallway. He appeared to have been waiting for several hours. The attendant introduced himself as Frank Williams. In their correspondence, Dr. Harrison had referred to Williams as "his enforcer." Dr. Peterson had always been afraid to ask why a physician, running a hospital that treated patients for seizure disorders, would need an "enforcer." Of course, the fact that Dr. Peterson feared the answer was probably one of the reasons why he was uneasy to be back at the Craig Colony.

"It's an honor to meet you, Dr. Peterson," Williams said, greeting Peterson as if they were lifelong friends. "I'm to take you to him."

"To *him?* Do you mean Dr. Harrison?" Dr. Peterson asked.

"Heavens, no. Harrison ran away yesterday."

"Then who are you taking me to?" Dr. Peterson asked.

"He is very excited to meet you," Williams said. "Please follow me."

"How did you even know that I was coming?" Dr. Peterson asked

"*He* said that you would come."

"*He* did? And how did *he* know?" Peterson asked, still trying to figure out who he was.

"All that he told me is that I should meet you in the lobby and bring you right to him," Williams said as he turned and walked quickly down the hall.

Dr. Peterson followed from a safe distance. The two walked silently through the seemingly deserted Peterson Hospital and then up the stairs to Costello's room. Peterson was shocked at the abandoned hospital. It was not devoid of supplies or equipment or furniture – just people. No doctors, or staff, or patients.

"Where is everyone?" Peterson asked.

Williams did not respond.

"I said, where is everyone?" Peterson repeated, raising his voice at the much larger man. "That is not your concern. You should prepare yourself, for in just a moment you will be in his presence. Now, follow me," Williams said, forcefully.

Williams then walked to the end of the hallway and stopped outside of a room. "You are to go in alone while I wait here and make sure that you are not disturbed," Williams relayed politely.

"Am I in danger?"

"You are in no danger," Williams replied, amused.

"How can you be so sure?"

"Just go in and meet him. You will understand. He's not here to harm us. He's here to save us." With that, Williams turned and stood at attention by the door.

"To save us?" Peterson repeated. But no other information was forthcoming; so, he took a deep breath to calm while approaching the door.

In his esteemed career, Dr. Peterson had spoken with all types of patients. He'd even authored a textbook on patient intake and evaluation, which was commonly used in hospitals across the country. *Certainly, I can interview one new patient, no matter how sick he may be.*

Peterson reviewed the patient's chart hanging on a clipboard by the door, giving particular attention to the diagnosis by Dr. Harrison.

"The patient has schizophrenia, delusions of grandeur, and a God complex, in addition to an extremely violent form of epilepsy," Harrison had written.

Dr. Peterson didn't agree that there was a "violent form of epilepsy," although he was aware that less sophisticated professionals had made the diagnosis on certain patients. *Harrison would subscribe to such a theory,* Peterson thought to himself as he took a deep breath and swung open the door.

Across the room, Peterson saw an enormous man sitting in the corner, his eyes closed.

"Hello. Are you Mr. Costello?" Dr. Peterson asked in a well-rehearsed, friendly tone, attempting to establish immediate rapport with the patient.

"Ni hao, Pai Ta-Shun," Costello responded warmly, in perfect Mandarin Chinese. Costello did not open his eyes, although he appeared to be aware of Peterson's location in the room.

"What did you just say?" Peterson asked, no longer smiling.

"I said, *Ni hao, Pai Ta-Shun.*" Costello replied.

"And why did you say that?" Dr. Peterson asked.

"I merely welcomed you by your Chinese name, Pai Ta-Shun," Costello responded.

"You speak English and Mandarin?" Dr. Peterson asked.

"We can speak any language you wish, Dr. Peterson," Costello said, his eyes still shut.

Costello had called him Peterson and Pai Ta-Shun, although they had never met before.

"Tell me, Mr. Costello. Why did you call me Pai Ta-Shun?" Dr. Peterson asked.

Costello rose and walked across the room. When they were two feet apart, Costello opened his eyes for the first time. "Because, Pai Ta-Shun, 'the ancestral voices are calling you and commanding you to do their will'."

"How do you know my words?" Dr. Peterson asked, visibly shaken.

"I know all Earth literature. Those words are from one of your most beautiful poems."

"But few people even know that I write poetry. Fewer still know my pen name, Pai Ta-Shun. My poetry was not even published in the United States. And I didn't tell anyone I was coming here today, or even introduce myself when I entered the room. So, why – how – do you know all this about me?"

Costello kept his silence. Dr. Peterson took a moment to regain his composure and asked another question. "Do you know why I am here?"

"Because, Frederick Peterson, I have summoned you," Costello answered.

"You summoned me?" Peterson murmured as he made notes. "And why have you summoned me?"

"I need your help completing my mission and, frankly, the Earth is running out of time."

That statement alone confirms Dr. Harrison's initial impression that Costello suffers from a host of psychological issues. Certainly schizophrenia, bipolar disorder, and delusions of grandeur are among them, Peterson thought to himself.

However, Costello's problems seem even more complex than Harrison recognizes. He appears to suffer from psychiatric problems that have not yet been identified by the medical community. To design a proper treatment plan, I will have to get him to fully describe his history.

"Tell me about yourself, Mr. Costello," Dr. Peterson asked, in his most empathetic voice.

"Where should I start?"

"Perhaps you could start by telling me why the Earth is running out of time?"

CHAPTER THIRTY-ONE

THE PRINCESS

Sonyea, New York
August 25, 1926

Dr. Peterson glanced at his watch. It was 2:20 p.m. He had been speaking with Costello in his hospital room through the morning and into the afternoon. Yet, despite Costello's candor about the events of the previous three months, it only reinforced the initial clinical impression that Costello was schizophrenic and delusional.

"I'm sorry, Mr. Costello," Dr. Peterson said. "I lost track of time. We skipped lunch."

"That is not important," Costello stated.

"Perhaps not. But please remind me again: why have you summoned me here?"

"I need your help with my mission."

"Of course, I will help you. But I still have a few details that I need you to clarify." Peterson kept his eyes on his notes as he spoke. "You believe that you trained a Medal of Honor winner, Major Mike Kelly to fight Jack Dempsey."

"That's right," Costello said.

"A Dempsey fight is usually all over the papers. Why didn't I read about it?"

"It was a sparring session in Saratoga. Major Kelly treated it like a real contest."

"And that is where you pointed a gun at the gangster 'Legs' Diamond?"

"Yes."

"What's Diamond like?" Peterson asked.

"A psychopath. A murderer," Costello responded.

"Do you think Diamond will visit you here?" Dr. Peterson asked calmly.

"I hope not," Costello said. "Diamond would not come here to visit. He would only come here to kill me. And since he doesn't leave behind witnesses, your staff would be at great risk."

Although Costello had just described a scenario that included the murder of Craig Colony staff, Peterson was not alarmed. Costello presumed that this was because Peterson did not take the threat seriously.

Peterson continued reading from his list of questions. "You said that Major Kelly is an officer in something called the New York Naval Militia?"

"Yes."

"But Kelly uses the militia as a cover for his rum-running business?" Peterson asked.

"Yes. To facilitate the smuggling of alcohol from Canada to New York City."

"Is Jack Dempsey also an officer in the New York Naval Militia?" Peterson asked in complete seriousness, testing Costello.

"Of course not. Dempsey is the world heavyweight boxing champion," Costello responded, losing his patience. "Dr. Peterson, you're not taking me seriously."

"Really? Why do you say that?"

"You've asked many questions, and I've patiently responded. But you have not asked the critical one."

"Oh?" Dr. Peterson leaned forward in his chair, excited that he had finally hit a nerve. *Maybe, at last, Costello would explain the cause of his delusions.* Peterson thought to himself.

Costello also leaned forward toward Peterson. "What can I say to convince you to assist me with my mission? Please, Doctor. The Earth is in grave danger."

"You can tell me specifically why the world is in danger."

"All right. I come from a planet several light years from Earth," Costello began. "I was sent here in advance of an Armada... "

This just keeps getting better and better, Peterson thought to himself. While Costello spoke, Peterson furiously wrote in his notepad. *I'll be writing books about this patient for years.*

Suddenly, with Costello in mid-sentence, the door swung open, and Nurse Cavell burst into the room. "I found her! I found her!" Cavell cried triumphantly.

An eight-year-old girl with long red hair trailed closely behind Cavell. Her clothes were tattered and dirty as though she had been wearing them for several days.

"I told you that I'd find her. And I found her," Cavell said as she guided the young girl to Costello for closer inspection. Cavell was so excited that she didn't notice Dr. Peterson.

When Costello saw the girl, he immediately dropped to his knees. "Oh, my... it *is* you. Welcome, Your Majesty," Costello said as he knelt before the little girl. "I am humbled and honored to meet you."

"Do you need this?" Cavell asked, offering Costello the light beam.

"No need, I am certain. *She is Princess Halana,*" Costello replied.

"She doesn't speak," Cavell whispered to Costello.

"Why are you whispering?" Costello asked, "If she doesn't speak, she must already know that she doesn't speak."

"Now I'm *really* confused," Dr. Peterson said. "Excuse me, Nurse. Why have you brought this child to Mr. Costello's room?" Peterson asked.

Cavell was so startled to discover Dr. Peterson that she failed to maintain her cover story. Instead, Cavell responded defensively, "Me? Yes, I am a nurse."

"I figured as much from your uniform. Why are you here?" Dr. Peterson asked.

"I'm – I'm with him," Cavell responded, pointing at Costello. Cavell and Costello both winced, painfully aware that her answer was not responsive to Peterson's question.

"Are you also from a planet several light years from Earth?" Peterson asked flippantly.

"*What?* You told him about us? You *told* him?" Cavell shouted at Costello, incredulous.

"I searched within him," Costello responded softly.

"You told him *who we really are* because you '*searched within him*'?" Cavell shouted, her anger growing the more Costello tried to explain himself.

"We need an ally. He has a deep capacity for good. I am certain that if we just tell him the truth, we can trust him, and he will help us," Costello said.

"Wait a minute. You – you both believe that you are from a planet several light years from Earth?" Peterson continued, "And Nurse, you are jointly engrossed in Costello's delusion? So, you both believe that this child is extraterrestrial royalty from across the galaxy?" Peterson scribbled furiously in his notes.

"Wow, I've read of shared psychotic disorders before, but this is the first time I have personally observed it," Peterson blurted out.

Costello, who was still on his knees, stood up at last and turned to Dr. Peterson.

"Dr. Peterson, we don't *believe* she is royalty; we *know* it." Costello said.

"That's enough, analyst! Say nothing further about our background or mission. *That's a direct order,*" Cavell shouted.

Suddenly, Major Kelly burst into Costello's hospital room wearing his combat uniform. Although it had been nearly ten days since his sparring session with Dempsey, cuts and bruises were still visible on his face.

"And who are you supposed to be?" Dr. Peterson asked, believing Kelly to be a patient.

"Major Mike Kelly. I'm here for Ryan Costello," Kelly snapped, and then saw Costello. "You're gonna need your uniform, Sergeant," Kelly barked.

"And I'm to believe that you're the war hero, Major Mike Kelly?" Dr. Peterson asked skeptically.

"Who the hell is this?" Kelly asked Costello, pointing at Dr. Peterson.

"I'm supposed to believe that you're Mike Kelly, the winner of the Medal of Honor?" Peterson asked.

"I don't give a rat's ass what you believe," Kelly said, growing impatient with Peterson.

"So please educate me, why is a national hero visiting the Colony today?" Peterson asked, wrongly concluding that the man in the combat uniform was a resident.

"To pick up Costello before 'Legs' Diamond gets to him," Kelly responded.

"How did you get those bruises on your face?" Dr. Peterson asked, less skeptically.

"Not that it's any of your business, but I got beat up by Jack Dempsey," Kelly snapped.

"So, you did fight Jack Dempsey?" Peterson asked, dumbfounded.

"Fight? Well, calling it a fight gives me more credit than I deserve," Kelly continued, "I got beat up. The only thing that saved me was Nurse Cavell and her remarkable healing powers." Kelly moved his hands through the air as though casting a magic spell.

"Does Mr. Costello really know the gangster 'Legs' Diamond?" Peterson asked.

"Unfortunately, we all do. That's why I'm here." Kelly turned back to Costello. "Diamond and Moyer tried to kill me last night. They know where you are. I think they are coming here."

"Diamond tried to kill you. And Moyer? Moyer is with Diamond now?" Costello asked.

"Yes. And I think they're on their way here," Kelly said

"You know that I'm with you," Costello replied.

"Great. Get in uniform and let's go," Kelly said.

"Before we leave, you really should meet someone," Costello said as he walked behind the child. When Kelly noticed the little girl, his demeanor immediately changed from a hardened military veteran to an empathetic, caring father.

"And who is this young lady?" Kelly asked, smiling at the little girl who appeared frightened and confused by all of the excitement around her.

Costello placed his hands on her shoulders as she faced Kelly.

"Major Mike Kelly, I'd like you to meet Nora, your daughter."

CHAPTER THIRTY-TWO

THE DAUGHTER

Sonyea, New York
August 25, 1926

"You'd like me to meet – my *daughter?*" Kelly asked, raising his voice. Cavell stepped between Kelly and the girl. Although Cavell didn't think Kelly would intentionally harm the child, she was too important to risk even accidental injury.

"Gentlemen, I understand that this is all quite sudden. But this discussion should be outside the presence of the child." Cavell stared at the three men, who stepped out of the room.

The three wandered the halls of the Peterson Hospital looking for a conference room. It had been twenty-four years since Peterson had worked at the Colony, and he was unable to locate anything. So, the attendant, Williams, lead them to the hospital cafeteria. Once alone, Kelly spoke first.

"I'd know it if I had another daughter." Kelly said.

"Besides, Ryan, you said the girl was royalty. If the Major is her father, how could she be royalty?" Peterson continued as he glanced at Kelly, "No offense, but you don't seem regal."

"None taken," Kelly replied.

"You want me to believe that you are not ill, then answer the question. " Peterson said.

"Costello, I am giving you a direct order, speak up, man!" thundered Kelly.

"Respectfully, sir, you were Ryan Costello's commanding officer in the 105th during the war. On this mission, you know my commander as Edith Cavell."

"Now I see why you keep writing 'delusional' in your notes. You should also write the words 'nuttier than a fruitcake'." Kelly whispered to Peterson.

Dr. Peterson ignored Kelly's comment, although he was concerned that the major had been apparently reading his notes as he wrote. "So, Costello, do you need Nurse Cavell's permission before you can tell us about the missing child?" Peterson asked.

"Exactly." Costello said.

Dr. Peterson rose from his chair and crossed to Williams, who was standing guard at the door. Williams listened intently to Peterson, nodded, and rushed down the hall. The three men sat silently as they awaited Williams's return. A few minutes later, Williams returned to the cafeteria accompanied by Cavell.

"Nurse Cavell, do come in," Peterson said, "Major Kelly and I are trying to understand how that young girl could be both royalty and his daughter. Our challenge is that you ordered Costello to remain silent. Would you please revoke that order? After all, if Major Kelly is, indeed, that girl's father, he has the right to know how she got here."

Cavell turned to Kelly. "Is that what you want?"

"Yes," Kelly replied.

"Even if the explanation will leave you with another child to care for?" Cavell asked.

"If she's my child, then I have an absolute duty to care for her, just as I care for my other children," Kelly stated. "But it's more than that. If she is my daughter, I *want* to care for her."

"See?" Costello said to Cavell. "It's what I've been telling you all along. He's a force for good. They both are. We can trust them both."

Cavell stared hard at Kelly and Peterson. After considering the matter for several seconds, she answered reluctantly. "All right, Costello. It appears that now that your powers are restored; you have access to your empath protocol. You're the empath. If you trust these two Earthlings, then I defer to you."

Costello stood and walked around the table, organizing his thoughts. "All right, gentlemen. What I am about to tell you, I have never told anyone else on this planet. You must swear that you will never tell another person."

"I swear," Kelly immediately responded.

Dr. Peterson looked at his copious notes and realized that an oath of silence would end the various books and treatises he was already contemplating.

"Just one more question. You said that you needed my help to get out of here. If you and Nurse Cavell are so powerful, why would you need my help to leave this hospital?"

"Two reasons," Costello answered. "First, you can get us out of the colony without any harm coming to those good people circling the hospital."

"Second, according to my database, in 1923, you published *The American Textbook of Legal Medicine and Toxicology*. So, you must be familiar with the drug phenobarbital, right?"

"It's relatively new, but yes, I'm familiar with it," Dr. Peterson said.

"Good. We need it to control Nora's seizures. We might need lots of it depending on how long we are stuck on this planet," Costello told him.

"I would not recommend it for seizures." Dr. Peterson spoke with an air of authority.

"I am not asking you to recommend it. And I'm definitely not asking for your professional opinion on the effectiveness of the drug. Just get it for Nora and for me. Can you do that?" Costello asked.

"Of course, I can. But I'm not going to prescribe it to a patient because you say so," Peterson said.

"After we are gone, if you want to commission a study on the efficacy of the drug to control seizures, that is up to you. Of course, after the drug is determined effective, you will have to explain the purpose of this dreadful place and your Colony Care Plan, since seizures can be controlled by medication. But that's between you, and your conscience," Costello said.

"All right, I'll help you," Peterson said reluctantly.

"Good. Go to the hospital pharmacy and get me phenobarbital," Costello ordered.

With that, Dr. Peterson exited the cafeteria.

"Costello, please tell me how you know that Nora is my daughter?" Kelly asked.

"Of course. Nurse Cavell and I come from a planet several light years from Earth."

"Stop right there. You come from a planet several light years from Earth?" Kelly asked.

"Yes. Does that frighten you?"

"No. But one question. What's a 'light year?'" Kelly asked.

"Just as it sounds. Since light travels at an extremely fast rate, your scientists use the term 'light year' to measure the very long distances between stars and galaxies. It is the distance that light travels in one Earth year," Costello explained.

Kelly was understandably skeptical that the man that he had spent so much time with was now claiming to be an alien from another planet. "Okay, please explain it so I can understand it.

"It takes approximately 1.2 seconds for light to travel from the Earth's moon to Earth. But my planet is so far away from Earth, that it would take light several of your years to travel from there to Earth." Costello said.

"Okay. See, I understood that," Kelly said. "Your planet is so far away; it would take a ray of light several years to travel from Earth to your planet."

"That's what I just said?"

"All right. So, now tell me how – and why – you believe the little girl is my daughter?"

"We are a race of explorers," Costello continued, "We have studied this galaxy and many, many others. Eight years ago, our leader, his wife, and daughter were passing through your solar system when there was a complete systems failure on their vessel. We have never been able to determine the cause. A decision was made to save the heir to the throne – an heir that you, in your language, would call the princess. The crew identified an appropriate host for the life force of the child – the princess. They selected a host that would carry the Princess's life force, until a rescue mission could be deployed to extract her."

"What happened to the crew?" Kelly asked.

"All were lost."

"I'm sorry. But what does any of that have to do with me?" Kelly asked.

"Mike, your daughter Nora is the host," Costello explained.

"The host of what?" Kelly asked.

"The host of the princess's life force," Costello said.

"You mean – you're saying the princess is inside that little girl?" Kelly asked.

"Yes. The life force of our Princess Halana has 'coupled' with your daughter," Costello replied.

"But I told you – I don't have a daughter named Nora!"

"Mike, you do. Nora was born August 10, 1917. You, were fighting in Europe."

Kelly just stared at him.

"But no one could have anticipated the side effects that the host, Nora, would suffer once the life force of the princess was in a human body," Costello continued.

"The seizures?" Kelly interjected.

"Precisely. The grand mal seizures," Costello said. "I mean, you've witnessed the remarkable physical benefits to a host when we couple with a human body."

"Costello?" Kelly said.

"Costello. But we are still studying what causes the seizures and how to control them."

"But how could all this have happened without me knowing about it?" Kelly said. "How could that child be my daughter?"

"From what Cavell and I have been able to figure out, while you were in Europe, Nora was born. At first, she was fine, but after a few months, Nora started having grand mal seizures. Mary tried very hard to care for the newborn. After a particularly difficult night, Mary consulted with the town doctor, who recommended what he understood was a highly specialized medical clinic for people with seizures. The Craig Colony," Costello explained.

Kelly was speechless. He sat and stared forward.

Costello placed his right hand on Kelly's shoulder. "Mike, search within yourself. You will know, that I am telling the truth."

Kelly thought of that morning in his kitchen when Costello asked about Nora. Mary immediately dropped a plate, and she never dropped anything. Later, in his office, Mary almost became hysterical. Kelly had rarely ever seen Mary get excited, but she certainly had when she heard the name *Nora*. And, the little girl looked like all the other Kelly children.

"She *is* my daughter," Kelly said, "I have another daughter," he repeated happily. "But why wouldn't Mary tell me?"

"You'll have to ask her that." Costello replied.

Dr. Peterson returned to the cafeteria holding a prescription bottle.

"She *is* my daughter. That little girl you are holding prisoner here is my daughter. And I will bring her home today, and I'd like to see you try to stop me!" Kelly said to Dr. Peterson.

"Let's not plan the escape just yet. I've got a few more questions," Dr. Peterson continued, facing Costello. "While it's certainly possible that Major Kelly is the father of that child, it's quite another thing to convince me that Costello is from outer space."

CHAPTER THIRTY-THREE
THE ARMADA

Sonyea, New York
August 25, 1926

"Costello, we have to go," Kelly said. "Diamond and his men will be here any minute."

"We need Dr. Peterson's help. We need that phenobarbital. And if we have to fight our way out of here, a lot of innocent people will die trying to stop us." Costello turned to Cavell, who was listening intently to the conversation between the three men. "Can't you just show him?"

"Show me what?" Peterson asked

"The danger that is fast approaching your planet," Costello replied

"Oh, yes. Please show me. Do you have photographs?" Peterson asked skeptically.

"All right. Since he's so eager, I'll show him," Cavell said, annoyed by Peterson's attitude.

"You'll have to sit down, Dr. Peterson," Costello said. "This won't hurt."

Peterson sat at the table. Cavell walked behind and placed her right hand on Peterson's shoulder. Within seconds, Peterson was teleported into what appeared to be outer space. Of course, since at this stage of the Earth's development there were no satellites or rockets, or even photographs of the universe, Peterson was not exactly sure what was now around him. He had a rudimentary knowledge of the prevailing theories of space; but although confident he'd recognize Saturn or Jupiter if he saw them, Peterson was moving too fast to recognize anything.

Suddenly, he heard Cavell's voice. "Do you know what you are looking at?"

"I don't know how you're doing it, but I presume this is a simulation of the universe," Peterson answered.

"You are partially correct. It is the system of planets inhabited by the Earth. But it is no simulation," Cavell told him. "While your physical body remains at the Craig Colony, your mind's eye is now able to see, in real time, the edge of your universe."

"Nonsense. No technology exists that would permit this!"

"No *Earth* technology. But as we have told you, we are not from Earth."

"Is this what you wanted to show me?" Peterson asked.

"Be patient, Doctor. The danger lies ahead," Cavell answered.

"What danger?"

"Please be patient."

Peterson waited for what seemed to him like several hours, although it was really only a few minutes. Suddenly, an immense saucer-shaped object entered the outer edge of the universe.

"This is what you've been waiting for," Cavell said.

"What is it?" Peterson asked.

"The first among many."

"Many what?"

"Vessels. On their way to Earth to extract the princess from your colony," Cavell said.

"That enormous object is a spaceship?" Peterson asked as he pointed at the saucer shape.

"One among many. But remain patient. There will be more. Many, many more."

Suddenly, scores of others came into Peterson's view. They were of varying shapes and sizes. Very few had the sleek saucer shape of the initial spacecraft. Some even appeared to still be under construction as the Armada lumbered through space.

"And those are all spaceships?" Peterson asked.

"Yes. And all on their way to Earth," said Cavell.

"Just so we are clear," Peterson said, "you keep using the word 'armada.' Do you understand what 'armada' actually means in my language?"

"A fleet of warships," Cavell answered.

"So those vessels are warships?" Peterson asked.

"Many of them. Others are support ships. Some are assisting with final construction of the Armada," Cavell affirmed. "Each one has a specific task."

"To invade my planet?" Peterson asked.

"Their mission is not to invade or to wage war. It is to rescue," Cavell replied.

"From what?"

"The princess is a prisoner in your Colony," Cavell explained.

"The Craig Colony is not a prison. It is a safe haven," Peterson protested.

"Dr. Peterson, as we see it, your Colony is a prison. To imprison the leader of another planet, is a universal act of war."

"What if we do not resist?" Peterson asked.

"Sir, look at those starships. Can you even imagine the massive damage to the Earth, if even one of those vessels is forced to land? Or the injuries caused by the flooding of your cities, like Chicago or Detroit, if just one were to land in the Great Lakes? Or the panic among your populace if just one were to appear in the Earth's atmosphere? I have run over a thousand simulations of the resulting harm to the human race if the Armada initiates its extraction plan. In each simulation, the princess is easily rescued. But in all, the collateral damage to the Earth is beyond catastrophic."

"What if there is resistance from our military?" Peterson asked.

"There is no possible favorable outcome if your military attempts to fight those vessels. We ran thousands of simulations of this possibility, and the immediate death and destruction to the people of your planet was incalculable. And that was only the first wave of casualties resulting from a violent extraction. A second greater wave of fatalities will result from the environmental and societal impact if the Armada enters your atmosphere and discharges our weapons on the planet's surface," Cavell said.

"And you believe that this extraction may occur?" Peterson queried.

"Dr. Peterson, none of this is theoretical," Cavell stated. "It's not that this destruction *may* occur. The Armada is on its way to Earth. I suspect the only thing slowing them down is those ships that are still finishing construction."

"Is there anything that we can do to stop it?" Peterson asked.

"That's why we are here. If Costello and I can remove the princess from the colony and reunite her with her host family, leadership of the Armada may call off the extraction. We will then take the princess to an isolated location and transfer her life force to a transport vessel and return her home," Cavell explained.

"Well, if there is even a chance, we have to try it..." Peterson acknowledged.

"I agree, Let's do it." Kelly interrupted.

When Peterson heard Kelly's voice, he opened his eyes. Peterson was shocked to learn that he was still sitting in a chair in the cafeteria. Peterson the skeptic was now a zealot in support of the rescue.

"Welcome back, Doctor," Cavell said.

"How many hours was I gone?" Peterson asked.

"Never. You were sitting here the whole time," Kelly said.

"How long?"

"About ten minutes," Kelly said.

Peterson looked at Costello. "How long until they get here?

"Assuming that the battle group is still traveling together, they could reach Earth in five and a half days," Costello answered.

"Five and a half days!" Peterson cried. "We have to act quickly!"

"Then let's go." Costello was now wearing the military fatigues that Kelly had brought for him. However, although this was his same uniform, it no longer fit him. In a matter of weeks, the recovery protocol had made Costello several inches taller and his muscles bulged out of his uniform. And only weeks earlier, Costello was so emaciated that this very uniform was too big for him and he had to cinch the waist with a belt.

"So, what's the plan? How do we get you out of here with all those police outside?" Peterson asked.

"Doctor, you leave that to me," Kelly said.

Kelly and Costello walked out the front door of Peterson Hospital in their U.S. Army uniforms. As planned, Billow and Feeney met them on the front sidewalk and saluted Kelly as though they were involved in an active military operation. This charade was entirely for the benefit of the local and state police. Kelly was certain that they would be watching, having encircled the hospital after being summoned by Dr. Harrison.

Billow and Kelly had arrived hours before. Once he saw the many policemen around the facility, Billow called as many former members of the 105th as were willing to make the eight-hour trip to Sonyea. Once there, they waited patiently in formation around the police. So, the military units that Dr. Peterson had witnessed upon his arrival at the hospital were actually Kelly's men. Although they carried military hardware, those weapons were for their inevitable fight with Diamond. The arrival of the local police effectively turned that weaponry into props, since it was inconceivable that the 105th would exchange gunfire with local law enforcement.

After saluting Major Kelly and pretending to speak about important matters for a sufficient period of time, the four approached what looked to be the command center of the police encircling the hospital.

"Excuse me! Who's in charge?" Kelly shouted as he approached three police cars parked fifty yards from the entrance of the hospital. Kelly surmised that this was the command center.

"Who am I talking to?" asked Sheriff Ray Flower of the Livingston County Sheriff's Department.

"Major Mike Kelly of the New York 105th Infantry Regiment and the New York Naval Militia!"

"You're out of your jurisdiction, Major," Sheriff Flower stated. "Unless you're here about the bomb threat."

"We searched the entire facility, Sheriff. There is no bomb," Kelly said.

"Good! We can all go home," the Sheriff replied.

"Except, I have another issue. Last night one of my top men was taken hostage in Albany by a gangster named 'Legs' Diamond. We then got word that Diamond and his gang are on their way to this hospital to kidnap a little girl. *My* little girl."

"Did you say *your* little girl?" Sheriff Flower asked, sympathetically.

"Yes, sheriff. *My* little girl," Kelly answered. "It's hard enough for my wife that my little Nora is a patient here. So, I think that you can imagine how she reacted when she heard that 'Legs' Diamond was coming here to take our daughter."

"Hell, I know what I'd do," Sheriff Flower growled.

"Me, too!" an officer piped in as the rest of them shouted and nodded in agreement

"I'm not proud of it, but I called in every favor I've ever been owed. I rounded up this group of friends and we drove through the night with every gun we had," Kelly said.

Kelly had won over the local police with his concocted story of a father rescuing his daughter from a gangster, so he pushed it. "I even called my daughter Nora's doctor, Dr. Peterson – "

"Like the hospital?" the Sheriff interrupted.

"Yes, Sheriff. The hospital was named after me," Dr. Peterson said, trying to assist Major Kelly. "I'm Dr. Frederick Peterson."

"Wow. It sure is an honor to meet you, sir," the Sheriff said.

"So, with Dr. Peterson's permission and, of course, with your permission, Sheriff, we will take my daughter Nora into protective custody. She will ride home with me in that vehicle." Kelly pointed to an armored military vehicle behind the police.

"Major, you're the girl's father. And this is still America. I don't think a father needs a lawman's permission to protect his child from some scumbag. But if you think you need it, hell, you've got my permission. Is there anything else we can do for you?" the Sheriff asked.

"I'd appreciate it if you and your men stay around the Craig Colony in case Diamond shows up," Kelly said.

"That's an excellent idea. And Godspeed to you and your daughter Nora."

"Thank you, Sheriff."

After obtaining permission from Sheriff Flower for the removal of Nora from the Craig Colony, Kelly, Costello, Billow, and Feeney went back into the hospital. Sheriff Flower was so engrossed in Kelly's story that he never realized that Costello was also an inmate at the Craig Colony, or that it was Costello who had threatened to blow up the hospital in the first place.

Moments later, the men reemerged, guns drawn, in a defensive military formation around Nora and Nurse Cavell. Of course, they were merely performing a show for the sheriff and his men. Once the civilians were safely in the armored car, the men of the 105th climbed into the remaining vehicles and drove away.

It would be an eight-hour ride to Granville. And at the end of that ride, Diamond and his men may be waiting.

CHAPTER THIRTY-FOUR

THE PHONE CALL HOME

Sonyea, New York
August 25, 1926

"We must convince leadership that the host family is stable and that the princess is in no danger. The moment their sensors identify Diamond and the danger he poses to the host family, the extraction team will be immediately launched to eliminate the threat," Cavell explained to Kelly and Costello as the three rode in the lead car with the girl.

"Would that be so bad? We let the Armada eliminate Diamond," Kelly said.

"But the collateral damage to this planet would be astronomical," Costello replied.

"Then what do you suggest?" Kelly asked.

"You eliminate the threat to the host family," Cavell explained.

"All right," Kelly said – and then it hit him that Diamond may have skipped the Craig Colony to head straight for Granville. He had to warn Mary.

Kelly found a payphone at a gas station on the outskirts of Rochester, but now had a different problem. The payphone would only accept coins as payment for the long-distance call. Although in his illicit business deals, Kelly regularly handled thousands of dollars in bills, he rarely carried loose change.

"Like I don't have enough to do today. On top of saving the world, now I have to find loose change out here in the middle of nowhere." Kelly said to himself as he flagged down his convoy of trucks to beg his men for coins. Meanwhile, Costello got a long-distance operator on the line. "I'd like to make a phone call to Mary Kelly in Granville, New York. Telephone number 1-133," Costello said.

"Please insert $3.45 for the first three minutes," the operator stated.

In 1926, the process of making a long-distance call was complicated. The caller would give the long-distance operator a phone number, and in turn the operator would quote the price for a three-minute call to the prospective caller. The operator would then remain on the line until the caller deposited the quoted amount into the pay slot. Only after the caller made the deposit, would the operator connect the call.

"Kelly, the call costs $3.45," Costello hollered.

"All right. I need $3.45 so I can call my wife to warn her about Diamond. Who's got change?" Kelly repeated to the men in the convoy. After collecting from his men, Kelly counted up the coins. There was $4.75.

Kelly held the money tightly in his hand as he ran back to the payphone. Costello handed the phone to Kelly, who heard the operator repeating the words "Deposit $3.45 for the first three minutes, please."

Kelly quickly complied, depositing the correct amount of coins into the payphone. Several seconds later, he could hear the phone ring on the other end – and after several rings, someone answered.

"Hello? Who is it?" Eight-year-old Mike Jr. had picked up the phone.

"Michael, it's Daddy! I need to speak to Mommy right away!"

"Mommy can't come to the phone right now," Michael said politely.

"Why not? Is everything all right?" Kelly asked, concerned Diamond had already struck.

"Yes. But Mommy is taking a bath."

"Okay," Kelly replied, relieved that there was nothing wrong. "Now, you run and tell Mommy that Daddy is calling, long distance. Tell her to come speak with me right away."

"All right, Daddy," Michael said. Kelly could hear Michael run off and yell with great urgency. *"Mom! Dad says to get out of the bath right now and answer the phone!"*

Mary Kelly shouted in reply, "Your father said *what?*"

To which Michael repeated, "Dad said you have to get out of the bath right now and come answer the phone!"

"Oh, that's what Dad said, did he? Okay. All right. You tell your father I'm getting out of the bath right now, just like he ordered me to. He may not like hearing the things that I've got to say to him, but I'm getting out of the bath right now!"

A few moments later, Michael was back on the phone. "Mom is out of the bath. She's coming downstairs to speak with you."

"I heard," Kelly replied.

"And I don't know why, but Mom seems mad about something," Michael said.

"I also heard," Kelly replied, and could not help smiling. In the background, he could hear Mary Kelly storming down the stairs and into the room.

"Here's Mom. Bye!" was all that Michael could say before Mary Kelly angrily pulled the phone out of her oldest son's hand and started speaking into it.

"Mike Kelly! What in God's name is so important that you told Michael to get me out of the bath to come downstairs to speak with you on the phone?"

"I don't want to alarm you, but you and the kids may be in danger."

"What?" Mary replied, her demeanor changed.

"I can't say much on the phone. I'll be there in a few hours, but you and the kids have to get out of the house. *Now,*" Kelly said firmly.

"And go where?" Mary had sensed the urgency of the situation and stopped arguing.

"I don't want to say the exact location. You never know who is listening."

"Mike, quit being so dramatic. No one is listening," Mary assured him.

Suddenly, the long-distance operator chimed in. "Your three minutes is up. Please deposit $3.45 for an additional three minutes."

"But I don't have $3.45. How much for one minute?" Kelly asked.

"One minute is $1.15," the operator replied.

After Kelly quickly deposited the $1.15 into the payphone, the operator said, "Thank you for using Bell Telephone. You have one more minute."

"We don't have much time. Here's what I want you to do. Take the kids to that place we built last summer," Kelly said.

"The place made of wood?" Mary replied.

"Right. And before you go, tell my men to take the personal supply out of the basement and stack it in that clearing in the Hollow. You know the one."

"All of it?" Mary asked, amazed that that much alcohol could even be moved.

"Yes, all of it."

"The clearing where the kids fly kites?" Mary asked.

"Exactly. And tell any man who helps move the personal supply, to take a case of whiskey for his trouble."

"Done. Anything else?" Mary asked

"Yes. Contact Father O'Brien. Tell him to meet me at the place made of wood."

"Got it," Mary said.

"One final thing, Mary." Kelly paused, not quite sure how to explain the next part.

"What, Mike? What is it?" Mary asked quickly. They had little time to waste.

"I'm bringing Nora home," Kelly said.

There was silence on the other end of the phone. "What did you just say?"

"Our daughter, Nora, I met her at the Craig Colony. She's beautiful. I'm bringing her home," Kelly said softly into the phone.

There was no response from Mary.

"I know she was born August 10, 1917," Kelly said quickly. "I know of her seizures. I know how hard it must have been for you when I was away in the war. I understand everything, Mary. She's been with me all day. She's our daughter, she's wonderful, and she's coming home."

He could hear Mary Kelly sobbing on the other end of the phone. "Mike, you don't know how many times I wanted to tell you. I was afraid that you'd hate me," Mary said, between sobs.

"Mary, I could never hate you. You are the most wonderful person I have ever known."

"And please tell Nora that I never intended to send her away for good. I thought it was a hospital, and those doctors at the colony told me that her seizures would be under control in two years. But they never got them under control, and they never said that she could come home. I was so ashamed. Too ashamed to tell you that I lost our child."

"Please deposit $3.45 for another three minutes," the long-distance operator interrupted.

"But I don't have another $3.45," Kelly replied.

"Then you will have to end your call," the operator said curtly.

"Did you hear that Mary? I have to finish. Now, you do all the things I asked, and I will see you and the kids in a few hours. I love you, Mary."

"I love – "

Click. The long-distance operator terminated the call mid-sentence.

" – you too, Mike," Mary whispered, aware that what may have been their final words had been cut off by Bell Telephone.

On the other side of the state, Mike Kelly was still holding the phone.

"Thank you for using Bell Telephone," said the long-distance operator, who then ended her connection with Mike Kelly.

CHAPTER THIRTY-FIVE
THE CABIN

Granville, New York
August 26, 1926

The convoy carrying Kelly and his men drove straight home from Sonyea. When they reached Granville, they split up. Six men, including Kelly and Costello, drove to the Kelly home to be certain that Mary wasn't still there. Once it was confirmed that the house was empty, Billow was left in charge of the men loading and transporting Kelly's "personal supply" to the clearing. Then Kelly rejoined Costello, Cavell, and Nora in the armored car, and the four drove off.

Just over the Vermont border, Kelly turned left onto Bullfrog Hollow Road. About a quarter of a mile further in was a small field on the left side. Kelly turned into the field and stopped the car.

"We walk from here. But first, help me camouflage the car," Kelly said, stepping out.

Using their hands, Kelly and Costello dug into the ground behind a tree stump and uncovered a tarp which the major had hidden for this contingency. They covered the car with the tarp, and then the four used branches to conceal it from anyone driving by. After about fifteen minutes, their work was complete.

"What next?" Costello asked.

"We hike up the mountain," Kelly told him.

"But there's no trail," Costello said.

"There will be," Kelly replied.

The four started hiking into the twilight. Sure enough, about fifty yards up, the thick woods gave way to a clear hiking trail, entirely hidden from the road below.

"Mary and the kids helped me clear this last summer. I feared that a time would come when I would need to lay low. Of course, I thought I'd be hiding from the law."

"Your family did all this?" Costello asked.

"This is just the beginning. There's another trail that starts about fifty yards behind my house. This is actually my escape route," Kelly said.

Costello and Cavell did their best to follow Nora and Kelly on the trail as they hiked a moderate incline up the side of a small mountain. Despite her youth, Nora was already quite athletic and appeared to navigate the rocky terrain easily. During the daylight hours, it would have been an enjoyable hike, but it was challenging in the twilight. After hiking for about forty minutes, they reached the ridge.

"We have arrived," Kelly announced, a small wooden cabin in the distance.

"You built this?" Costello said as they carefully approached the cabin.

"Last summer," Kelly said proudly. "No one other than Mary and the kids know of it."

"So, this is where you intended to hide from the police?" Costello asked.

"If I ever needed to. We even ran a phone line up the trail," Kelly replied.

"So, what exactly is your plan? You're going to hide up here for the rest of your life?" Costello asked.

"Because that plan won't work. If the Armada's sensors confirm that the host family is in danger, they will intervene." Cavell continued, "You have to handle Diamond."

"Of course, I'll 'handle' Diamond. And I'm not the one who's hiding up here," Kelly replied, unlocking the door to the cabin. Mary's and the children's belongings were strewn throughout, which is what the major had hoped to find.

Michael Jr. jumped out from behind a corner by the bedroom. "Mom, it's all right! It's Dad and Uncle Ryan!" Michael shouted. Mary Kelly and the children rushed out, relieved that their father was home.

"Is it over, Mike?" Mary asked, holding her husband's revolver which she had removed from their bedside table.

"Give me a couple of days," Mike Kelly replied as he held his children tightly, "It will be."

CHAPTER THIRTY-SIX
THE INVASION
OF THE CONTRACTORS

Granville, New York
August 27-28, 1926

The response to Diamond's call for mercenaries exceeded his expectations. He anticipated hiring between ten to twenty contractors. He figured that those hitmen, supplemented by his crew and the remaining members of the Monahan gang, could handle the Kelly family. But in his anger and haste to kill Kelly, Diamond had placed no limit on the number of mercenaries that could accept his offer. A big mistake. Almost overnight, Diamond's biggest worry was not Mike Kelly but whether he had enough money to pay the hundreds of mercenaries who had accepted his offer.

Diamond's newly formed army of contractors was a diverse bunch. As he had expected, experienced hitmen for the New York City mob accepted the work. But Diamond didn't anticipate the level of response. Hardened contractors from as nearby as Albany, Schenectady, Syracuse, Utica, and Buffalo and as far away as St. Louis, Pittsburgh, Kansas City, Missouri, and New Orleans eagerly accepted the contract. Many were young, up-and-coming murderers who were hoping to one day make it to the big time. Still others were small-time criminals who just needed the money.

In all, 345 mercenaries accepted Diamond's open call. Although they were from very different backgrounds, they all shared a willingness to commit mass murder for one thousand dollars per day, plus expenses. In 1926, it was an extravagant fee for that line of work and would be, by far, the most substantial payday that most of them would ever know – assuming they lived to collect it and, of course, that Diamond could pay it.

Although this caused him great stress, Diamond decided to take a positive approach. He'd hire them all to kill the Kelly family, and if he played his cards right, over half of his new contractors would be wiped out in the process. Then, if he was lucky, he may have just enough money to pay the survivors. Besides, it wasn't as though Diamond had personnel files on the contractors' next of kin.

If they didn't insist on getting paid upfront, it's their own fault. I've double-crossed actual living mobsters. I'm certainly willing to stiff the surviving family of some hitman killed by Mike Kelly, Diamond thought to himself, considering his new predicament.

After calmly reflecting on his plan, several different problems emerged. The public was already growing tired of the violence associated with the bootlegging trade. The sheer number of people Diamond intended to kill would force an FBI investigation and public prosecution. The murder of decorated World War veterans and their family members – even those involved in the rum-running business – would be wildly unpopular with the public and could adversely impact Diamond's prospects to control the upstate New York liquor trade. Indeed, the mass murder of Kelly, his family, and the members of his crime family may so alienate suppliers and customers that they may never do business with Diamond again, thereby undermining the very reason for murdering Kelly.

On the other hand, even if Diamond did try to call it off, the contractors would insist on payment. And once they killed the Kelly family, Diamond could use the money and liquor recovered from Kelly to help fund the surviving contractors. He could also steal Kelly's vehicles. If enough money was recovered, Kelly would finance his own demise.

The decision made itself. The hit would proceed. Unless, of course, Kelly could offer Diamond something of even greater value. Something that would get them both out of this mess.

Each morning at 7 a.m., Bobby Billow walked to his barbershop on Quaker Street. Billow was a creature of habit. Nothing was going to change that routine. Despite repeated warnings from Kelly, Billow intended to be open for business as usual.

He had considered closing that weekend, but Saturday was his busiest day. Besides, it was the week before Labor Day weekend, and his regular customers needed him to ensure that their hair was looking its best for the annual Labor Day Parade. Historically, he had two of his most profitable days of the year on the two Saturdays preceding Labor Day. So, despite the obvious personal risk, Billow decided to open.

Strangers had been pouring into town since Thursday. Although summer tourists are a welcome tonic to the local economy, these visitors were not in town to sample maple syrup or see the changing foliage. They were heavily armed, and many drove fancy cars, the sort of vehicles not often seen on the streets of Granville.

Once Kelly was sure that Mary and the kids were safe in the cabin, he went back into town to prepare for Diamond's arrival. When the first few visitors came on Thursday, the numbers seemed manageable. But then, on Friday, over one hundred additional strangers blew into town. Every little motel and boarding house in the area was suddenly booked solid.

On Saturday, at least another one hundred fifty men arrived in Granville. Assuming that they were all with Diamond, his army now outnumbered Kelly's men by at least twenty-five to one – and additional mercenaries were arriving by the hour.

Naturally, this worried Billow. But he was concerned for Kelly and his family, not his own well-being. After all, Billow was a sniper. His targets, like the men who died in the alley behind the New Kenmore Hotel, were shot from a vast distance. Billow killed in anonymity. His victims never saw his face or knew his name.

Indeed, few people would ever imagine that the jovial town barber, who Mike Kelly had easily pummeled on the night of Memorial Day, was one of the most lethal members of the Kelly crime family. Not even the recent betrayal of Kelly by Jim Moyer had shaken Billow's resolve. So, despite the heightened tension and the influx of dangerous men who were undoubtedly in town to murder Mike Kelly and his family, Billow still felt that he could safely open his shop.

At least, that is what the barber believed as he walked to work on August 27, 1926. Like clockwork, Billow unlocked the door at 7:45 a.m. to prepare for the arrival of his first customers at eight. Billow didn't bother with appointments. Everyone in Granville knew his hours. He would simply turn the sign in his front window from "closed" to "open," and in a manner of minutes, his shop was filled with customers.

But on this day, when Billow opened his front door, he instantly knew that something was very wrong. Inside his shop, four men were already waiting for him. As he entered, Billow immediately heard a familiar click. Then another. And another. Click. Click. Billow knew only too well that the sound was the cocking of multiple revolvers. Without bothering to look, he knew that those handguns were all aimed at him.

One man, who was already seated in his barber chair, spun around. It was Jim Moyer, a pistol in his right hand.

Billow quickly scanned the room. As he suspected, three other men were spread out in the shop. All were pointing weapons at Billow.

"Good morning, Jim. You need a haircut?" Billow asked bravely.

"I'm here to save your life," Moyer responded.

———•———

Father Thomas O'Brien loved Saturday morning Mass. It would begin promptly at 7 a.m. and – if his sermon was brief and he maintained a quick, steady pace throughout the remainder of the ritual – he could breeze through it in, at most, thirty-five minutes. The priest's absolute record was twenty-nine minutes, but that was on a day when he was also scheduled to officiate two weddings, one baptism, and two funerals.

Today was one of those rare Saturdays when O'Brien had absolutely no other events scheduled and so, like everyone else, he could enjoy a well-earned day off.

As was common, it was O'Brien's practice to bid farewell to his parishioners on the front steps of the church after each mass. This day was no different. Just as he had bid farewell to the last member of his congregation, a large black sedan pulled up in front of the church. The car remained parked for a few moments until the occupants were satisfied that he was alone.

O'Brien, utterly oblivious to the trouble brewing in town, stood trustingly on the steps. He was eager to see who owned the extravagant car and why they would be in this little town, parked outside his modest church.

After a few moments, Diamond stepped out of the vehicle. He was followed closely by two large, ominous-looking men.

"Father, you don't know me –" Diamond began.

"I know who you are," O'Brien interrupted, contempt dripping in his voice.

"Good. I know who you are, too," Diamond continued. "I'm in the market for some good wine, and I hear you're the proprietor of a local vineyard licensed to sell sacramental wine."

I let Mike Kelly use my name on the license to market his wine, but I never imagined that hoodlums like Diamond would learn of my involvement in obtaining the license – let alone approach me as a customer, O'Brien thought to himself, stunned.

"I'm sorry, sir. I don't know anything about a vineyard." O'Brien said.

"Sure, you do. I saw your application." Diamond replied.

O'Brien was speechless. Guilt rushed through his body.

"Father, do you live with the Kelly family?" Diamond asked, feigning ignorance.

"Of course not. I live in the home adjacent to this parish," O'Brien said indignantly.

"I thought it was a mistake. Because for some reason, Mike Kelly's home is listed as your home address on your sacramental wine vineyard application," Diamond said, still feigning ignorance. O'Brien was dumbfounded. After allowing O'Brien to stammer for a few moments, Diamond continued.

"So, Father, are you in business with Mike Kelly?" Diamond inquired.

"In business with Major Kelly! Don't be ridiculous," the priest replied, visibly ashamed.

"Well, I'm certainly relieved to hear how ridiculous that is," Diamond said amiably. "And since I am a great benefactor of the Catholic Church, I'm gonna straighten this mess out for you, *gratis,* so nobody gets the wrong idea. Come on, Father. Get in the car. We'll go over to Kelly's house and make sure that you are no longer listed on his fraudulent vineyard license."

When O'Brien didn't move, Diamond hollered threateningly. "I said, get in the car!"

Although O'Brien's instincts told him to stay out and run for his life, his fear of Diamond and his shame over his involvement in Kelly's sacramental wine sales were too much for him. O'Brien climbed into the car, followed by Diamond and his men.

———•———

Owen Feeney's Saturdays were reserved for tending to his garden. Actually, as a result of his hard work, it was much more than a garden. It stretched over two acres of land, and Feeney was now proudly growing seven different crops, including ten ripe pear trees. What had once been his parents' home was now a small farm. To earn his living, Feeney would toil in a slate quarry all week, counting the minutes until he could be back, alone in his garden. Although he also greatly augmented his income working for Mike Kelly, Feeney's happiness was found in this garden.

After returning from the World War in 1918, Feeney could no longer abide most people. He found himself spending more and more time alone in his garden. Indeed, on certain nights in the summer, he would "camp out" among his pear trees. Some would say that Owen Feeney lived a sad, solitary life. Perhaps. But it was the life that he was able to make for himself upon his return from the war.

Feeney was up bright and early on Saturday, August 28, 1926. This day, his pear trees were finally ready to harvest. Feeney had patiently waited through the warm days of August, fighting the daily urge to pick the pears too early.

Kelly had instructed all of his men to lay low that weekend while a plan was formulated to deal with the huge influx of strangers in town. As a loyal soldier, Feeney would do as ordered and hide out, but his pears wouldn't wait for the crisis to end. They had to be harvested this weekend, or many would overripen and fall from the trees.

So, although he was holed up in a fortified location within his house, Feeney decided to sneak out and commence early Saturday morning, just before daylight. He would work quickly, at the break of dawn, and have his pears off the trees before Diamond's men were out of bed. The night before, Feeney collected the few tools he would need – a ladder, gloves, and several wicker baskets – and left them by the back door. Feeney would pop out to the garden before dawn and be back inside again before anyone knew the better.

Except for the three contractors that Diamond had sent to Owen's home, armed with shotguns. They had been waiting for him in his back-yard since 4 a.m. Feeney rose at five, quickly dressed, and, filled with the excitement of the harvest, rushed out his back door.

It was a short day for Owen Feeney. As he lay dying under one of his beloved pear trees, he looked up at the ripe fruit waiting to be picked.

CHAPTER THIRTY-SEVEN
THE SANCTUARY

Granville, New York
August 28-29, 1926

By Saturday evening, all 345 contractors were in Granville, ready to work. Diamond's army was at full strength. Augmenting the army were ten men from Diamond's crew and ten more from Monahan's. In all, that brought Diamond's army to 368 men, including Diamond and the two Monahan brothers.

By contrast, Kelly had fewer than twenty at his disposal… and Billow and Feeney were still unaccounted for.

Father O'Brien was also missing. No one had seen the priest since Saturday morning mass. Still, Kelly figured O'Brien was safe. Not even Diamond would flout organized crime mores so far as to harm a priest.

It was the fact that Billow and Feeney were missing that concerned Kelly. Billow had not been heard from since Saturday morning. Feeney had not checked in since Friday night. Sure, they could have skipped town. But they were two of Kelly's most loyal soldiers. Together they had survived the German Army. Kelly was certain that they wouldn't run out on him now.

At 6 a.m. Sunday, Kelly received a call from O'Brien. Although the priest claimed that nothing was wrong, there was tension in his voice.

"Mike, Diamond wants a sit-down," O'Brien said.

"All right. Where?"

"Basement of my church. Today. After eleven o'clock mass," O'Brien relayed.

"Fine," Kelly said. "I will meet him in the basement of St. Mary's. However, a non-negotiable condition is that the Kelly family and Diamond – and all of Diamond's men – have a truce until that meeting is over. Both sides will honor the concept of sanctuary while our men are in the church, both for the mass and for the sit-down."

"Hold on a minute. I'll ask him," O'Brien said. Kelly could hear a conversation in the background and then, suddenly, Diamond was on the line.

"Kelly, you know who this is?" Diamond asked.

"Yes."

"We have a deal," Diamond said. "My people won't do anything until after the meet."

"One more condition," Kelly said.

"For a man who's about to die, you make a lot of demands," Diamond said. "Go ahead."

"Let Billow, O'Brien, and Feeney go," Kelly said.

"Well, I can give you back the barber and the priest, but we don't have the farmer."

"Are you sure?"

"Positive. But I'm told that he's lying peacefully under a pear tree," Diamond said.

Kelly swallowed hard. "Please release the barber and the priest. I will see you after mass. Until then, we have a truce. You have my word."

"See, Kelly, how easy things are when you play nice?" Diamond said. Fifteen minutes later, Billow and O'Brien were dropped off in front of St. Mary's.

————•————

Kelly's meeting with Diamond was set to follow eleven o'clock mass. The church was filled to capacity that day. Many of the contractors were Catholic, as were members of the 105th. But this was no ordinary Sunday service. For the faithful about to die in battle later that day, this mass would be their last chance to make peace with God.

Mike Kelly was in attendance. He had mixed emotions about the vast number of Diamond's contractors present. On the one hand, their sheer numbers would have intimidated even the most loyal members of the Kelly family. On the other hand, since so many of Diamond's men were in the church, "Legs" couldn't set it on fire.

Why did Diamond want a meeting, anyway? Diamond has so many men. Why would he ever negotiate away that advantage? Kelly thought to himself.

During his sermon, Father O'Brien alternated his gaze on Kelly and Diamond for several seconds and then spoke.

"And as the Lord said in his sermon on the mount, 'Blessed are the Peacemakers, for they will be called children of God,'" O'Brien preached dramatically. "Blessed are the Peacemakers."

Father O'Brien paused as he again stared at Kelly and Diamond. After glaring at each, O'Brien backed away from the podium and sat down. It looked as though the power of his own words had drained O'Brien of his strength. Either that or the power of bad amateur acting.

"Looks like the priest is trying to get us out of here quickly today," one contractor whispered to the man on his left.

"Good. I need to clean my guns before tonight," the other contractor responded.

Fifteen minutes later, the mass was over, and Father O'Brien stood beside the front door of his church, bidding farewell to his parishioners. Diamond was one of the final members of the congregation to leave.

"Powerful words, Father. Powerful." Diamond said.

"I'm counting on you to be the peacemaker," O'Brien said.

"I will do my best, Father," Diamond responded in mock earnestness.

After the congregation had left, O'Brien took Diamond to the front of the church and down an interior stairway to the church basement. There, Kelly sat waiting alone.

"Now that I've brought you peacemakers together, I trust you to work this out?" O'Brien said.

"I'll do my best," Kelly said.

"Me, too," Diamond said.

"Fine. Then I'll leave you to it." O'Brien left the room, pleased that his powerful sermon had had such a profound effect on the two bootleggers.

"What a putz," Diamond said as soon as the priest was out of earshot. The two laughed heartily.

"So, Mr. Diamond," said Kelly. "Why did you ask for this meeting?"

"Mike, I don't want to kill you and your men. Killing is bad for business. Just turn your assets over to me, and come to work for me as my second-in-command, and all is forgiven."

"Well, I certainly want to live. But I'm not gonna take orders from you," Kelly said.

"Come on, Kelly. You were in the Army. I bet you took orders from a lot of people you didn't respect," Diamond said with a smile.

"I can't argue with that. I just don't want to be in the business anymore. What if I promised to disappear forever?"

"Without the war hero, Major Kelly, your organization has no business," Diamond said.

"Then why kill me? What do you gain?" Kelly asked.

"I have to pay these damn contractors," Diamond blurted out.

"What?" Kelly asked.

"These contractors. I hired way too many. Now I can't afford to pay them. And if they kill you, all your suppliers and contacts die with you. I thought that Moyer would be able to replace you, but he's just a big lummox. But if I cancel the contract on you, they will still want to get paid, and I don't have that kind of money. If I tell them not to kill you because we've settled, they'll *still* want to be paid, and I *still* don't have that kind of money."

"Wow, that's a tough position you're in," Kelly said, trying to keep a straight face, and realizing that this was the opening he'd been waiting for. "Is there anything I can do to help?"

"Yeah. You give me $345,000 so I can pay these contractors, and I'll let you walk away," Diamond replied.

"You know that I would, but I don't have that kind of cash." Kelly said, flippantly.

"Huh. Then I guess we're going to have to finish it tonight," Diamond said.

"I'll do it tonight on one condition," Kelly answered. "We fight outside of Granville, so we don't hurt any civilians."

"You agree to show up tonight so I can stop the meter on these damn contractors, and I'll have the fight wherever you want," Diamond told him.

Kelly nodded. "Fine. Tell Moyer that we'll meet in the large clearing off Bullfrog Hollow. He'll know the one. Tell him we'll be there at seven."

"And Kelly, be warned, if you don't show up, my men will burn this town and everyone in it," Diamond warned.

"Don't worry, I'll be there."

CHAPTER THIRTY-EIGHT
THE FINAL CONFESSION

Granville, New York
August 29, 1926

Father O'Brien arrived at the Kelly home amid a flurry of activity. The busy workers barely noticed him as the final cases of Kelly's personal supply were being loaded onto trucks. Two other men were loading cases marked "TNT" into a separate vehicle. The trucks, jammed full of crates and kegs, lined the driveway of the Kelly home.

"What can I do for you, Father?" Billow asked hurriedly after spotting the priest.

"It's what I can do for you. I'm here to hear confession from any men who will be involved in that matter later tonight," O'Brien answered.

"Thank you, Father. I know that I am one of at least four of the men who need your services. And when you're finished with us, I'll take you to see Major Kelly."

"Thank you, Bobby."

Twenty minutes later, O'Brien had completed the sacrament for the four men who, in turn, left to transport Kelly's personal supply to the clearing. Billow then led O'Brien out through the back door of the Kelly home and into the woods for the hike up to the cabin.

On the trail, they were met by Mayor James, who was carrying a .22 caliber hunting rifle.

"Why, Mayor, what are you doing up here?" Billow asked.

"This is *my* town. If you men are driving that scum out, I want in," James said.

"You'll get no argument from me, Mr. Mayor, sir. Come with us." Billow hiked on ahead with his sniper rifle strapped over his shoulder.

—·—

Kelly and Costello sat outside the cabin, looking down on the clearing below. They both understood that in a few hours, that idyllic forest would be ablaze. Although Kelly had hoped that alumni of the 105th would rally against Diamond, only a few had arrived for the fight.

Who can blame them for staying home? Diamond has an army of mercenaries, Kelly thought to himself.

Mary and the kids would spend the evening in Whitehall, safe in the armory. There they would be guarded by members of the National Guard. In the morning, Kelly would either join his family, or he would be dead. As for Nora, she would be safe with Cavell, hidden away at a secret location. In the morning, they would also join Kelly at the armory. From there, they would sail north on the *Victory* to a rendezvous with ambassadors from Dagan on Valcour Island.

If Kelly did not survive the battle, Mary Kelly would still board the *Victory*. Captain Edwards would sail to Montreal, where Mary and the kids would catch a train and disappear west. Unless things changed quickly for Kelly, it certainly appeared that his children would be growing up fatherless in Canada. So far, the only recruit with Kelly at the cabin was Costello.

"We're going to die together tonight, and I don't know your real name." Kelly said.

Zho hesitated. One of the primary warnings in the Transference Protocol Manual was not to disclose one's actual identity to the native species. Still, given all they had shared, he felt that he owed Kelly this much.

"Tashan Zho," Costello said, in Zho's voice.

"Tashan Zho. Well, Tashan, have you ever killed anyone?" Kelly asked.

"It appears that Costello did in your World War, but Tashan Zho has never killed another living thing," Zho replied in his voice, through Costello's mouth.

"Well, I have. I've killed so many – too many – and I've ordered the deaths of so many more," Kelly said as he reflexively started to rummage through various liquor bottles he had brought with him to brace himself for the evening.

"Aren't you a war hero? Isn't that what you were supposed to do?" Zho asked.

"Still, it never gets any easier. I'll tell you one thing I've learned. If you have to order the deaths of a bunch of people, don't overthink it. Just grab the nearest bottle, drink up, and say the words," Kelly said as he settled on a bottle of Canadian whiskey. Kelly stared at the bottle as though he was fighting himself.

"After all your good work on your sobriety, you're gonna throw it all away tonight?" Zho asked.

"Zho, why are you still here, anyway? You've got your princess. You notice that Cavell is nowhere to be found. There is no reason for you to die with me tonight. Diamond wants to kill me," Kelly said, fumbling with the top of the bottle.

"I gave you my word. I'm with you until the end," Costello said in Zho's voice.

"Well, at least somebody is," Kelly murmured.

"So, why are you going to drink? This fight is a lot bigger than the

Dempsey match. There are so many people counting on you tonight to make the right decision at the right time. Don't they need a sober Mike Kelly?" Zho said, still using his own voice.

"You really want to help me? Then leave me alone and let me get ready to do the only thing in life I'm really good at!" Kelly yelled as he walked over to the cliffside, above the clearing and stood, waiting.

Minutes later, Billow and James arrived with O'Brien. The major greeted his friends and offered them each a bottle. Although they probably would have accepted anyway, tonight they really needed to drink.

"How many men do we have?" Billow asked.

"Counting the three of you, twelve, …. maybe," Kelly replied.

"You don't know the exact number?" Billow asked.

"I'd guess there's about twelve still hanging around these hills," Kelly continued, "You know Diamond only wants me. The rest of you don't have to stay here to be slaughtered."

Father O'Brien was particularly despondent. He had been Kelly's friend for over fifteen years. He had officiated at Kelly's wedding and had baptized all of his children. And now, at far too young an age, O'Brien was going to hear his friend's final confession.

Although Kelly doubted that his small band of men could defeat Diamond's army, at least the battlefield was to his liking. Kelly had the high ground, which almost any student of military history understood was a great advantage. Kelly knew that his only chance of survival was to lure Diamond and his army into the clearing below. When Diamond agreed to meet there on August 29, it was a moral victory for Kelly. Even if Diamond's sheer numbers made the advantage somewhat academic.

But at least, since they were outside of town, no civilians would be injured.

At 7:10 p.m., Diamond's army appeared in the clearing below.

"This is it," Kelly yelled, mostly out of habit. Other than four men within earshot, there was really no one else listening. In the World War, he would have commanded thousands of men as they prepared to face down the mighty German war machine. By this point in battle preparations, he would have already consumed an entire bottle of Jack Daniels. On this night, however, with only a few brave men under his command, he had not broken the seal. Kelly threw the unopened bottle aside and drew his revolver from his holster. Standing alone on the cliffside, Kelly peered down at the army approaching below.

CHAPTER THIRTY-NINE

THE BATTLE

Granville, New York
August 29, 1926

Diamond didn't consider tactical advantages or battlefield positions. The sheer size of his army made him overconfident. Besides, Diamond was rooting for Kelly to kill at least half of his men in the battle. Why not give Kelly the better position? The more mercenaries that were killed, the better the chances that Diamond could pay the survivors and send them home.

Diamond's army began shuttling by truck to Bullfrog Hollow at 5 p.m. Diamond calculated that he'd need two hours to transport all of his men, so he showed up just before seven. He was met by Moyer, who proudly informed his new boss that the army was assembled a whole ten minutes early.

"Excellent work, Mr. Moyer. As a reward, you may lead the men into battle tonight," Diamond said.

"You mean from back here with you?" Moyer replied hopefully.

"Of course not. You'll lead from the front," Diamond replied.

"From the front? But I'll be slaughtered!"

"C'mon, Jim, what kind of attitude is that for a soldier? You survived the Great War. No one is more qualified than you to lead our men.

Now, go and lead!" Diamond said as he gestured to three of his men, who each pointed a shotgun at Moyer. Wisely, Moyer made his way to the front of the troops.

As Moyer passed his men, it was obvious to him that Diamond had placed the "cannon fodder" in the front lines. The contractors had been told to supply their own weapons, and some had only brought handguns. A six-shot Smith & Wesson was certainly reliable for committing crimes at close range, but it would be of limited use in the type of firefight about to occur.

In fact, Diamond viewed this as a partial solution to his overstaffing problem. So, he placed those contractors armed with handguns in the front ranks, together with the less experienced hitmen. The most experienced contractors would be held in reserve to guard him. After all, it was the Manhattan contractors that would be of most use to him when he made his move to reclaim his position in the New York City mob.

Precisely at seven, Moyer ordered Diamond's army to move out. The clearing was about the length and width of a football field. It was a classic valley, surrounded on all sides by hills. If Diamond had cared at all about military tactics, it would have been obvious that Kelly had lured them into an indefensible position.

Night was falling, and, understandably, the men were on edge. Moyer tried to reassure them that Kelly would not strike until after dark. Although it was late August, the summer air was still warm, and the evening was brightly lit by the setting sun.

Suddenly, Moyer ordered the men to halt. "Mr. Diamond. Mr. Diamond! There's something up here you've got to see!" Moyer hollered.

Diamond, who claimed to be strategically stationed in the back to defend against rear attacks, pushed his way to the front.

There he saw Kelly's personal supply, abandoned in the middle of the clearing. Once outside the underground warehouse, the supply was even more enormous than Kelly realized. It contained over eleven thousand cases of Canadian whiskey, hundreds of large wooden crates holding scotch or wine, and hundreds more kegs of beer.

Pinned to the outside of one of the crates was a note which read as follows:

> *Mr. Diamond, if you accept the truce, you can have my entire personal supply. Just take it, or use it to pay your men, and go home. You will never see me again. –Mike Kelly*

Once Moyer was out of earshot, Diamond turned to the Monahans. "Great. We've got Kelly's stash. Now we kill him, his men, and their families. All of them. Is that clear?" Diamond said.

"Clear, boss," the Monahans replied in unison.

"And if Moyer survives this battle, you put one in his head."

"With pleasure," Red Monahan replied.

Moyer and the contractors waited in the clearing as night fell. It was a beautiful summer evening. While two groups of men were preparing to fight to the death, a few short miles away, families were enjoying their weekend on Lake Saint Catherine.

Suddenly, a solitary man stepped out from the forest opposite the mercenaries. Several contractors raised their guns and aimed.

"Hold your fire. It's a priest!" Moyer yelled.

Father O'Brien, adorned in his formal vestments, walked slowly toward the contractors. As a man of God, he was considered no threat and, in fact, was welcomed by them.

When he was thirty yards from the personal supply, O'Brien stopped and stood opposite the contractors. Many had taken defensive positions on and around the crates. Either it hadn't occurred to Diamond that there was no cover for his men in the clearing, or more likely, since he was primarily interested in thinning their numbers, he didn't care.

Kelly's few men were expertly hidden on the high ground. They had to be. Diamond's army, now supplemented by the Diamond and Monahan crews, outnumbered Kelly's men almost thirty-five to one.

"Where is Diamond? I must speak with "Legs" Diamond," O'Brien shouted.

"Have you come to give Last Rites to my men, Father?" Diamond inquired after confirming that it was O'Brien and making his way to the front line.

"I've come to tell you to leave Mike Kelly and his men alone," O'Brien began sternly.

"Take it easy there, padre. You're not a target tonight, but I could always add you to the list," Diamond said, pointing his gun at O'Brien as he spoke.

"Diamond, what in God's name are you still doing here?" O'Brien said. "Look at the amount of alcohol behind you. Kelly will give you everything he has. All you have to do is leave."

"I've already got everything he has," Diamond said, motioning toward the personal supply. "And you are way out of line telling me how to handle my business. Now, do your job: perform Last Rites so we can get this shindig over with, and I can go home."

"I'm not performing a holy sacrament for you or any of your men. If you harm just one of Kelly's men, I *guarantee* that you'll spend an eternity burning in Hell," O'Brien hollered defiantly at Diamond as he removed his clerical collar.

"You guarantee, huh?" Diamond laughed. "And how are you going to do that?"

O'Brien closed his eyes and raised a gold crucifix into the sky with his right arm. It appeared that, through the power of his faith alone, he was attempting to summon the wrath of God upon the Diamond army. At first, the true believers among the contractors were frightened. After all, it isn't every day that a Catholic priest looks to Heaven and asks God to unleash his wrath upon you. But after several seconds, nothing happened. Undaunted, O'Brien stood firmly, holding the crucifix high in the air. Still nothing. At first, only the most cynical of Diamond's men laughed, albeit nervously. But as O'Brien continued standing defiantly, holding the gold cross above his head, laughter spread throughout the contractors.

Still, O'Brien stood before them, supremely confident that the power of his faith alone would strike down Diamond and his army.

"Enough padre, you're embarrassing yourself. God isn't coming here to save your friends," Diamond said.

"Who said anything about God?" O'Brien replied.

Suddenly, flames rained down on the contractors. As each fireball hit the Earth, the ground shook violently from the resulting explosion.

Anyone nearby was killed immediately, and each blast unleashed a devastating chain reaction. As the inferno spread to Kelly's personal supply, the cases of Canadian whiskey and other spirits within caught fire. With each explosion, flames and shrapnel shot in every direction, killing all in their path.

Many of the most experienced contractors, who had foolishly taken cover among the crates, were among the first victims. Those members of the Diamond army who were lucky enough to survive this first wave of explosions thought that the resulting wildfire was God's righteous intervention. Naturally, this caused widespread panic among Diamond's men, many of whom began running wildly in all directions, trying to escape the apparent wrath of the Almighty.

But as Father O'Brien had candidly admitted, God had nothing to do with it. From a farmer's field over one mile away, several 75mm howitzer artillery guns, "borrowed" for the evening from the Whitehall Armory, were shelling the contractors' position. Although the howitzers had an effective range of nine thousand feet, Kelly had elected to place the cannons about half that distance away, near a phone line. This allowed the major to communicate with the howitzer crews in real time. Kelly, using his cabin phone line, relayed targeting adjustments to the crews throughout the battle. The same active Guardsmen who had accompanied the 105th on several missions, including their journey to northern Vermont, were now manning the howitzers, assisted by gunnery veterans of the 105th.

Kelly's personal supply had been carefully stacked in the clearing earlier in the day. This gave Kelly plenty of time to ensure that the howitzer crews had precise targeting coordinates for the crates. Kelly gambled correctly that those crates would be irresistible to the contractors, who would try to use them as cover.

To maximize the explosiveness of the liquor within, Kelly's men had also layered hundreds of pounds of dynamite inside certain crates. In their rum-running business, Kelly's men had unpacked thousands of cases of liquor. Kelly knew that the contractors would have neither the time nor the desire to check the contents of an entire crate before the start of the battle. Although the whiskey itself was highly flammable, when dynamite was layered among the crates, it created an entirely new level of destruction.

The Guardsmen stationed at the Whitehall Armory were a highly trained howitzer company. The howitzers, 75mm cannons which had devastated the German infantry in the World War, were transported to Wells, Vermont from Whitehall earlier in the day, hidden on the back of dump trucks.

The gold crucifix, which Father O'Brien volunteered to bravely hold in the air, was the perfect fixture to reflect light, allowing Kelly to better coordinate the targeting for the howitzer crews.

After the first explosions began, heavy machine gun crews stationed in each corner of the hills above the clearing, opened fire on Diamond's men below. Four "nests" of two men each operated the Browning M1917 machine guns, which were also "borrowed" from the armory. Each M1917 fired .30 caliber rounds at a rate of 450-600 per minute.

Volley after volley of artillery shells poured down on the contractors' position. All the while, machine-gun fire streamed down continuously from each corner of the clearing. Although a few of the contractors tried to return fire, they couldn't even locate a target. Kelly's men were expertly camouflaged on the high ground, hidden from sight. The onslaught was so utterly swift and complete that most of the contractors in the Diamond army never even realized that they were being shelled by an artillery company.

As the fire and explosions continued to rage around him, Father O'Brien stood motionless, still holding the gold crucifix high above his head. Two of the contractors tried running toward O'Brien. It wasn't clear whether they intended to harm the priest or simply to use him as cover; whatever their motivation, neither got within twenty yards before being taken down by a bullet from an M1903 Springfield rifle.

Billow was hidden on the rise, seventy yards behind O'Brien. His orders were to ensure that no harm came to the priest.

From the cabin high above the clearing, Costello watched the slaughter with binoculars while Kelly methodically, soberly relayed orders to his men below. As each stage of the one-sided "battle" unfolded, Kelly gave additional orders either by telephone or to runners, who would relay his orders to the men hidden on the hillside.

A mere ten minutes into the "battle," the clearing was a killing field. Each of the four howitzer crews had fired over 280 artillery shells, which meant that a total of over 1,120 artillery shells had landed on and around the contractors. The four machine gun nests had each fired over four thousand .30 caliber bullets.

The entire length of the clearing in front of O'Brien was ablaze. There was no sign of movement from the contractors.

"Reload and fire again," Kelly said into the phone.

"No. Hold your fire!" Costello shouted.

"What did you just say, Sergeant?" Kelly asked, shocked that anyone would dare to countermand his order.

"Mike, quick, tell your men to hold their fire," Costello said.

"Why?"

"Look!" Costello said, pointing at the clearing below.

Kelly raised his binoculars and saw that his daughter, Nora, was wandering onto the battlefield. She was sobbing and trembling as she surveyed the carnage around her.

"Where in the hell did she come from? I thought Cavell was watching her? Hold your fire. Hold your fire!" Kelly screamed into the phone. Within a matter of moments, the roar of modern warfare that had been rocking the clearing was replaced by silence, save the crackle of burning flesh.

Nora walked up to the priest, who still stood frozen, his right arm locked in the air, apparently now shell shocked by the ferocity of the onslaught. O'Brien appeared to be the only living thing remaining in the clearing. When Nora took his left hand, O'Brien looked down at her. Nora shook her head, mouthing the word *"enough."*

Nora then turned and stared up at Kelly and Costello. She had not been provided with their location atop the mountain, and there was no way she could have known that they were watching her at that very moment. But somehow, it was clear that she knew.

Nora turned back and looked at the flames and carnage around her and grew angry. She again looked up at Costello and Kelly. "I said *enough!*" Nora shouted. Her voice sounded far more mature than one would have expected from an eight-year-old girl. It was the first time that anyone had ever heard a sound from Nora's mouth, and what a sound it was. When Nora shouted *enough,* the ground trembled, and the wind blew with such force that the fire in the clearing was immediately extinguished, revealing charred and mangled bodies strewn the length of the clearing.

Nora again viewed the carnage around her and shook her head several times. Once more she looked up at Kelly and Costello's position and shouted, "Enough." This time, a teenage voice echoed through the mountainside.

"I've seen enough," Nora said softly. But with these three words, the clearing returned to its lush, natural state. Nora, still holding the shell-shocked priest by the left hand, led O'Brien off the field of battle.

"All right. I'm shutting down the simulation," Costello said in Zho's voice. Interior lights illuminated, revealing Costello, Kelly, and Cavell sitting in the holodeck of a starship. The holodeck was now empty and looked like a small warehouse.

"That thing is amazing," Kelly said. "Even though deep down I knew that it was simulated, it was like we were right on the battlefield. And Zho, it was in one of these things that you learned so much about boxing?"

"Well, we call it Skiirmiishing, but yes. I have spent much of my life in simulators like this," Zho replied.

"So, now you know that my plan will work," Kelly said confidently.

"Major Kelly, respectfully, this was a simulation. It is one possible outcome. By our calculations, there are thirty-seven different possible outcomes of your plan, and not all of them will work out successfully for you," Zho explained.

"Thirty-seven? Tell me the worst possible one," Kelly demanded.

"The howitzers miss their targets and hit the forest, causing an uncontrollable wildfire and wiping out most of your beautiful town." Zho continued, "There is another possible outcome in which Diamond holds back half of his men until after your artillery runs out of ammunition. Both scenarios end with Diamond hunting down you, your men, and your families."

"Major, there is something else we need to discuss," Cavell said. "We know that you are just trying to protect your family. However, we simply cannot allow the level of brutality in your battle plan."

"You cannot *allow*?" Kelly said, "I'm not asking you to allow me to do anything."

"The princess instructs you to find another way. She cannot permit this level of death and destruction," Cavell said.

"She cannot 'permit' – " Kelly began.

"*Find another way!*" Cavell barked.

"If your princess is so powerful, why do you need me anyway?" Kelly asked.

"Major, the battle between you and Diamond is your fight, not ours. We cannot get involved," Cavell said. "So, please quit wasting time arguing. Just find another way – a way that doesn't require you to murder almost 350 people and place the residents of your town at risk."

CHAPTER FORTY
THE BETTER WAY

Granville, New York
August 29, 1926

Although no longer simulated, the battle had proceeded just as Kelly had foreseen. After discovering Kelly's personal supply abandoned in the middle of the clearing, the contractors assumed a defensive posture around the crates. O'Brien appeared from the forest, dressed in his formal vestments. The contractors did not consider him a threat.

"Hold your fire, it's a priest," Moyer ordered.

"Where is Diamond? I want to speak to 'Legs' Diamond," O'Brien yelled.

"What do you want, padre?" Diamond hollered back from behind a line of men.

"I want to demonstrate the power you will be facing tonight," O'Brien said.

"All right, everyone, the priest is going to show us his power. This should be good," Diamond shouted.

"I want every gun aimed at that priest. If he tries anything, you shoot him down," Diamond yelled. All guns were trained on O'Brien, as he faced the contractors, closed his eyes, and raised a gold crucifix to the sky. He appeared to be summoning the wrath of God upon the Diamond army.

As he remained safely behind his army, Diamond shouted, "Father, you can put the cross down. God isn't coming to save your friends."

"Who said anything about God?" O'Brien replied.

Suddenly, flames began pouring down from the heavens above. The surprised contractors stood helpless as fireballs rained down all around them. The 75mm howitzers had already fired two volleys each, and the artillery shells were barreling down on the mercenaries huddled below. When the fireballs became visible in the night sky, under Kelly's orders, the four machine gun nests opened fire at will on the contractors below.

As the artillery shells and bullets approached, some tried to run, but it was too late. They were sitting ducks. Then something completely unexpected happened. O'Brien, who had been holding the crucifix in his left hand, raised his right hand and spread his fingers open, as though he was now summoning the power of the Lord to stop the projectiles. And, to everyone's surprise, it worked. When the fireballs and bullets came within fifty feet of their targets, they simply vanished.

"Did you see that? The priest stopped them," a cry went up from one contractor.

"It's a miracle," another contractor shouted, falling to his knees.

While spontaneous cheers broke out around him, O'Brien stood humbly. The contractors believed that with the power of his faith alone, the priest had stopped the fire raining down from the sky. Father Thomas O'Brien had performed his miracle.

But as O'Brien would have candidly admitted, if anyone had ever dared to ask him, God had nothing to do with it. Instead, a Galaxy Class starship from the planet Dagan was hovering, in stealth mode, fifty feet above the contractors' position, completely undetected by the Earthlings below. Just as the artillery shells and bullets were about to hit the contractors, the projectiles' energy was absorbed into the starfighter's shields.

"I thought you could not get involved in the Earthlings affairs?" Zho said to Samson, as they sat in the cockpit of her galaxy class fighter.

"I did not get involved in their dispute. An important part of my mission was to determine if the Earthlings weapons were capable of penetrating the shields of a galaxy class fighter. That issue was very important to Chairman Dondor. What better way to find out? And now I can conclusively report that those weapons cannot penetrate our shields," Samson replied.

"But isn't the fuel on our starships extremely harmful to the Earth's atmosphere?" Zho asked.

"If you buy that cheap fuel produced by Hoaon Industries. The fuel required to be used in all government ships as mandated by Council law. I use bootleg, organic fuel. Perfectly safe on Earth," Samson replied.

"If you had a starship, then why did you even need me on this mission? Why am I here?" Zho asked.

"I told you before, I am a soldier. I follow orders. And that's all I am going to say," Samson replied.

As soon as the second volley disappeared above their positions, Diamond and the Monahans ran down the trail behind the clearing, leaving the contractors to fend for themselves. They climbed into Diamond's car and sped off, north toward Albany. Once the third and fourth volleys from the howitzers had vanished, absorbed by Samson's ship, Kelly gave the order to cease fire, leaving O'Brien and the shell-shocked contractors standing in the clearing.

As the contractors tried to regain their composure, Mayor James walked up to their position, carrying a white flag of truce in one hand and his trusty acoustic megaphone in the other. When reaching the center of the clearing, about ten yards from the contractors' position, he stopped and raised his megaphone.

"Gentlemen. I am Jim James, the Mayor of Granville. I am here to assure you that everything that you are about to hear is true. If you accept Major Kelly's offer tonight, it will be reflected in a legally binding contract. Before I continue, I just want to stress that those howitzers and machine guns are reloaded and aimed directly at you, so if anyone shoots at me, Father O'Brien won't be motivated to save you this time."

The contractors looked on in disbelief. The priest had stopped the bombardment, and now James and O'Brien were standing in the clearing, completely unarmed. And James sounded like he was simply trying to negotiate a business deal.

"Gentlemen, I'll make this quick, so we can get out of here before those cannons start firing again. We know that you traveled a long way to earn money for your families. I'm sorry to tell you, but Diamond never had enough money to pay you," James said.

There was a gasp from one of the contractors. Then certain others started yelling, *"What do you expect from a lawyer? He's a liar. You're a liar!"*

"I'm not lying," James continued. "Think about it. There are 345 of you. He promised you over $1,000 each, but he doesn't have $345,000 to pay you. He was counting on most of you to die, tonight. Now ask yourselves, although you're all here, where's Diamond?"

The contractors stood in silence. They were already badly shaken by the ferocity of the howitzers. Now, their trauma was heightened when they learned that Diamond had been lying to them all along.

"And now to Major Kelly's offer," James pulled out a sheet of paper from under his coat and began reading the proposal.

"Today, a case of Canadian whiskey sells for between seventy and one hundred twenty dollars per case, depending on the city. Kelly offers to hire each of you as distributors in his highly profitable liquor distribution business. Each new distributor will receive a free starter kit of thirty cases of Canadian whiskey. If you choose to sell it, you can keep all proceeds as profit. We estimate that you will earn between $2,100 and $3,600 for the resale of the thirty cases." James finished reading and said, "Any questions?"

"And we don't have to pay you back? Bull!" a contractor holding a rifle yelled out.

"Not on the first thirty cases," James replied.

"Why would you just give us thirty cases of whiskey?" another man asked.

"Because I'm investing in every one of you that signs on with the Kelly family," Mike Kelly said as he walked into the clearing and stood next to James. "But that's not all. If you accept my offer tonight, you are going to drive that whiskey home in a new truck. And my people, expert rum runners, will modify that truck so that your thirty cases are well hidden. In return, you swear loyalty to me and agree that the Kelly family will be your exclusive supplier."

"That's it? And then we'll be your distributors?" a contractor yelled out.

"That's it. And after you sell that booze back home, all you have to do is drive your new truck back to Whitehall, where we will sell you as much liquor as you want to buy," James said.

"This sounds too good to be true!" a contractor in the front row yelled out.

"So, what's in it for you?" a contractor from Buffalo shouted out.

"What's in it for me? Well, there's a lot in it for me. I don't have to watch some of my friends die. Did you ever watch a friend die? I lost a lot of friends in the war. Let me tell you, it stays with you. It stays with you. So, that's one thing that's in it for me.," Kelly said.

"But you know what else is in it for me. I won't have to order my men to kill you. I mean, I'll do it if you make me. But I'm not ashamed to admit that I'm tired of all the killing. We came home having won the war, only to find that the government had created an entirely new issue for us all to fight over. And that's all we've been doing these last eight years. Well, I've fought and killed enough people in my life. It took my daughter to teach me that there's a better way," Kelly said.

Various contractors started applauding and yelling. "That's for sure."

"So, that's my pitch. It's a free country. It's your choice," Kelly concluded.

He turned and walked into the woods, and not one contractor tried to stop him. Just as he reached the edge of the clearing, he looked back. "One final point. Unfortunately, Prohibition won't last forever. You have to think about your future," Kelly said, and then walked off into the forest. All 345 contractors signed on as distributors with the Kelly family.

Kelly won the battle without firing another shot. He had found a better way.

CHAPTER FORTY-ONE
THE AFTERMATH

The Hudson River, New York
August 29-30, 1926

The Lake Champlain branch of the New York Naval Militia was now more important than ever. Presumably, the most ambitious of the new distributors would return to Whitehall in a matter of weeks seeking more liquor. If this expanded venture was to succeed, the product had to be ready for pickup.

Kelly's newly formed company, Major MJKelly Imports, Inc. was entirely the brainchild of Mayor Jim James. The attorney had been pestering Kelly for months to expand his business, and when given the opportunity, James ran with it. To an outsider, providing each of the new distributors with thirty cases of Canadian whiskey seemed like a bad investment for Kelly. However, since most of it was from his "personal supply," which he had intended to weaponize during the final battle anyway, there was minimal out-of-pocket loss.

The other selling point for each new distributor was the latest Ford Model T truck. It was a bit of legal sleight of hand that allowed Kelly to afford to give a new truck to each contractor. James had failed to explain that the distributor's use of the vehicle was "for the duration of their distributorship with Major MJKelly Imports, Inc." In fact, Kelly did not *buy* each contractor a truck; he *leased* it. The distributorship agreement expressly provided that Kelly was "only obligated to make the first month's lease payment." Thereafter, the contractor was required to continue making payments from his profits. If he missed a payment, the contract provided that that was an issue to be resolved entirely between the distributor and Ford's leasing company.

Of course, it didn't matter to most of the contractors. They were driving home with a brand-new truck and thirty cases of Canadian whiskey hidden within.

The Lake Champlain Auxiliary set sail on its most critical mission on August 30, 1926. The *Victory* would travel north on the Hudson River to Valcour Island. There, Kelly and Costello would meet with ambassadors from Dagan. If all went according to plan, Princess Halana, the soon-to-be Queen Halana, would be reunited with her people.

The entire Kelly family – Mike, Mary, and all the children – would accompany Nora on her journey north. Colonel Samson had previously arranged for the separation, or "uncoupling," to be held about ninety miles north of Whitehall on Valcour Island.

When Kelly found the *Victory* docked in Whitehall on August 29, he was delighted to see his old friend Captain Edwards on deck.

"Where are we heading, Major?" Captain Edwards asked.

"We have an important meeting on Valcour Island. Can you get us there?" Kelly asked.

"Of course. It's straight up the Hudson into Lake Champlain, and then on to Plattsburgh. Are we waking up the good folks of Plattsburgh again tonight?"

"No. This is a stealth mission. How long will it take to get there?"

"Why? You in a hurry?"

"No, but the folks that we're meeting are," Kelly said.

"Just a few hours," Captain Edwards responded.

"Perfect," Kelly said.

The *Victory* rarely ferried passengers, but the Kelly children were heartier than most, and they were excited to be taking this trip with the entire family, particularly their new sister, Nora.

Costello and Mike Kelly were on the deck of the *Victory*. Once they were certain that they were alone, Kelly spoke.

"I hope that your people can find the rendezvous point," Kelly said.

"Our navigation systems brought the Armada across the universe to this location. I'm informed that we currently have multiple vessels orbiting the planet. I think they can find Valcour Island, even without your coordinates." Costello said.

"This procedure tomorrow. This uncoupling, as you call it..."

"We use that term for your benefit."

"Whatever you call it. I need to hear that Nora will be all right."

"Your daughter will be fine. Now, get some sleep."

After Kelly left the deck, Samson appeared. She had been waiting to speak with Zho.

"Tashan, I owe you an explanation and you're not going to like it," Samson said.

"You're going to tell me that you did something worse than knocking me unconscious and sticking me into a starship on a mission to Earth, where my actual body was destroyed by a killer drone." Zho said.

"I don't know if it's worse than that. That sounds pretty bad." Samson replied.

"Samson, It's fine. I'd do it all over again. After all, we saved the Earth." Zho said.

"That's what I've got to tell you. The Earth was never in any real danger."

"What?"

"There never was an Armada." Samson said.

"I don't understand. There was no Armada?

"It was all a story to plant you here."

"What do you mean plant me here?" Costello replied.

"I have strict orders not to tell you. Please talk to the ambassador."

"What about?… The extraction force?"

"There never was an extraction force. Well, except for me. I'm the extraction force. I mean, we were the extraction force." Samson said, trying to bolster Zho's role in the rescue.

"*We were the extraction force.* What did I even do? Why was I sent here?" Zho asked.

"To save Princess Halana." Samson said.

"But you did everything. You saved Halana. You found the Craig Colony. You located her while we were in there. You even found a way to fly a starship safely into the Earth's atmosphere. What did you even need me for?"

"You were my ticket in," Samson said sheepishly.

"So, my entire contribution to the mission, was that I had a seizure."

"To be precise, I gave you a seizure. But it was part of your mission." Samson said.

"So, my contribution to the rescue was that you gave me a seizure so that you could use me to get inside the Craig Colony disguised as my nurse?"

"Exactly. But, there's one more thing I need to warn you about." Samson said.

"There's more."

"You're not gonna like the way you are treated tomorrow. But please stay calm. The ambassadors we are meeting with will act friendly, but they are killers."

———•———

Kelly rose the next morning at 4 a.m. The *Victory* was off the coast of Valcour Island, and it would take Kelly at least thirty minutes to row a dinghy to shore. Once on land, they would hike to the agreed upon location. Joining Kelly were Costello, Billow, and Nora. Mary Kelly stayed behind with her other children, confident that her family would be reunited before the others arose.

The journey to the meeting went off without a hitch. They hiked until they were three hundred yards from the meeting area. "You can set up right here," Kelly said to Billow.

"The high ground?" Billow said.

"Always choose the high ground," Kelly replied.

Billow began assembling his rifle and scope.

"What are you doing?," Costello said. "You won't survive a battle with them."

"I just like knowing who I'm meeting with," Kelly replied, looking through the scope.

"Nothing yet," Kelly said as he scanned the area. Kelly didn't know what he was looking for, so he just kept looking for anything unusual.

"Do you see anything?" Billow asked.

"Not a thing," Kelly replied.

Suddenly, a light shot past their position and stopped about one mile away, hovering in the air. It slowly descended to Earth.

"I've got movement about one mile away. I can't make it out yet. Wait, something is coming straight for us. It's moving fast," Kelly said.

"How many are there?" Billow asked.

"Two, I think. They look human," Kelly said.

Within seconds, the ambassadors were at the agreed upon position, standing across from Kelly.

"Good morning, Major. I am High Councilmember Arixn, and this is High Councilmember Hoaon."

"I apologize for my appearance. When meeting a new species, we generally try to project an image familiar to them. I had intended to appear as your George Washington in full Army uniform. We searched our databases for everything that we know about Earth and concluded that your General Washington is your most likely match. But my Washington avatar was deemed inaccurate," said High Councilmember Arixn.

"That's still quite a compliment," Kelly said. "And even if you made a mistake on replicating Washington's appearance, it's the thought that counts."

"It's the thought that counts—what a beautiful philosophy. Are you a philosopher on this planet, Major?" Hoaon asked.

"I sell alcohol for a living, so I hear the opinions of a wide variety of philosophers," Kelly said with a grin.

"That sounds like a most rewarding life," Hoaon said. "Is Princess Halana with you?"

"Why don't you tell us?" Kelly replied.

Without saying anything further, Hoaon walked past Kelly while removing a box about the size of a baseball from his pocket. Hoaon placed the box at Nora's feet and bowed.

"Princess Halana, I would be honored to introduce you to your loyal subjects," Hoaon said as he activated the device.

In one motion, the princess stepped away from Nora, leaving Kelly's eight-year-old daughter still standing in place. Princess Halana did not look at all alien, but instead took the form of a fairytale princess, like Snow White or Cinderella. She turned to Nora, who was standing close to her father.

"Nora, how could I ever repay you for these last eight years," the princess said.

"Why would you ever have to repay me? You're my best friend: my only friend. I will miss you desperately," Nora replied, utterly unfazed that an alien princess had just stepped out from within her body.

"I will miss you, too. I will miss our bedtime talks most of all." the princess said.

"Me, too," Nora replied, smiling at the princess.

"All of Dagan owes this child a great debt. Thank you, young lady. Now that that is settled, we must deal with the criminal, Zho." Councilmember Arixn said firmly.

"What do you mean, 'the criminal Zho'?" Kelly replied. Costello was standing a few feet behind Kelly, clearly concerned that he would not be greeted as warmly by the aliens.

"The being that you know as Costello, is named Tashan Zho, an anthropologist on our planet. Unfortunately, Zho has broken many of our most sacred laws," Arixn firmly stated. "Please turn him over to us. I give you my word that he will be dealt with most severely."

"You mean, punished? But why? It's because of Costello – or Zho – that you have your princess back. And he did it without harming the Earth, which you apparently were more than willing to do," Kelly said forcefully.

"Major, I'm afraid it's not that simple," Hoaon said.

"Of course, it's that simple," Kelly said. "Zho is a hero. Why would you punish him?"

"Because even if Professor Zho was well-intentioned, he has altered the development of your planet. One of our most sacred laws is that we will never intentionally alter the development of any of the planets that we observe," Hoaon explained.

"Look who we have here." Arixn said, walking up to Costello. "Just as I predicted. What is the Earth expression? We planted an acorn , and now our Dr. Zho is a mighty oak."

"You planted an acorn? Project Acorn. *I was Project Acorn.*" Zho said out loud, angrily.

"Listen to that simmering rage. That aggression. The Acorn Protocol is working perfectly." Hoaon said, as he looked Costello over as though examining a specimen.

"Dr. Zho, are you hearing an inner voice urging you to commit violent acts?" Hoaon asked.

"You did this to me? It's because of a protocol that I am hearing voices?" Zho said.

"Don't be so dramatic Striker, we are trying to help you." Hoaon said.

"Do you have anything to say in your defense, Striker?" Arixn asked Costello.

"No Councilmember, I do not," Zho said as he tried to regain his composure, struggling to control his growing anger, "Everything you said about me is true. I broke my oath. My actions here have likely altered the evolutionary development of this planet. But, in my defense, you lied to me. I believed that I was preventing an extraction plan that would have killed millions," Costello said, "I thought that Samson and I were stopping you from destroying this planet."

"You and Samson?" In her report to the Council, she said you admitted that you had little to do with rescuing the Princess. Guards surround the prisoner. Colonel Samson front and center." Arixn shouted sounding more like a trial judge than the friendly Merriment Industry representative that Zho had met at the High Council meeting.

Within a moment flashes of light appeared, and four armed guards surrounded Costello. Another flash and Samson stood next to Costello.

"Colonel Samson, you interrogated the prisoner about his role in the rescue of Princess Halana. Please play back what he said." Arixn asked dispassionately. Without making eye contact with Costello, Samson projected a hologram recording of the conversation that she had with Costello the previous evening.

"We were the extraction force? What did I even do? Why was I sent here?" Zho asked.

"To save Princess Halana." Samson said.

"But you did everything. You saved Halana. You found the Craig Colony. You located her while we were in there. You even found a way to fly a starship safely into the Earth's atmosphere. What did you even need me for?"

"You were my ticket in," Samson said sheepishly.

"So, my entire contribution to the mission, was that I had a seizure." Zho said.

"To be precise, I gave you a seizure. But it was part of your mission." Samson said.

Samson turned off the hologram at that point in the conversation. She remained at attention, unwilling to even make eye contact with Costello. Suddenly, Councilmember Hoaon interjected.

"Councilmember Arixn, I truly feel sorry for Dr. Zho," Hoaon said, turning to Arixn, "I believe that he thought he was doing the right thing. I humbly beg you to show him mercy. Please accept the criminal Zho into community service with the Merriment Industry. He can spend his sentence entertaining the mere citizens of Dagan."

"Entertaining? I already told you that that I am retired from Skiirmiishing," Zho said.

"Don't be rash, Striker. Imagine, an entirely new type of Skiirmiishing where the competitors face off, live in an arena. Daganians will eat it up. Think of the numbers we will get, the credits you will earn. Besides, it certainly beats doing hard labor on a rehabilitation planet," Arixn said.

"And it will be completely risk-free. We will have a Transference Protocol system ringside. When a Skiirmiisher is near death, we will beam his or her life force out of the dying host into an entirely new host. Just think of the possibilities. No matter how powerful the opponent, or gruesome the match, you will live to fight again!" Arixn raved.

"Sounds dreadful," Costello said.

"It sounds like a blockbuster. The great Tashan Zho, animating the body of an enhanced human, Skiirmiishing all challengers. The ratings will go to the stars." Arixn said.

"Well, I won't do it," Costello said.

"You will after my tribunal finds you guilty of all charges and sentences you to lifetime service in the Merriment Industry," Hoaon said.

"Councilmembers. There will be no tribunal. It is my decision," the princess declared.

"With all due respect, princess, you are still a child," Hoaon replied.

"This child is to be Queen, and your Queen has made her decision," the princess said.

CHAPTER FORTY-TWO

EPILOGUE

Albany, New York
December 18, 1931

At 4:30 a.m., Diamond staggered into his Dove Street boarding room. He had been celebrating since the previous day. Diamond had been found not guilty of kidnapping and torture of one Grover Parks, a truck driver for a Diamond competitor.

Five years earlier, Diamond had been warned that his final day on Earth was fast approaching and that he should become a force for good. Rather than heed that advice, Diamond embarked on the most violent period of his already bloody career. Diamond had always murdered fellow gangsters, but he had now killed several innocent bystanders, too, so that they could not testify against him.

The trial was held from December 13-17, 1931. After the jury rendered its "not guilty" verdict on December 17, Diamond celebrated into the early morning of December 18.

By the time Diamond staggered home to the boarding house, he was so drunk he could barely walk. After falling into bed, he realized that he couldn't move. Not a muscle. It was as if something was holding him down. A power he had never felt before.

Then he heard a strangely familiar voice.

"Congratulations on your acquittal, Mr. Diamond," said the soft, almost monotone voice.

"Who's there?" Diamond shouted.

"Think, Mr. Diamond. You know who I am."

"Why can't I move?"

"I am not the cause of your inability to move."

"Then why can't I move?"

"Because it is your time," the voice responded.

"What do you mean, my time?" Diamond said.

"I warned you to prepare for this day. You really should have done something to redeem yourself."

"Costello!" Diamond yelled out, as though he had solved a riddle.

"Yes, Mr. Diamond," Costello answered.

"Costello, it's really you?" Diamond said, feigning relief. "Man, it's good to hear your voice. You had me worried there for a minute. Okay, you can let me up now."

"Mr. Diamond, I already told you. I am not the reason that you cannot move. But I am also not permitted to interfere in today's event, even if I were inclined to do so; and I am certainly not inclined to do so."

"Then, why are you here?"

"I volunteered to return as a witness."

"A witness?" Diamond cried. "A witness to what?"

"To your final moment. As long as it occurs today at the scheduled time, I will report that our 'interaction' from five years ago did not alter your predetermined timeline."

"*What are* you?" Diamond asked.

"I told you long ago: never mind what I am."

"Costello! I know you. Hurting people ain't your style. And I'm in pain here. Real pain. Please, please stop hurting me and let me up!"

"Mr. Diamond, I already told you. I'm not the one holding you down," Costello stated.

"What?" Having finally understood Costello's words, Diamond twisted his neck and looked behind him, and saw an enormous man holding him down.

"Who the hell is that? What do I do?" Diamond yelled.

"I suppose you should pray," Costello responded.

"I'm not afraid!" Diamond shouted.

"Perhaps you should be," Costello said calmly.

A second man, who had already removed a revolver from his coat, fired three shots into Diamond's head and back, killing him instantly. As the men left the room, leaving Diamond's lifeless body on the bed, they shared a laugh about the way Diamond had met his maker.

"Man, I never expected "Legs" Diamond to scream like that," the enormous man said.

"I know. And who the hell was he talking to?" the second man answered. "It was kinda interesting. Part of me wanted to let him keep talking so I could hear the rest."

The two men quickly they left the room. From their perspective, the drunken mobster's final moments were spent talking to himself. They were completely unaware that Costello had witnessed the shooting.

To this day, the murder of Jack "Legs" Diamond has never been solved.

———•———

Mike Kelly sat behind his desk in the Albany branch of Major MJKelly Imports, Inc. Like every morning, Kelly was working long before the arrival of his burgeoning staff. Business was far better than anything his father or grandfather could have ever dreamed. In August of 1926, Kelly added 345 regional distributors. Although not all panned out, enough did that Kelly's company was now the fastest-growing illegal liquor distributorship in the country. Kelly had since added distributors throughout the Western United States.

The Board of Directors had recently voted to adopt a name change. The new entity would remove the Kelly name and be branded MJK, Inc. The lawyers unanimously recommended that by dropping the Kelly name, the MJK brand would be more easily marketable internationally. Since Prohibition would be repealed in 1933, the company was positioning itself to become one of the leading distributors of legal alcohol in the country. Mike Kelly was now the Chief Executive Officer of a major international corporation.

Costello opened Kelly's door without knocking, ducked his head so that his now seven-foot, six-inch frame could fit through the doorway, and sat down across from Kelly.

"Costello? Zho?" Kelly asked, surprised. "Look at the size of you." Costello, the host body, was far bigger and more muscular than their last encounter five years earlier. "What are you doing back here?"

"Today was Diamond's last day," Zho responded through Costello.

"Please Zho, not in here," Kelly said.

They took an internal staircase from Kelly's office up to the roof of the newly renamed MJK building. There, they stood silently on the roof, watching the sun rise. Each appeared to be waiting for the other to speak.

"So, it's done?" Kelly finally asked, breaking the silence.

"It is," Zho replied.

"Then your work here is also complete?" Kelly asked.

"My friend, my work here will never be finished," Zho replied.

"Why?" Kelly asked.

"You know my sentence. I am in the custody of the Merriment Industry until I can verify scientifically that my visit to your planet did not change its development. With all the things that Earthlings observed five years ago, how could I ever confirm that? So, I am effectively their prisoner," Zho explained.

"I know how you feel. I'm basically stuck in this office for the rest of my life running MJK, Inc., a glorified liquor store." Kelly continued, "And although I am now much wealthier, I am racked with guilt. I've recently commissioned a study on the effects of alcohol on the human body. We don't have any medical data yet, but I'm beginning to suspect that drinking alcohol may not be very good for people."

"You don't say?" Zho replied.

"Really. Yet we keep producing it anyway, day after day after day. My company is now multinational and is becoming so rich and powerful that I fear that we will end up causing more human suffering than Diamond could have ever inflicted."

"Wow. That's some insight. So, do you still think about Diamond?" Zho asked.

"Every day," Kelly replied.

"Me, too. But he's finished now. So, we don't have to discuss him every time we see each other?" Zho said.

"I can talk about other things," Kelly offered.

"You can? Like what?" Zho asked.

"Like, …. you know who I saw the other day? The G-Man," Kelly said.

"You don't say. Where did you see G?"

"He came to the office. He was campaigning. He's running for Congress," Kelly said.

"The G-Man in Congress. Sounds like a perfect fit. That's one job he could do where it wouldn't matter whether he was drunk or sober," Zho said.

"He told me to remind Ryan Costello that you still owe him two bucks."

"It just goes to show that not even the dead can escape a debt owed to the G-Man," Zho said. The two shared a laugh and then stood silently on the roof for several awkward moments, struggling for something else to discuss.

"How long do you have?" Kelly asked.

"I was given one week to return to Earth, witness the end of Diamond, and report back to the Merriment Industry."

"So, Arixn still has you fighting live Skiirmiishes?" Kelly asked.

"Yes. And since the ratings keep getting higher, the Ministry keeps changing the rules to increase the level of brutality."

"Sounds horrible," Kelly said, after a pause. "But remember you do have another option."

"I do." Zho responded.

"Do you still have access to your Earth database?"

"Reading is one of the only things that keeps me sane," Zho replied.

"Read about Spartacus. If you really can't take it anymore, that may be your option."

The two stood in awkward silence for several more minutes. Although Kelly had said that they could talk about things besides their struggle with Diamond, they really had little else in common. Now that "Legs" had reached his final day, they both understood that this was farewell.

ACKNOWLEDGMENTS

Writing a novel takes many people. I would be remiss if I didn't recognize all of them.

First, I must acknowledge my extraordinary wife. Sarah was there for me as a loving and supportive partner, and in the fine tuning of at least two drafts of this work. It was not always easy, but at least for me, it was wonderful. Thank you my love.

Second, I must thank my editors. And I had a dream team. The developmental editor was Jeff Seymour. A published author of multiple works, Jeff gently walked me through the first two finished drafts of the book. Although The Lady Melanie sprung from my mind, it was Jeff who repeated the mantra "the inciting incident must be in the first chapter." Janeen O'Kerry, also a multi published author, was the copy editor. Janeen pushed me to better integrate the science fiction and alternate history elements, vastly improving the story. Alison Howard was the ideal line editor. She put the finishing touches on the dialogue and greatly improved the text. I am grateful.

Third, I want to acknowledge my beta readers. Sarah Brown, Tim Brown, Chris Morano, and Samantha Brown. Each saw a different draft of this novel and each provided me with valuable advice for the next draft. Thank you.

Fourth, thanks goes to the wonderful staff at Canoe Tree Press and DartFrog Books, particularly Gordon McClellan, Suanne Laqueur and

Simona Meloni. Canoe Tree and DartFrog do wonderful work and I could not be happier with them.

Fifth, I want to thank the cover designer Ricardo Montaño Castro. Every person who has seen your design has loved it. Richi, you made my book better, and I am grateful.

Finally, I am humbled that all of you chose to read my words. I hope you come back in the Spring of 2021 to read Book Two as we learn more of Lady Melanie and follow Tashan Zho as he attempts to navigate the world of "Live Skiirmiishing."

ABOUT THE AUTHOR

Philip Raymond Brown lives in Colorado with his fabulous wife, four beautiful children, and two good dogs. He has a B.A. in History and Political Science from Le Moyne College and a J.D. from Washington & Lee University School of Law.

Writing fiction is Philip's lifelong dream, and is his second career. In 2017, he walked away from a highly successful career as a trial attorney to pursue this dream. While writing STRENGTH, he devoted his time to his family, coaching little league and youth basketball. This year, while his heroic wife, the fabulous Dr. Sarah Brown, was on the front lines of the battle against COVID-19, Philip was homeschooling their four children.

As a trial attorney, he received numerous accolades, including being named to Best Lawyers in America, attaining the highest ethical/ability peer review rating ("AV") in Martindale-Hubbell, and being listed in Super Lawyers.

The yet-untitled sequel to STRENGTH will be released in the Spring of 2021.

Philip's website may be found at https//www.philipraymondbrown.com/. His social media may be found on Instagram, Twitter and Facebook. Links to those accounts may be found on the website. Philip's email is philiprbrown33@gmail.com.

CPSIA information can be obtained
at www.ICGtesting.com
Printed in the USA
LVHW080803160820
663144LV00013BA/163/J